The One's THAT Write Themselves

a novel

SYDNEY BOLEN

This is a work of fiction.

A few well known real people, organizations, and places are mentioned in this book but all the facts and events are fictional. Other than that, all the characters in this book are fictitious, as are their actions and occupations, and any resemblance to actual persons or to real events is purely coincidental.

First paperback edition 2023

ISBN 979-8-8635-8812-4

Sydney Bolen is an established writer and interviewer, as well as the creator of The Female Main Character, an online resource that encourages people of all shapes and sizes to find magic in their everyday. She currently lives in a flatshare in London in a room that is quickly filling up with books. You can usually find her at a local coffee shop or concert, FaceTiming her cats in the US or getting into, honestly, very little trouble with her friends.

The Ones That Write Themselves is her first novel.

"We all have stories we are living and telling ourselves."

-Bruce Springsteen

To whoever is reading this,
I hope it makes you feel a little more seen.

(If that happens to be 2020 me: we did it, bestie.)

Songs are written in many different ways. Sometimes they start as concepts. Sometimes, as melodies you can't get out of your head. Sometimes a line comes from something you overhear or from a moment in a dream. Some songs never see the light of day. Some take months to perfect. There isn't a formula to follow to guarantee success or even reliability. But, for me, the songs I'm proudest of, the ones people seem to connect with the most, are **The Ones That Write Themselves.**

1

Laurel

FEBRUARY

I enjoy another sip of this month's Winc, a Chardonnay I was considering re-purchasing before the evening went south. However, now I'm sure Cherries & Rainbows will be forever banned from all current and future Avalon households.

"I'm – so – sorry." The words arrive staccato, broken by sobs and stifled against my stomach. "This – ruined – our – roomie – date." From where she is nestled in my lap, the sodden mess of rumpled clothes and running mascara that resembles my best friend wipes its nose on the hem of my pajama shirt.

I distract myself from this by running a comforting hand through her hair.

"Shh," I croon, "No self-blaming allowed for the next 48 hours. There will be plenty more Winc's deliveries, which means plenty more dates, plenty more rom-coms, and plenty more gossip sessions. You have nothing to apologize for. Judah, on the other hand..."

My attempt to lighten the mood doesn't land. A new wave of hysteria breaks over Taylor. With a grimace, I peel her fingers from the stem of her empty glass and replace it with the original container. "Here. Drink this. It'll help." I watch as she contemplates attempting the feat from her current position.

"Just this once, I'll let you try that if you want, but I wouldn't recommend it," I warn. She frowns up at me, and her hazel eyes narrow into slits, but eventually, she props herself up on her elbow and raises the alcohol to her lips.

"I should have known." She coughs out as she transitions into a full and upright position. "The second he said he was busy on Valentine's Day, I should have known there was someone else. He was a full-time street artist!

Why would he need to work on Valentine's Day?!" She groans and takes another drink.

The presumably sentimental holiday was a week ago, but Judah hadn't been available until earlier this evening. Over wings and a King's game he couldn't miss, he mistakenly gifted Taylor a card with a different name and lingerie that was nowhere close to her size. She had returned home in a red-hot fury that slowly abated into a miserable mix of self-pity and rejection.

"Oh, my god. I'm so stupid. What if it's multiple 'someone else?' You don't think there were more than two of us, do you?" Her gaze sweeps over the shock on my face, which she interprets instantly. "You do! Laurel!"

I swallow the liquid in my mouth as fast as I can. "I didn't say that. I just–," I start, but before I can explain, Taylor flops into a nearby cushion and screams. When she rises, her demeanor has completely changed.

"Alright. That's that," she declares, tucking her bob behind her ears, "I am swearing off men until further notice." I watch in stunned silence as she relishes another pull of wine. "Enough about me. Laurel Cole, how is your love life?"

Taylor's last sentence was spoken into the Chardonnay as if it were a microphone. She holds it out to me, awaiting an answer.

I take it from her and drink. "Ha. Ha."

"I'm serious!" She whines, "What happened to the guy we met at Runyon?! I liked him."

"You liked that he went along with your lie about me twisting my ankle." I chastise, "I still can't believe you let him carry me all the way back to the car."

Taylor smiles dreamily. "It was romantic."

"It was embarrassing, given that I was fine. I don't understand how you expected me to build an entire relationship on a lie." I counter, teasing her.

"He totally knew you were fine. That was the entire point." She snatches the Winc delivery back. "It's called flirting. God, he was so into you and so hot. Your loss."

I throw a decorative pillow at her head. "Hey! You're supposed to be on my side."

"Always. Through every crush and every daydream." Taylor promises, all melodrama. "What about that guy Olivia knew?"

I pick at my cuticles as I consider the man I went on a date with a few weeks ago. "I don't know. I just wasn't feeling it. He was nice, but in that way that's kind of fake and annoying. If that makes sense?"

Taylor shocks me by throwing up her hands so fast droplets of Cherries & Rainbows slosh out and land in her hair. "There's always an excuse with you! Always an easy out. I swear you have one foot out the door before it's even been opened all the way."

I can't help but scowl, even though it's a fair assessment. "I like the life I've built. I'm happy. I haven't met anyone who makes me want to jeopardize that." I end my thought there, worried that talk of a potentially broken heart will remind my friend of hers.

Thankfully, she doesn't seem to notice.

"Complacency is the thief of joy," Taylor states noncommittally.

"I don't think that is the saying, but go off, Aristotle." She chokes briefly on the swig she was taking from the quickly dwindling bottle. As she wipes her mouth, it transforms into a grin.

"Do you want to know what I think?"

"Oh, please. Do tell." I say, leaning forward and snatching the wine from her grasp. I smirk at her from around the rim, pleased she's still distracted.

"I think–" She obliges, the intensity of her brandished finger undermined by her hiccups. "one day you're going to meet someone–who makes–" My eyebrows rise in incredulous anticipation, but, to my surprise, Taylor falters.

"You know what? No. You're too stubborn for my insight. For your own good, I'm keeping my mouth shut." I open mine to protest, but she cuts me off by dropping back into my lap. " Just know I can't wait to meet him."

2

Laurel

AUGUST

"Laurel, I love this song, but it is way too early and way TOO LOUD!" The shout is accompanied by three loud bangs directly behind my headboard, the epicenter to my own personal earthquake. I groan, rubbing the sleep from my eyes, entangling my fingers in the mess of dirty blonde hair that has escaped my ponytail before propping myself on one elbow and tossing the portion that managed to survive the night over my shoulder. Still more than groggy, I absentmindedly feel around my bedside table, searching for the alarm clock that is causing an affront on my longtime roommate's senses.

The song. What is this song?

The music blaring from the small machine isn't of the usual genre with which we start our mornings. In fact, our days usually began with the first shift KLOS DJs announcing with great punctuality, and in Taylor's opinion much creduli-ty, the arrival of 7:00 AM.

My hand finally finds my mini radio and tugs it, chord straining, toward my face. My confusion only doubles when I discover it isn't going off.

As my eyes struggle to focus on the LED display, Taylor sends an aftershock through the wall.

BANG! BANG! BANG! "LAUREL!" *BANG! BANG!*

At long last, the numbers form a crisp 6:32. I sit bolt upright. *The record player!*

I fight to untangle myself from the nest of green and mustard bedclothes encasing me and dart, as well as I can dart, across my rug-covered hardwood floor, down the hall-way and into the den. Careful to not overturn the red-wine-stained glasses left out from the night before, I scale the small mountain range of pillows stretching across the middle of the room and finally reach my target - my 'mint condition,' vintage, 1973 record console with an art deco exterior.

Thirty six years old by the time it was gifted to me, the record player had been a constant in my childhood. On the eve of my thirteenth birthday, while my father cleaned every nook and cranny, my mother, and her knowledge as a mechanical engineer, outfitted the staple piece with a few new features. While I was overjoyed to learn the player could now hold more than one disc at a time, much to my teenage chagrin, it had also been modified to act as an alarm clock. While I have begged, pleaded and attempted bribery via Venmo, to this day, my mother refuses to tell me how to disable this component. As a result, any time vinyl is left in the console overnight, it begins playing again at 6:30 AM.

I turn the volume down on The Aces' *When My Heart Felt Volcanic,* the selected soundtrack to the roomie date Taylor and I had last night, and make my way back to my bedroom. As there isn't much of a point in trying to fall back asleep now, I bang on the wall in the exact way my friend had.

"Do you want coffee?" I ask.

"I'm trying to sleep," she returns, clearly miffed that she was not just unceremoniously woken but is also being expected to converse.

I lean against my still-warm mattress, careful to allow a single solitary knee back into its waiting embrace, and reach to switch off my 7:00 AM wake-up call. "You have to get up in like thirty minutes anyway. Do you want coffee from home or not?"

It's quiet for a few beats, but I know she's not asleep. "Yes, please."

I thought so. I bang on the wall one more time merely to be annoying (and to show her I love her).

On my way into the kitchen, I grab the leftover wine debris from the den and turn the record up enough for the hushed sound to follow me. Even though it's early, the famous Los Angeles sunlight streams through the window of the small mint room, creating spotlights on the burnt orange tile that I purposely step in as I deposit the bottle in the recycling, set the glasses in the sink, and power up the coffee machine. Dusting my hands on the shorts of my striped cotton pajama set, I pause for a moment and let my head droop against the teakwood cabinet, closing my eyes and stealing a minute to process my unexpected morning. As the aroma of freshly brewed coffee grounds me, I open my eyes and smile to myself knowing Taylor will see this "rude awakening" as an omen for the upcoming weekend - though good or bad, only she can say.

3

Laurel

Taylor climbs into my 1962, orange, convertible Volkswagen Beetle at 8:07 AM, collarbone length black hair still damp, per usual, mid-sentence.

"...and I know it's not your favorite place or your favorite crowd, but please come. I know you don't want to, but I think you should given the morning we had. It's a sign we, or rather *you*, since it was *your* turn to make sure the record player was empty–" here she pauses and throws me a very pointed stare before proceeding, "–need to do something unexpected. If you don't, who knows what the weekend could hold?" I scoff and roll my eyes as I hand her the to-go mug I'd grabbed from the kitchen table. I presumed we had finished talking about this in the house, but clearly, I was mistaken.

Planning to ignore her, I back out of the driveway and begin to wind through the Hollywood Hills, but she tries again.

" I really, really, really, really want you to be there. What if I buy all your drinks?"

I toss my phone to Taylor so she can choose the music as I half whine, half sigh.

"You know how I feel about nightclubs. If the party was at a bar or a lounge or a speakeasy, I'd be there. But clubs are…"

I can't come up with the right word, so I hope the expression on my face properly communicates my disgust.

"Oh, come on! They are not that bad. You're being a baby." Taylor huffs, crossing her arms and overall affecting a pose that greatly resembles a pouting toddler.

For the record, I am not being a baby. I have a whole list of reasons why I loathe clubs, each one added based upon a valid and not so pleasant personal experience.

1. I am not a fan of crowds, for obvious reasons, and clubs are *always* crowded.

2. I prefer to not be groped by random men, and dancing with your friends at a club seems to invite that.

3. Drinks are *always* more expensive at a club.

4. Intoxicated people at clubs seem to be more "messy" than intoxicated people in bars.

5. 9 out of 10 clubs give me a headache within 30 minutes.

6. You can't have any decent conversations in clubs because of the headache-inducing level of the music.

7. It's harder to find a seat or even a wall to rest on in a club.

8. For some awful reason I will never understand, going to a club means the night doesn't even begin before 10:00 PM. Once I'm out, I'm good to go as late as the night does, but not starting until 10:00 PM? Insane. I feel tired just considering it.

We stop at a red light. The heat waves ascending from the asphalt give the passing traffic a mirage-like quality. I grab my phone from the cup holder and tap out a familiar pattern on Spotify. "You don't have to take my word for it," I say, turning up the volume on *Shape Of You*. "Take Ed's."

"Shut up," Taylor huffs, lightly shoving me. But, I see the barest hint of a smile flit across her icy exterior as I put the top up and indicate to merge onto the interstate.

Taylor and I don't work together, but our offices are close. We carpool because on the days we need to utilize the highway, it cuts 30 to 45 minutes off our commutes. The ride today is quiet due to the fact Taylor is racking her brain for a way to convince me to attend her ~~shallow socialite wannabe~~ coworker, Mckenna Clayton's, 27th birthday party tonight: a party I was not specifically invited to, but for which I fall into the 'friends welcome ~~but solely so it seems like I have more friends~~' category, a party that is being held at Nightingale Plaza, an "exclusive VIP' club on La Cienega Boulevard, self-described as "the next step in elite Hollywood nightlife, where refined elegance meets tastefully crafted technology," which to me translates to everything I hate about a typical nightclub dressed up in that highly sought after faux-elusive Hollywood glamour. I mentally chastise myself for being mean, but then I remember all the times I've been around McKenna, and I don't feel that bad.

As I navigate off the freeway, I roll down the window, letting in the sounds of the city. There's a light breeze now that we're out of The Valley that causes the tips of the passing palm trees to gently sway.

In only 5-10 minutes, depending on traffic, I will be dropping off Paramount Studios' newly promoted Media Relations Associate. Her near-constant sighs and posture adjustments warn me she is preparing to state her case one final time. I brace myself for the forthcoming argument.

"Laurel, please come! Please. I want you to be there."

Her words come out as such a desperate plea that I'm caught off guard, causing us to sit in more than a few moments of extremely awkward silence as I contemplate how to respond. As the first refrain of *Galway Girl* sounds through the speakers, it hits me.

"Taylor," I probe, as sweetly and innocently as I am able. I catch her immediate wince out of the corner of my eye and know I have hit the nail on the head, "what is the real reason you want me to come tonight?"

"Because I don't want to be with my co-workers and McKenna's influencer friends alone," she tries. But her delivery makes the words contestable.

"Nope. Try again." I shake my head, unsuccessful at keeping mirth from my voice.

Taylor groans and puts her head in her hands. "Because Jeremy is going to be there, and I may... you're my best wing woman! Happy?!"

Holy Hell. I knew this was about a guy, but Jeremy?

"A bit," I offer, fighting the urge to pull over and dance down North Gower Street.

Jeremy is the only one of Mckenna's usual invitees whose company I genuinely enjoy. We met around a year ago when he attended one of her gatherings as a friend of a friend (maybe even of a friend). Despite being a complete stranger, he spent most of the evening in our company and, although we all automatically hit it off, it was more than fairly obvious he drifted in our direction because of Taylor.

In my humble, yet highly-valued opinion, Jeremy is the perfect guy for Taylor. He's everything she needs in a man. The quiet to her crazy, the calm to her storm, a good listener, steady, sincere, kind, and unabashedly obsessed with her. Yet, she has always maintained the relationship could never be anything but platonic. A declaration I found devastating but true, as I nursed and comforted her through a slew of his antitheses: dark, brooding, stoic, Doberman men who I felt never deserved my friend. I never hid these sentiments, but agreed she was an adult capable of making her own decisions. Since her swearing off of men back in February, I have been hopeful the dark days were behind us, but I never entertained the idea that when we emerged into the light, the next stop would be Jeremy.

I don't speak a word as I ease up to a vacant meter outside the historic studio and throw on my hazards. By the time Taylor cranes her neck in my direction, I'm grinning from ear to ear.

"Well, it sure took you long enough."

"Oh shut up," she says, shoving her door as wide as the hinge allows, prepared to be angry with me for the rest of eternity. As she crosses to my side, mumbling under her breath, I lean out of my window.

"What time are we leaving?"

My friend rotates around so fast I'm afraid she may get whiplash. "Are you serious?!" she exclaims, her hazel eyes wide with surprise.

"Yes, but," I hold up my hand so I can emphasize my stipulations with my fingers, "you have to: one- buy all my drinks, and two- promise we won't be out until 2:00 AM. We have to cover the store in the morning."

Taylor is beaming and nodding as she walks backward across the street. "Ok, yeah! That's fine. Of course."

"Bye, honey! Have a good day at work!" I call enthusiastically, something we trade off doing every day. She blows me a kiss and practically skips across the street. As she reaches the gated entryway, I realize she didn't answer my question, "Hey!" I yell after her, "What time do you think we should get there?"

"10:30!" she shouts back without even a glance over her shoulder.

4

Laurel

I enter the Capitol Records' employee parking lot ten minutes later, exchange Friday morning pleasantries with Daysie and Paul, the bright-eyed receptionist and totally-in-timidating-but-actually-very-nice security guard, respectively, and head straight to the cafeteria on the fourth floor. I had planned to dine on a breakfast of a dark chocolate, nuts and sea salt KIND bar from my desk drawer stash, washed down by a cup of break room coffee while checking emails, but I have thirty minutes until I need to clock in. Add this to the fact I am now going to a party tonight (with all alcohol courtesy of Taylor's debit card), and I have no choice but to indulge in a "real" breakfast.

I am not the kind of person that can go out drinking on a whim. At less than an inch over five feet and somewhere around 110 pounds, I am the textbook definition of a lightweight. I have to prepare. I weave my way around the circular tables and red and white chairs to join the short line at the head of the commissary. The breakfast burritos here are the best. I find myself salivating, merely anticipating eating one. I stuff a tortilla with hash browns, vegan cheese, Beyond breakfast sausage, avocado, and spicy ketchup. Heaven wrapped up to-go in under ten minutes.

One more ride on the pristinely clean elevator to my floor, and I'm seated at my desk, coffee within reach, and my food plated in front of me. I'm skimming today's schedule when someone knocks softly on my desk.

"What did I tell you about getting here so early, kiddo?"

I look up from my computer to see Jenny perching herself on the faux-wooden surface, green eyes already bright with mischief. I attempt to smile in return, doing my best to recover from the extremely large mouthful of breakfast she caught me taking.

Jenny is my boss, genuinely one of my most beloved friends in Los Angeles, and the reason I even have this job in the first place.

I met her six years ago when I was a junior at UCLA, sightly over halfway done with my Bachelor of Arts in Music History and Industry and completely unsure what kind of career I wanted. Going to gigs was my favorite. Many of Los Angeles' iconic venues felt like my second home. I considered a career in touring, but eventually decided I wanted something slightly more stable. I knew my father could get me a job in music journalism with his eyes closed, but I also knew I wanted to play a more hands-on role in the business of music itself.

Taylor and I were waiting to pay for our drinks at the El Rey's showroom bar in between the secondary and headlining acts, discussing the recently ended set.

Bracing myself against the counter and prying my shoes off the already sticky rubber floor mats, I said, "I'm telling you, everyone will be talking about that band soon." Taylor, the tiny segment of her stiletto heel easily dodging the fifth, grabbed both our drinks from the bartender as she replied.

"I mean, I'm glad you liked them. I didn't really expect this show to be your cup of tea."

Pop Punk was not my cup of tea then and is not my cup of tea now. But when it comes to live music, I'm pretty much down to see anyone.

"Oh. I didn't love them for me, but they had a good stage presence, which I can appreciate, and I didn't even see one side conversation in the crowd. LA crowds never watch the opener. You know that!"

Taylor sighed, passed me my tequila sunrise and placed her free hand on her hip, "You and your weird thing with watching the audience. You paid to watch the band, stupid."

"I know," I laughed, squeezing in a quick sip before we wound our way back to the space commandeered and guarded by our other friends, "but I like to. It's interesting to me to see how other people respond to the artist and their songs."

"Excuse me."

I twisted toward the hand that had been laid on my elbow and was met by a woman in an eggplant colored pantsuit waiting for my attention. She had long braids, a few of which were multi-colored, and dark red lipstick, but what I fixated on was the neon blue all-access wristband fastened around her right wrist. Graciously, she pretended not to notice as she stuck out her hand.

"I'm sorry if this is weird, but my name is Jenny Colteur."

"I'm Laurel," I said, shaking her offered introduction. "This is my friend Taylor." Taylor's ultra-sized eyes met mine over the straw hanging limply in her mouth as they exchanged short greetings.

"Laurel," Jenny resumed, focus back on me, "I don't know what you do or what your professional interests are, but I'm the A&R Manager at Capitol Records. In all honesty, I was eavesdropping on your conversation and wanted to say if you don't work in A&R, you should."

As this was not what I was expecting from this interaction in any way, my brain automatically chose a response that had great potential to ruin the conversation: it powered down. For longer than is socially acceptable, I did not respond at all, mouth agape. Finally, my mental reboot kicked in, ending my silence with an incomprehensible stammer of what was meant to be gratitude.

Fortunately, Jenny found this amusing. Pulling a pen out of her purse, she said, "The headliner is going on soon, so I need to get upstairs, but if you're in school, you'd like a career change, or you're simply curious about what a job in A&R would entail, give me a call." She handed me her drink napkin, which now had her cell phone number scribbled across it, and confidently walked away.

"What the actual hell just happened?!" Taylor practically hissed in my ear as soon as the industry professional was far enough from us. "Did your life just become a movie? Did we uncover a glitch in the matrix? Next week you and I are going to go have lunch near all the major film studios and talk about PR. Maybe an exec. will walk in and offer me a job." I shook my head, still awestruck, as I folded the napkin and tucked it into my pocket.

Five years later, I have been promoted up the A&R hierarchy position by position, eventually landing the job Jenny initially held when I met her. She, in turn, is now the Senior Vice President of the department.

Nowhere near the age of my mother, Jenny has called me "kiddo" ever since she was my internship supervisor, and I accidentally referred to her as "mom."

"Hey, Mama Jenny," I respond as soon as I swallow. "How are you feeling today?"

Jenny sighs and places my hand on her rounded, just-over-eight-months-pregnant stomach. "Your younger broth-er–"

"or sister," I interrupt casually.

Jenny narrows her eyes at me as she finishes her sentence. "Your younger *brother* has the hiccups and is driving me crazy."

I focus on the hand pressed to her belly, and sure enough, on almost a rhythm, I can feel a tiny pulse a few times a minute. I meet Jenny's eyes, my brown ones wide, and we break out into giggles.

♥

The workday passes without much incident. I answer emails. I run through what needs to be done next week, noting if I'm set to attend any recording sessions or have any artist team meetings. I order a Hollywood Bowl from Sweetgreen for lunch with extra rice. I consume my body weight in ounces of water. I listen to the demos that have made it past the rest of our team and do some cyber-stalking of the artists or bands. As I go, I sort them into four piles:

1. Demos from artists that already show strong potential to grow an audience, but that I don't personally connect with

2. Demos from artists that already show strong potential to grow an audience and that I would add to my Spotify playlist

3. Demos from artists that do not have a big following as of yet, but I think could potentially gain a following with some assistance

4. Demos from artists that I feel aren't a good match for our company

The first two categories are technically one, but Jenny likes to know which bands I would be a fan of.

By the time I finish, it's 5:30 PM. On a Friday, that is sufficiently late enough to end the workday. I swing by Jenny's office on the way out to officially hand off my three categories of passing demos. When I knock on her welcomingly open door, she's packing up her things.

"You all set for while I'm gone?" she inquires, taking a break and resting her hand on her abdomen.

"I feel pretty good," I affirm, leaning on the doorframe and ticking my list off on my fingers. "I've got calendar reminders scheduled for all the meetings on my phone. I've triple-checked that we have studio space booked for when we need it. Morgan and Nessa are all set to go see that possibly promising band at the Fonda so I can be here for Halsey's album Release Concert and check in with her day-to-day team about upcoming promo and marketing, and new demos are already making their way to me."

In response, Jenny exhales, marginally relaxing her posture, "Well, I can't think of anything you didn't say, so I guess that's good."

I move across the room, set the discs on her desk and place my hand on her shoulder. "Jenny," I state, imbuing my voice with reassurance, "it's going to be fine. Between Irene and I, we've got this, I swear."

Jenny and her wife are leaving late tonight for a business trip turned babymoon. Anytime Capitol adds an artist to our roster, Jenny likes to see them perform wherever they currently generate the biggest fan base. That way, we can see what we need to work on with the artist, what their fan base is already responding to, and what they naturally do well. Yes, there is a lot about the music business that is a numbers game. Still, in today's world, especially when developing new artists, one of the most important things is how they connect with their fans. Usually, this means the two of us tag-teaming various shows around Los Angeles. Sometimes Jenny gets to fly to New York or somewhere in Canada. But three weeks ago, Capitol signed a locally established Irish band, & Then Some, so Jenny is being flown out to attend their Dublin concert. The trip was initially set to be three days (fly-in, see the show, fly back), but then Jenny got approval to book her returning flight for a week later. She and Pam will be "living it up," as she puts it, for ten days in Ireland before coming home and "going full parent beast mode."

Since Jenny became SVP, she has never taken more than a day or two off at once. This Celtic excursion has her gone seven to eight business days, some of which she will hopefully be off the grid enjoying some last moments of pre-baby peace with Pam. I understand why she's nervous to hand the reins over to her assistant and me.

"I know, Laurel," She squeezes the hand I've placed over her arm. "I just can't believe it's time to do this babymoon thing already. Sometimes I feel like the pregnancy went by so fast, even though I know I complain about it feeling like forever a lot of the time."

I laugh. "You know she isn't going to be here as soon as you get back."

"True," she admits, rubbing her stomach, "This is making it feel real, I guess. I hope we're ready," she makes eye contact with me and grins as she adds, "for him."

"You are," I respond, beaming back, happy for her. "I've seen the nursery, all the books you've read. You guys will be amazing parents." Jenny scoffs and tries to wave off the compliment. But, when her gaze meets mine again, I notice her emerald eyes are watery.

"Don't mind the pregnancy tears," she requests, pushing up from her seat, "but I have to give you a hug."

I break the silence a few seconds into the embrace by saying, "Hey Jenny," and pushing away so I can see her, "you're going to Ireland tonight." The hint of a smile crosses her lips as she blinks away any remaining moisture.

"I am!" The excitement I was hoping for is back in her voice. "Actually, I better get a move on. I need to do one last packing check and make sure Pam hasn't forgotten the bag she's supposed to bring with her when she drops Jagger at the kennel."

I grab my tote so we can walk out together. "What time's your flight?"

"11:15 PM. Hopefully, we'll be able to get enough sleep on the plane, so that we don't feel like zombies when we land.

After the elevator announces its arrival with a cheery *"ding!"* I ask, "Is the gig that night?"

"It's Sunday, so luckily, we can get settled beforehand." She wrinkles her nose. "Maybe even shake off some jet lag."

I chuckle, knowing how hard simply traveling to the east coast is for her.

We've reached the doors now, so I give her a departing hug. "Have so much fun, and know I am beyond jealous! Text me how the band is, but otherwise, please forget we all exist over here for a few days."

"I'll try, but I make no guarantees," Jenny says genially, heading to her car. "Have a good weekend, and don't miss me too much."

5

Laurel

"What are you doing with the top still up!?!" Taylor practically screams half an hour later as she slides into my car and presses the convertible's release button. "And no music on?!? Who are you? It's pre-game time!"

I feel a rush of energy from her tangible excitement followed by an undercurrent of affection in knowing she's going overboard for my benefit.

"I was on the phone with my mom. Any requests?"

"Why are you even asking? The Party Playlist!"

The Party Playlist™ is a playlist curated carefully by Taylor and myself as the perfect companion to getting ready for a great night out, emotionally, mentally, and physically. Created on a night such as this: me going to a club, where it should be noted, it is almost assured I will not love the music as DJs aren't my favorite, theme nights excluded. (I should add this to my list of why I hate clubs.) Way too long to need ever be repeated on any given evening, this particular playlist features any and every pop, rock, rap, country or hip-hop song to ever put one or both of us in a good mood.

I locate and select *The Party Playlist*^TM on my Spotify and set it to shuffle. *Best Song Ever* by One Direction blasts through the speakers. Right on cue, we face each other and scream the opening lyrics. I can't help but giggle.

Increasing the volume, Taylor suggests, "Let's take the canyon home. We can keep the top down." She's still beaming as I indicate and pull into the not quite bumper-to-bumper traffic.

♥

By 9:00 PM, Taylor and I are in the final stages of getting ready for the evening. We arrived home after encountering a lovely lack of evening commuters along Laurel Canyon, dined on mind-blowing proportions of boxed mac 'n' cheese, each showered, shaved, exfoliated, waxed, plucked, moisturized, blow-dried, and styled and are now finally ready to begin covering, coloring, plumping, sparkling, highlighting, dressing and accessorizing. I'm sitting at my vanity, wearing an oversized patterned button-up I stole from my dad back in high school and putting the final touches on my carefully crafted smokey eye by dabbing sparkly cream eyeshadow onto my eyelid's inner corners when it happens.

As Niall Horan's *Heartbreak Weather* fades out, the familiar introductory riff of *Life In The Fast Lane* shoots through our sound system's speakers. I take advantage of my socked feet to dramatically slide into Taylor's room, grabbing her door frame to keep upright, and mime singing the first few lines into an invisible microphone. I release the doorframe and point to her reflection in the mirror. She twists around in her desk chair and lip-syncs the end of the sequence back to me, batting her recently applied eyelashes. We leave the rest of the song to The Eagles, chortling at our antics.

I sit down on Taylor's cream and blush pink bed, completely at ease amid the preparation chaos. Clothes are strewn around her room, some laying as if they were perhaps paired together, others left alone in a heap on the floor. Various makeup items are out of their usual living spaces, and tissues adorned with rejected lipstick color kisses litter the area around her trash can.

"Have you decided on what you're wearing?" I question, guessing her current ensemble of pushup bra and red PJ shorts is not her outfit of choice.

"My silk cheetah print mini dress with the cowl neckline and black heels." Her left eye winks at me as she lines the right, "You?" I smile back.

"Not yet," I confide, sliding the clips from their place in my hair. "Are you bringing a jacket?" LA days in August are warm, but the nights can get pretty chilly.

"I think I'll wear my black blazer. They have a coat check we can use. Can I borrow your curling wand? The little one?"

"Of course. I'll grab it." I answer as I slide back out of the room. This time, accidentally.

Treading more carefully as I return, I hand the smallest barreled of my three curling irons to Taylor. After she plugs it in, she stops dividing her hair into sections and faces me.

"Thank you for coming. Seriously," she says, her tone unexpectedly somber, "I know last time we went to one of McKenna's parties, *The Incident* happened.

Ah, yes. *The incident.* Eight months ago, during McKenna's family's private NYE party at Skybar LA, I had ventured to the bar alone around 1:00 AM to order Taylor and myself waters for the road. While I was waiting, an aggressively drunk man in a wrinkled suit and a fading cologne that belied an over-exaggerated sense of self-importance decided he had the winner of all introductory icebreakers.

"So, what happened to you? You're too pretty to be crippled."

It was so far from what my female intuition had mentally prepared for when I clocked him staring, my gut reaction was to inquire if I had misheard him. As it turned out, I hadn't. Unfortunately for him, Taylor had heard as well. The realization she had joined me dawning when I watched her fist collide with his face. In the end, one of my first memories of the new year, was feeling both proud and horrified as I tried to calm my creative-insult-and- profanity-spouting best friend while the bouncers dragged her from the premises.

Remembering the occasion, my answering grin is nothing but sincere. "Next time, lead with the real reason you want me to come. I'll need less convincing."

Her reflection rolls its eyes at me as I leave the room.

When I'm through the door, she calls, "You should wear that bodysuit I like. You know the black lace one?" She can't see me, but I still snort and shake my head. Taylor always wants me to wear my black lace bodysuit. She bought it for me. While I finish my makeup, I run through outfit ideas in my head.

A handful of songs further into the playlist, my room in the same state of disarray as the one next door, I remove the aforementioned item from my closet and give it a once over. My plan was to wear a dress, but maybe?

I step into the bodysuit, easing it over my hips and snapping it closed before drawing the elastic straps over my arms. I grab my high-waisted, tight-legged black pants and a thick belt from my dresser, my God-sent black sandals with a wide kitten heel from my closet, and my leather jacket from the back of my door. Checking out my final ensemble in the mirror, I can't help but feel pleased with what I see. To Taylor's credit, this does make my boobs look really good. I embellish the outfit with my favorite hoop earrings, three necklaces, and a dark red lipstick and finally feel ready to go. With one last glance in my mirror, I gulp down some water through the straw I've stuck in my cup. Maybe Nightingale will surprise me. Maybe it won't be so bad after all. Maybe.

I add both the red lipstick and one of my go-to pinks, in case I get tired of reapplying, to my jacket pocket alongside my ID, debit card, and spare house key and head to the den to discover Taylor already there and ready to go. Her dark hair is in tight, brushed-out curls, the top layer pinned back away from her face. She's gone for a glossy nude lip. The saturation of the cheetah print in her dress perfectly complements her skin color and brings out the cool tones of her eyes. I gasp, 100% overselling it, right as she sees me and does the same thing.

"Look at you, you absolute babe!" I say.

"Holy shit, Laur! I knew that top would be a great idea. I'm warning you now, you *will* be hit on tonight!

I laugh, enjoying the praise. "Stop it."

"Are you sure this is OK, though?" she asks, suddenly uncharacteristically shy.

"Oh my gosh, yes! Jeremy won't know what to do with himself. I promise."

The pink of Taylor's blush deepens. "I don't know why I'm so nervous. We know he likes me."

"It will be great. Don't worry," I insist, giving her hand a soothing squeeze.

She squeezes mine back, "Maybe he'll bring a friend."

"Don't start. Tonight is about you, not me."

"It could be about us both!" she exclaims, exuberant personality back in full force. "You never know."

I decide to concede. "Ok, true. You never know, but I really feel like the odds of meeting someone I want to date in a club are slim to none."

"Well, with that attitude, they are." Taylor frowns.

My phone buzzes on the table. Saved by the Uber. Or at least that's what I assumed.

As I pick it up, it keeps vibrating. It's Jenny. I smile to myself, accepting the call. She should be on the way to or at LAX right now. I wonder what she needs to make sure I don't forget.

"Hi, Jenny!" I say.

A different voice responds to my greeting. "Hey, Laurel. It's Pam. There's been a slight change of plans. Jenny's in labor."

"Oh, my goodness! Is she ok?" I notice Taylor has stopped doing last minute touch-ups in the foyer mirror, and is honed into my conversation, body language on alert.

"Yeah, yeah, yeah, sorry! She's fine, all good–"

I hear Jenny interrupt. "Put her on speaker. I can talk to her. It's only childbirth." The phone clicks over. "Hey, Kiddo. I'm going to need you to do me a favor, ok?" Jenny's voice is pained, but not more so than I expect.

"Ok," I answer.

"You have a valid passport, right?"

"I do," I state quietly.

"Okay, good, I was right. Listen, I need you to go to Ireland for me. I don't want to reschedule on the band. Plus," she chuckles. It's light, but it's there, and it comforts me. "It's too late for us to get a decent refund on the flights or the room, so someone should use them. Irene is currently chang-ing–" she stops, groans, and concentrates through a few deep breaths before speaking again. "Sorry, contraction. Irene is currently changing everything to your name because I took a gamble on you having a passport. Ok?"

"Ok," I swallow

"I need you to say, 'Jenny, I'm going to Ireland,' so that my labor brain will register it and hopefully remember you will be there in my place."

She's half teasing, so I do my best to appease her. "Jenny, I'm going to Ireland." As soon as Taylor hears this, she disappears down the hall.

Jenny sighs in relief, "You're a lifesaver, kiddo. And hey, don't worry about me. The doctor thinks we will both be fine. I'm 34 weeks, and this guy has been ahead of all the big gestational checkpoints."

"I'll try, but I make no guarantees," I'm smiling now more for her benefit than because I'm feeling it. Have Pam keep me updated, ok?"

"I will," Pam cuts in, and I find solace in the steadiness of her voice.

"Of course," Jenny says as she groans through another contraction.

My head is spinning as I hang up the phone. I stand still, close my eyes, and go over the things I know: Jenny is in labor six weeks early. I was over two months early. Jenny said the doctor said everything would be fine. I was also ultimately fine. Jenny needs me to be on a plane in 90 minutes. I need to help Taylor pack my suitcase.

6

Laurel

I am the kind of person that is two hours early to the airport. So this Home Alone 2-esque mad dash to my gate from security is not doing anything to help my personal stress level.

In an amount of time I am sure qualifies us to be in the Guinness Book of World Records, Taylor and I "packed" my suitcase- threw every item of clothing, accessory, beauty supply, and toiletry we thought I would ever need or possibly want inside-, sped to LAX-Taylor bobbing and weaving around the late-night traffic on the 405 like a champion F1 driver, while I transferred the things I would need from my bulky work bag to a backpack small enough to slide under an airplane seat and called my bank, credit card and phone companies, and, while circling departures to get to the American Airlines terminal, ran through a necessities checklist: Phone? Check. Laptop? Check. Chargers? Check. Passport? Check. AirPods? Check. Finally, as I pulled my bulging bag out of her backseat, Taylor and I exchanged rushed thank yous, goodbyes and other well-wishes. Somehow, we had done it. I had 30 minutes to get to the plane.

Once through the doors, I ran straight to a desk clerk to drop off my luggage, not even bothering with the self-check-in kiosk and rushed up the escalator to security. Last year, Jenny and I had gone to a business conference in NYC. Because she was already registered, she suggested I join TSA Precheck, which I thank my lucky stars I did. My passport scrutinized, and my boarding pass approved, I emerged into terminal 4 and double-checked my gate on the closest LED board. Gate 47A. Which gate was I near? 41. Of course.

Now, I tighten my backpack straps and take off in a full-on sprint down the white and blue scuffed tiled floor, apologizing to the travelers I disturb as best I can at a run. I make it to the gate with literal moments to spare, arriving as I hear my flight's final call over the intercom. The attendant smiles at me, chipper for 11:00 PM.

"I was hoping you'd make it," she says, flattening my crumpled boarding pass.

As she waves me through, I huff my thanks, attempting to rub out a cramp in my side while tramping across the jet bridge.

Finally, gratefully, I slump down in my seat and press my head against the cool plastic of the window. For what feels like the first time since my phone rang, I deeply and fully exhale. I give myself a minute to breathe, trying to rid some of the worry from my body, before situating to comply with the flight attendant's instructions. As I switch my phone to airplane mode, I check my messages one more time—still nothing from Pam. I consider reaching out to her, but I don't want to be a bother.

A fun fact about me is I was born two and a half months early, and as a result, I have cerebral palsy. To this day, doctors are not sure why this is. Most likely, I had a seizure at some point in the birthing process, but this obviously cannot be proven. I have a semi-mild version of CP known as spastic diplegia. This manifests itself in a few physical ways. Due to my weaker and tighter muscles, I walk with a varied gait, and I find tasks that require a more intricate level of hand coordination more difficult than an "able-bodied" person would. Other than that, I am pretty much your average 26-year-old American woman. I love Jenny and Pam, and I know as long as the mother and baby are okay, their family will adapt where needed if necessary. But, while having cerebral palsy has never really bothered me, it's not something I want for Jenny's child.

I say another prayer for them while I put my headphones in my ears and fluff the provided pillow, creating as homelike a space as possible for my body, mind, and soul to crash after the stressful events of the last hour and a half.

Making sure the seatbelt is fastened over my blanket, I put on one of my more mellow playlists, *Cup of Tea*, full of songs from Taylor Swift's *Folklore*, Maisie Peters, Gavin James, Lewis Capaldi, and others, and snuggle into the wall of the plane.

7

Laurel

I wake to a gentle nudge from the elderly man next to me. A stewardess is expectantly gesturing in my direction and moving her lips. It takes me a minute to register that I can't hear her because music is still playing through my headphones.

"I'm sorry," I stammer, withdrawing an earbud and shifting to attention. "What did you say?"

I catch the trace of a grimace before she repeats herself in a pleasant British accent, "My apologies for having to wake you, but we're descending. I just need to check your seatbelt."

"Oh, yeah. Here." A glance down reveals the top half of my blanket has fallen over the strap and buckle.

The stewardess nods as I unfold the covering. "Thank you. Sorry again."

When she's gone, I give myself a moment to get my bearings, stretching as best as I can in my seat. If we've begun our descent, we should be landing in about 45 minutes, which means I miraculously slept for nine and a half hours, give or take. This recognition makes me aware of three things:

1. I'm hungry

2. I'm thirsty

3. I need to pee.

I gather that with our descent comes a halt in the food and beverage service, so I'll have to suffer through until we land, but I can at least go to the restroom. Luckily, the bathroom nearest my row is unoccupied. I unclasp my belt and tap on my neighbor's shoulder.

As soon as the automatic light pops on, I instantaneously lock eyes with the unbelievably haggard individual staring at me from the other side of the tiny room's smudged mirror. I waste a solid minute refusing to claim my reflection and then use the next 5 to 7 to come to terms with the truth presented to me. My perfectly styled hair is now a tangled mess. My brown eyes are tinged red and puffy from sleeping in my contacts. And my face is not only somehow both dry *and* oily but also features what is 100% dried spit in the corners of my mouth. I didn't know it was possible to sleep this hard on a plane unmedicated. After washing my hands, I splash my face with cold water then pat it dry with a paper towel before trying in vain to comb through the knots formed from last night's curls, which can now be generously classified as "matted waves." The eye issue is a lost cause, my saline and lens case being in my checked bag. C'est la vie, I guess.

When I return to my seat, I can see a teeny tiny version of the London skyline through the window. My stomach does a little flip. I'm actually here. *I'm in London.* Maybe it has to do with its association with my favorite Richard Curtis rom-coms, but seeing the metropolis makes me feel like something magical is bound to happen, like I'm going to have a Sherlock Holmes-style adventure or meet my very own Graham Simpkins from *The Holiday*. My imagination is running wild with this scenario when I recall that, upon Taylor's insistence that comfort was a necessity worth the three minutes it would take to change, I am currently adorned in blue pastel joggers and an over-sized Selena Gomez T-shirt which had been discarded on my bedroom floor. The items do match but, when paired with my grey puffer jacket and the UGG ankle boots I swear I only keep ironically, are not my first choice for an international business trip debut. I'm definitely giving off more Bridget Jones vibes than Amanda Woods. If a man notices me in this state, I will marry him on the spot.

I watch tower bridge and the surrounding landmarks grow exponentially in size. As they disappear from view, a garbled voice breaks me from my reverie.

"Ladies and gentlemen, this is your captain speaking. The time in London is currently 17:35 or 5:35 PM. We did arrive a few minutes ahead of schedule. The weather is currently overcast, typical British skies, with a temperature of 17°C, which is 62°F. On behalf of all the crew, thank you for choosing American Airlines."

Moments after he finishes, one of the flight attendants commandeers the speakers.

"Good evening, ladies and gentlemen." I can tell he is trying to sound upbeat, but the time in the air has taken a toll on his stamina. "In a few minutes, we will be landing at London Heathrow. If this is your final destination, you will be able to reclaim your baggage at belt number seven. If you are traveling on from London today, we will be arriving in Terminal 5. Please keep in mind, you may need to use the shuttle to transfer to another terminal."

While he continues, I locate my passport and check the LHR-DUB boarding pass I crammed inside. My connection to Ireland doesn't leave for another two hours. I sigh with relief over the fact I don't have to rush anymore.

Moments later, the familiar thump of landing gear emerging from its holding area sounds through the plane. As my body recovers from the typical jostling of touchdown, I try to connect to the Heathrow Wi-Fi. On my fourth or fifth attempt, the plane is close enough to the airport that I'm successful—a text from Pam dings in, the sound almost swallowed by the metallic clicks of dozens of passengers unclasping their fabric restraints.

SENT 12:01 AM PST:

Mama and baby doing fine :)
No complications.

The next message I receive is a picture of Jenny, absolutely glowing, holding a tiny pink bundle. Followed by one of a big-eyed, light-skinned baby girl with a mess of dark curly hair. It's captioned:

Meet Addison Juniper Colteur-Lansin (AKA: Juni).

Tears well up in my eyes, and I have to cover my mouth with my free hand to keep any noise from escaping. She's beautiful.

As I'm typing a response, a text from Jenny comes through.

Don't forget to use the company card.
This is a business trip ;)
Keep me updated and have fun, kiddo.
I owe you one.

My tears morph into laughter. I send back:

> CONGRATS! (sent with confetti).
> Juni is absolutely breathtaking!!!! Will do!
> (You absolutely do not owe me anything.)

I start to put my phone into my purse when it vibrates again. Taylor has also text me.

> So are you there?!? Are you in Ireland?!?
> Now that all the craziness is over,
> I might be super jealous...maybe?

Then, in a separate message:

> UPDATE ME!!!!(sent with slam)

Followed by:

> I also want the record to show I was
> right about something unexpected
> happening this weekend ;)

I chortle and roll my eyes.

> I literally just landed in London. Calm down.
> You got lucky, and you know it.

She responds immediately.

> I refuse. Don't worry about the store.
> We both know I can cover it myself,

> *but I may have already hired your replacement ;)*

> *I did not. I am part psychic. I feel it in my bones.*

I barely stop myself from physically smacking my forehead. I completely forgot about the store.

The small two-bedroom home off Laurel Canyon Boulevard in which Taylor and I now live was purchased by my father in 1976 as a wedding present for my mother. My parents met in high school and bonded over a shared obsession with the Laurel Canyon music scene. As the story goes, when they were eighteen, my father was willed a large sum of money. Most of it was caught up in the stipulation that it fund his education, but with the rest, he purchased two things: the house, with its original furnishings, and an engagement ring. They married that June.

When unpacking boxes, they realized the pooling of their individual record collections led to a) an overabundance of duplicate recordings and b) multiple machines on which to play them. Once they were settled, what was meant to be one or two weekend garage sales slowly morphed into an extremely small boutique buy-sell-trade music store that has run on most weekends for as long as I can remember. It's a hobby of which neither of my parents have ever grown tired.

The only condition of Taylor and I living there, rather than my parents renting it out as an AirB&B, is that we run the store on weekends they can't. It's an easy gig considering the hours are 10:00 AM-3:00 PM. While there isn't a lot of random foot traffic, we do get a steady amount of people coming to collect items they purchased off the online catalog I helped set up in high school, in addition to a few loyal regulars.

I write back:

> *You star! Jeremy?????*

She replies:

> *Calm down.*

Her mimicry makes my smile wider.

> *I refuse. I take it the party went well, then?*

Her text comes in as it's my rows turn to stand.

> *It could only have been improved if you were there.*

Then:

> *Call me when you get to your hotel.*

It dawns on me that we're assuming I'm staying at a hotel. I don't really know any of the details of this trip except that the concert is tomorrow.

♥

An hour has passed before I'm as comfortable as I can be in the minimally padded plastic chairs outside my final gate, my backpack tossed into the seat next to me. I dip a "Rustic Roll" into the Moroccan Lentil Soup I purchased from a place called PRET, while thumbing through some in-flight reading I grabbed at a giant WHSmith's, along with a packet of what seem to be chocolate-covered cookies strangely called *Digestives*. The more food I consume, the more I feel like a real person again. By the time the wax-lined container is empty, I'm finally able to truly process where I am and what I'm doing. Now that I know the *three* Colteur-Lansins are all happy and healthy, I allow myself to feel the excitement that anxiety was holding at bay. I may currently be a pajama-clad banshee, but I'm about to spend a few days in Ireland! Not to mention, get paid for it.

I check my emails to see if Irene has sent over Jenny's travel plans and reservations. Marked as important at the top of my inbox, in classic Irene fashion, is a single email with all the information I'm looking for easily accessible, complete with all required and referenced attachments.

> *Hi Laurel!*
>
> *I just finished putting everything in your name. Below you will find Jenny's itinerary. I went ahead and left a couple things I couldn't get a refund for or that Jenny thought you'd enjoy. But, she wants you to know you do not have to do any of it if you do not want to.*

My brows knit together. Maybe Jenny and Pam were planning on having a nice dinner after the & Then Some show, but surely I'm not...

I pull myself out of my head and skim the rest of the email.

> *The hotel room should be ready when you arrive. The location and details are attached. Jenny will send any other materials she received from them if needed.*

As my lodgings are no longer my number one priority. I jump farther down the page.

> **Below is an overview of each day:**
>
> **F-August 25** - *LAX-LHR*
>
> **S-August 26** - *LHR-DUB*
>
> **Sun-August 27** - *& Then Some Show @ The Olympia -*
>
> *Name is on the list. Show info attached.*

I'm expecting the next date to read 'DUB-LHR-LAX,' but it doesn't. The rest of the email reads:

M-August 28 - *Free*

T-August 29 - *Guinness Factory - Tickets (2) and info attached*

W-August 30 - *Free*

TH-August 31 - *Bus Tour - Tickets (2) and info attached*

F-September 1 - *Free*

S-September 2 - *Free*

Su-September 3 - *Dinner reservations for 2 at VCC - info attached*

M-September 4 - *DUB-LHR-LAX - info attached*

My adrenaline spikes as my cerebral cortex processes the extended schedule. Why in the world would I stay the full ten days that Jenny and Pam were set to? I'm not sure I can even afford to.

A three-day business trip, sure I can do that, but a week out of my own pocket? I haven't saved for this! I didn't put in a time-off request at work?! Granted, that would need to be approved by Jenny, so it's a non-issue, but still. I know my boss doesn't want to waste her money, but this surprise week-long vacation has thrown me. This can't be right.

I open the attachment that has my return details. It's a ticket for British Airways flight BA 845 at 10:45 AM on September 4. My breath becomes shallow gasps. I expected

Accounting would approve a fee to change the date I flew home. I presumed they had.

As people shuffle and chat around me, voices quick with excitement or harsh with stress, I check the world clock tab in the pre-downloaded app. It's 11:00 AM in Los Angeles. I tap out the sequence necessary to call Jenny via FaceTime Audio, presuming she's awake, but hesitate over the final button as I currently don't trust my deductive reasoning skills. Instead, I text Pam.

> *How are you guys?! How is Juni?*
> *Is Jenny awake?*

My question is answered in the form of a video call.

"Well, hello, London!" Jenny proclaims as soon as I connect. Behind her, I can see the top of a hospital bed. She's beaming, "Don't you have a flight to catch?"

"It boards in 15 minutes," I reply. Scanning my friend's exhausted yet glowing features, my query suddenly doesn't seem as pressing. "Is she there?" I ask quietly, gently, like I'm in the same room.

The maternal pride is evident in her eyes as she responds, "She's sleeping, but I can give you a peek." The camera rotates to reveal a small swaddled body, rosy pink lips parted for content snores, curly hair falling into her face.

"Oh Jenny," I exclaim as she flips the camera back onto herself, "she's incredible. I can't wait to hold her."

"Oh, I've already told her all about you. She's a huge fan. I don't want to embarrass her, but she's definitely counting down the days until you come home."

"About that," I begin, watching Jenny's smile adopt a Cheshire-Cat-like quality, "I know you didn't want the trip to be wasted, but I didn't think I was staying all ten days. I mean, thank you, and I absolutely would love to, but I don't know if I can. I assumed I was only coming to cover the gig." I've glanced at the departure screen as I talked, but can tell Jenny is shaking her head.

"You can absolutely stay," she declares.

"But what about the office?!" I interrupt as I've just ascertained I was the one covering for her while she was gone, and it's not as if she will be back in the office on Monday. Now, she'll be on early maternity leave.

"Everyone will survive," she states calmly. "Nessa and Morgan are splitting our workload. It'll be good for them to try out shouldering some bigger responsibilities."

"But–" I try again. Jenny holds up a finger.

"No, buts. I've taken care of it. You have plenty of paid time off, Laurel. I checked. You have used fewer vacation days since you started at Capitol than I have in the last five years, and this was my third. Take a break. Enjoy my baby-moon."

Somewhat reluctantly, I let a grin grow across my face. She's right. Amidst my panic, I had forgotten about my PTO. If I'm getting paid, I can afford to stay longer.

"Thank you," I say.

Jenny shrugs off my gratitude. "Don't thank me, thank Juni. She's the one who decided you should go."

I laugh. The early stages of a queue has collected near the gate agent desk.

"Thank you, Juni!" I call quietly, standing and hauling on my backpack. "We're about to board, so I should go, but I will keep you updated." Jenny blows me a kiss. As I go to hang up, I add, "Send me tons of pictures!

8

Laurel

The Uber I ordered drops me off in front of The Dean, a boutique hotel in City Centre, around 11:00 PM. I expected a barrage of light and music to be streaming down from the rooftop restaurant called *Sophie's* and obvious exterior indicators of the modern/retro vibe they seem to be aiming for based on the photo I saw at the top of the confirmation email, but from where I'm standing, my hotel is almost indistinguishable from the terraced houses encasing it on either side. The sole visible identifier is two narrow vertical signs mounted between the ground floor front windows on either side of the door. As I lug my suitcase toward the entrance, I note the tile in the walkway also bears the hotel's name, though it's hard to make out in the dark.

I get in a fight with the door, insisting it's a push while it wants to be a pull, or maybe it's inconveniently heavy. Eventually, the clerk, unsuccessfully stifling a giggle, comes to my aid. She looks to be around my age, if not younger, with sparkling amber-tinted green eyes and long jet-black hair tied into a high ponytail.

"You'd be surprised how many people mill with this door," she says as she opens it for me. I am pleased to see I was correct. It was a push, just extremely heavy. "My name's Rosie, and I can get you all checked in right over here." She leads me right, toward the front desk, past a plush loveseat and matching armchairs, and between the round wooden tables that line the nearest wall and a freestanding shelf of somehow coordinating nicknacks. There's a blue neon sign in cursive script above the reception area that reads, "I fell in love here." Across from the desk, now behind me, is a bar. In the corner adjacent to it, a darkened doorway promotes access to a full coffee shop during daylight hours. Overall, the lobby is rather cozy. As she rounds the desk and wakes up her computer, Rosie inquires, "Name?" Her voice is light, and her accent gives it a whimsical quality.

I stifle a yawn, "Laurel Cole."

To my shock, she gasps. "You're the friend of the lady who had the baby." She exclaims, "That story's made its way around to all the hotel staff today. Is she ok? Is the baby doing well?"

"Yes," I say, touched by the sincerity in her face. "They're both great. Thank you for asking."

The hostess seems delighted at the tale's happy ending. "Right. Let's get you squared away then," she insists, tapping a black folder a few times on the white marble top before addressing it. "You'll be in this room here." She's laid out a smaller envelope labeled 'Dylan Suite' that must hold my room key.

Back at Dublin airport, as I waited below signs written in both English and Gaelic indicating baggage reclaim, I had finally checked the hotel attachment. The Colteur-Lansin's had spared no expense with this holiday. I'd audibly gasped as I'd scrolled through the booking. Below the typical numerical data was a brief description of the room's amenities.

Antiqued oak floor. Supersized handcrafted bed. Walls of art. Balcony. 50" Samsung Smart TV. Netflix. Marshall Speakers, Rega RP1 turntable. Classic vinyl. Martin & Co. Limited Edition guitar. Vintage drinks cabinet. Irish munchies. Loaded full-sized SMEG. Nespresso. Buckets more.

I'd let out a small squeal then and there. Not only was I going to have my own balcony, but there was also a turntable and vinyl included in my room! I may never leave it. I'm not as excited about the guitar because I can't play, but I mentally pledged to stare at it lovingly. It's the kind of accommodation I never would have gotten for myself but have always wanted to splurge on. I had been so caught up daydreaming about my future, drinking coffee on my private balcony as *Joshua*

Tree played softly on the record player inside, that I'd almost missed my suitcase coming down the belt.

I'm placed back into reality once again, by Rosie's cheerfully delivered directions.

"You can access the room by taking the lifts behind you to the second floor. You can't miss it. I'll let you get up to bed," she proceeds pleasantly, "but inside this folder is information on the hotel, Sophie's, the rooftop restaurant, and a map of the area. Please don't hesitate to ask if there is anything else you need."

"I won't," I say. "Have a good night, and thank you for your help." Now that I'm actually in the building, it's all I can do not to repeatedly press the call button in anticipation. When the Art Deco doors slide apart, my reflection is mirrored back to me in the colored glass surfaces of the walls and ceiling. I can't help but laugh out loud. This *would be* how I arrive in Ireland.

Rosie wasn't lying. When I alight on the second floor, directly to the right of the elevator bay, on a small landing between two short sets of stairs is a grey door with the words Dylan Suite painted in typeface near the top. My excitement causes me to fumble for a moment with the keycard, but then I'm inside.

I abandon my bag by the door, jaw-dropping free in awe as I commence my initial exploration. The room is large. In actuality, it's two rooms, a lounge area and a bedroom. Directly to the right of the entrance is the door that leads onto the balcony. Across from it, to my left, is the living space. A peek inside establishes it does indeed feature everything promised, plus an orange sectional, gray chair, and three small hexagonal wooden tables. I run to the room next to it and pounce on a large fluffy bed with a grey pillowed headboard. Two orange chairs have been placed at the foot, along with a white version of the hexagon tables from the lounge. Then I recall my favorite part of any decent hotel room: the bathroom!

I push myself up off the mattress and slide over the rolling door that makes up one wall. Stretching so that I can place one hand on either side of the newly made entryway, I inhale sharply. In front of me, on white granite floors that match the walls and countertops, is a large black flat-bottom tub with a white interior. On the wall to my right is another door that must lead back to the hallway. The opposite wall is filled by a massive glass shower and the toilet, partially hidden by a partition. Behind the tub is a window looking out onto the balcony and his and her sinks. Mouth still agape, I fly to my purse, grabbing my phone from its depths. Mind on autopilot, I FaceTime Taylor.

The second I think she's not going to answer, her face appears on the screen. In lieu of a typical greeting, I announce, voice hushed by my budding frenzy, "This room!" I access the back camera and carry her around, noticing other details as I do. Upon inspection, the fridge is indeed "loaded," but we don't waste our time delving into exactly what it entails. And there is a stack of 7-10 vinyl on the shelf underneath the record player, but I don't notice the specific albums. There are collections of books on the varying shelves. In the bedroom, there is a decent-sized closet across from the bed I hadn't spotted originally. And, when I test it, we discover the bathroom shower head is one of those super fancy "rainforest" kinds.

When we've both had our fill of my room, and the elation found in screaming at each other has died down, Taylor demurely admits she needs to go. In my enthusiasm to show her my lodgings, I had completely forgotten about the time change. It's just past three in the afternoon in LA.

"Oh my gosh," I gasp, " I'm so sorry." Then add, at a whisper, "Is he there?"

She blushes and grins, "Yes. He's waiting in the den. We're going to grab food and then watch *Leap Year* in your honor."

"Taylor, you shouldn't have taken my call." I gently chastise.

"I know. But, I wanted to see so that while I'm living vicariously through your real-life *Leap Year*, the visuals are accurate."

"You're annoying, plus I'm not here to propose to anyone, and that is key," I tell her.

"So are you, plus we both know it's Declan who is really the key in that film," she replies, "Call me later though! I need to fill you in!" She's positively glowing but doesn't say more as FaceTime beeps to a close.

It's only then that I register how grimy I feel. Not having the energy to fully commit to a bath, I retrieve my toiletries from my luggage and take a shower. It's heavenly. The provided locally-made soap has a calming lavender scent. My energy seems to wash off my body with the dirt. By the time I'm done with my typical routine, the perfectly plumped comforter is so inviting I have no choice but to crawl underneath it and fall asleep.

9

Laurel

The first thing I see when I open my eyes is a digital clock face blinking a bright 6:24 AM back at me. I'm not sure if it's due to the jet lag or my eagerness over a full day in Ireland, but I don't recoil back into the recesses of the mattress. A tiny sliver of light is straining to peek over the tops of the buildings I can see from my bedroom window, so I stretch and kick my feet out from under the covers, deciding to use this extra time to get settled and investigate what from my belongings actually made the trip. First things first, however, I need coffee.

There's a Nespresso machine in the lounge. So I head that way. It proves easy to operate, and the SMEG is helpfully stocked with both milk and non-dairy creamer. While my cup brews, I step out on the balcony to bask in the early morning sunshine and take in my surroundings. The hotel really is in the middle of the city. It's not on a main road, but down below me, there are already cars and people getting a jump on the weekend traffic that is sure to come. To my surprise, a tram trundles down the asphalt lane. As it carries on its way, I make note of the track line that rounds the bend, filling my lungs with a deep breath and smiling to myself. The weather isn't bad. With a pair of socks and light flannel pajamas, I'm comfortable.

When the coffee machine beckons me with a gentle beep, I return inside and set to work on the mess that is my suitcase. I'm usually a very organized packer. I have various sets of CALPAK Packing Cubes. But there is no rhyme or reason to what lies before me. In our haste, my things were haphazardly shoved inside. I covered toiletries and medicines while Taylor handled clothes, so I'm counting on her to have managed some complete outfits. In preparation for the needed excavation, I tap into my notes app so I can jot down anything I may need to buy.

When I'm finished, I have one thought and one thought only: Taylor Avalon is a goddess among women. I have every piece of clothing and shoe I would have wanted and then some. She not only packed me full weather-appropriate outfits but also made sure I had options from casual to dressy and everything in between. I snicker when I realize I have all three pairs of my matching PJs, as well as the full contents of my underwear drawer. I think she may have actually dumped it on top. She even had enough of her wits about her to pack some of my jewelry in a small box, which she tucked inside an ankle boot. Am I overpacked? Absolutely. But is having nothing to wear an added stressor? Not at all. My shopping list is short as a result:

Power adapter for my curling iron

A few pairs of socks

Some sheer tights in black and nude

A bath bomb (or two) :)

With nothing left to do, and because the noise from the environmental hustle and bustle is now pouring through my unlatched window, I decide to get dressed and venture out for something to eat.

Leaning on the century-old stonework of St. Andrew's church, watching other tourists gawk at the religious attraction or pose for photos with the bronze rendering of Molly Malone, I readjust my shopping bags and do my best to trap my phone between my shoulder and my ear. This morning, as I was getting ready, I had sent my parents a series of texts.

SURPRISE! I'm in Ireland! (sent with confetti)

And Jenny had her baby! (sent with love)

Call me when you wake up.

The time after had passed quickly. I left The Dean with no real plan but to head in the direction of the river since my map app informed me two of the stores I needed were across the Liffey. Another online search had shown me Whelan's, an iconic concert hall, was literally two blocks away and en route, so I set off toward it, grabbing a scone and a second coffee at a quaint mom-and-pop bakery called Gerry's on the way. Outside the club, I stopped to snap a photo of the upcoming gigs, planning to listen to the artists when I got back to the hotel in case there was one I wanted to catch. As the day wore on, the gray sky had brightened to a cheerful blue. The only indication of a breeze, the wispy clouds being carried across it. Essential errands done, I had crossed back over the dark teal water and found lunch. As I exited Nando's, stomach and heart full, I felt my pocket vibrate. I veered out of the central path and extracted my phone to answer what I knew would be a call from my mother.

"Hi, Mom!" I chirp cheerily.

Practically over top of my greeting, she says, "You're on speaker so your dad can hear. Please explain how you are in Ireland."

As briefly as I can, I recount the events of the last 48 hours. My parents occasionally interrupt with a few questions about Jenny, Juni and Pam and react in the places I expect them to. I can hear coffee being poured in the background, so I offer to leave them to their routine.

"No, we'll let you go," Dad chimes in, voice still gruff from sleep, "You're definitely the one being held up here."

I chortle as my mother adds, "Have a good time, Sweetheart. Update us whenever you get a minute."

"I will," I assure her.

Cell stored back in my purse, I head down Suffolk Street toward the LUSH I searched for while eating my lunch. I plan on full-on pampering myself ahead of tonight's concert as it is a) the first time I have ever acted as the **sole** record company representative at a show for a newly signed artist. I go as point for local unsigned artists all the time. But in these situations, if they are local and I get to go, I'm always Jenny's plus one. b) It's my first international gig, and if you can't pamper yourself then, when can you? and c) It's really just an excuse for me to take full advantage of my newly acquired influencer-worthy bathtub.

As I round the corner onto Grafton Street, I notice a small crowd gathered to the side of the walkway. When I get closer, I can hear the sounds of a busker at their center. I'd seen a few already, but none of them had garnered enough onlookers to pool into the main thoroughfare, so intrigued, I slide into a free space near the edge. From a distance, I could have sworn the tenor vocal was singing *Adore You* by Harry

Styles, but now that I'm really listening, it's definitely Taylor Swift's *Cruel Summer*. This perplexes me, but as my hand finds my phone to set a reminder to get my ears checked, the performer shifts effortlessly back into the *Fine Line* single. By the time the song ends, having switched between the two hits a few more times, I'm beaming. The gathering cheers and then thins slightly, allowing me to move to the front. The musician is young - my age, maybe a few years older, casually dressed, but not lazily so. His washed-out t-shirt sleeves are cuffed so they stretch snuggly across his biceps, his jeans relaxed but not baggy. Their length allows his complementary patterned socks to peek out from above his low-cut Converse. He has wavy brown hair that curls around the top of his ears and across his forehead, a kind mouth, and on the cheek nearest me, the beginnings of a dimple forming as he converses with his audience. As they leave, a few people throw coins or smaller notes into the vacant, velvet-lined but well-loved guitar case at his feet, cruelly reminding me I have no physical money to offer.

I turn to go, hoping to get away before the next song when the busker addresses me.

"Don't leg it just because you don't have any cash." At first, I don't apprehend I'm the intended recipient of these words, but then he waves to get my attention, his bright blue eyes crinkling at the corners when they finally lock onto mine.

"Sorry. What?" I stammer, flustered, mortified because I feel blood rushing to my cheeks. *Geez, Laurel. Calm your tits.*

He repeats himself with a laugh, "It's ok. You can stay."

Unbelievably, I do nothing but stare back at him. I have genuinely no idea why he is telling me this and am considering whether or not fleeing the scene would be more or less embarrassing when he chuckles *again* and continues.

"You were eyeing at my guitar case very forlorn, like. I guessed you were a tourist and didn't have any money with you. I usually have a Venmo code, but I forgot it today."

"Oh." That is all that passes through my lips, the word 'oh.'

"Practically no one tips anymore anyway, so don't fret about it." His eyes are twinkling. He's enjoying this, and it annoys me. "American?" he guesses with a grin that is the definition of cheeky.

"Mmhm." I nod, trying to hold my head up while also aware there is a 98% chance it is now tomato red.

"Okay then," he says, strumming his guitar. He gives me a once over, his whole body still brimming with mischief, and steps toward his microphone. Almost instantly, I recognize the opening of Tom Petty's *American Girl.*

The progression of chords triggers my fight-or-flight reflex. Immediately, my brain goes into overdrive. While this is very flattering, I did not ask to be singled out. I wasn't prepared for the extra attention, and I'm not sure I like it. I can sense people staring at me. I bite my tongue purely for something to do, forcing myself to not take my eyes off the singer while my brain tries to figure out if I want to kiss or kill him. I'm doing pretty well until he gets to the second verse, prior to which he brings his full focus back to me, winks swiftly, and Changes. The. Words. The lyrics from the 1976 classic become:

It was kind of warm that day

She stood alone on Grafton Street

She could hear the cars roll by

Out on R811

Like waves crashin' on the beach

The new rendition trips a mental wire, bringing my sanity back in full force. I definitely want to kiss him. However, he is probably flirting this blatantly because while *I* may not have any money, other people watching do, and they are eating out of his - well, *our* now that he has made me part of this narrative - hands. The audience has doubled in size since he started talking to me, and the guitar case is filling much faster than during the mashup.

If I was scouting him as a potential Capitol artist, I would mark that his crowd work was exceptional, and, whilst it did send me into a momentary tizzy, the fact that he changed the lyrics, even as basic as those changes were, on the fly, could mean he's also a songwriter.

As the final notes play out, the busker looks at me again, a smirk plastered on his face. Then, so does everyone else. I have the upper hand here. When the cheers, claps and whistles die down, everyone wants to know what I am going to say, how I'm going to react.

I wait a beat. "Clever," I answer, smiling, "but I don't really like Tom Petty."

This is a lie, of course. I love Tom Petty. He knows it's a lie too, because, while I can guarantee most of the people in attendance didn't notice my Tom Petty & The Heartbreakers 1987 RockNRoll Caravan Tour T-shirt, he definitely did. As I take my leave, he's shaking his head and laughing yet again.

10

Laurel

There is a small possibility I went a little too hard in LUSH. The damage, a significant dent in my bank account, is physically represented by four various-sized black paper bags on the bathroom counter waiting to be unpacked. I have roughly three hours until I would like to leave for dinner, and I plan to use that time to live my best boutique hotel suite life. I've connected my phone to the in-room speaker system but haven't decided what to play. A bottle of wine I purchased on the walk home, not wanting to charge one to my room, is chilling in the fridge.

While I wait for it to be an appropriate drinking temperature, I deal with what I'm going to wear. This is a professional outing, which for my industry, means I should dress business casual. After about twenty minutes of holding items up in front of the mirror, I settle on a black satin midi dress, topped with my cropped leather jacket and my go-to black sandals I had planned to wear to Nightingale. I then lay out a few accessory options. Outfit sussed, I move on to the fun stuff.

Back in the den, I finally assess the snack situation and learn the previously referenced "Irish Munchies" indicates locally branded, typical hotel room fare. I pluck the Keogh's Crisps and the Cadbury Dairy Milk bar from the tray, then open the SMEG to check on the wine. It needs a few more minutes, so I head to the bathroom.

I deposit my snacks on the table I've placed beside the bathtub, run the water, and sort through my LUSH purchases. Removing my shirt so I can transition into The Dean's dream of a bathrobe, I snort to myself, remembering the busker from earlier. His eyes beset my subconscious musings, and I shake them off. Best to not let the mind wander. *Oatifix* smeared all over my face and a timer set, I drop the add-ins—half of a *Big Comforter* bubble bar, a *Groovy Kind of Love* bath bomb, and a *Double Vitality* bath oil—under the water flowing into the now nearly full tub. The bath bomb begins to fizz as I sneak a crisp and turn off the tap before bouncing into the kitchen to procure my glass of wine.

My first bath in this city may be the best of my existence. During the next 45 minutes, I feel like a queen. I change my face mask, wash with rose-scented soap and relax as Picture This, Dermot Kennedy and other artists on Spotify's & Then Some radio serenade me. By the time the water drains, the snacks and glass of Moscato long gone, I'm convinced I am a goddess.

The effect lessens when my emergence from the depths of the tub does not play out as gracefully as it did in my head. But when I'm wrapped in my warmed robe, feet coated in *Volcano* to soften, lips scrubbed and balmed, face toned, moisturized and primed, it returns in full. I can't think of anywhere else I'd rather be.

11

Laurel

I don't get nervous until I'm queued at the box office window at Olympia Theatre. About an hour ago, a taxi dropped me off at a local Mexican restaurant around the corner. I was craving the cuisine, and while 777 was not outrageously expensive nor traditional, I allowed myself the pleasure of charging one "fancy" meal to my company card. In the midst of a vintage car mosaic, a tower of melted candle wax, and a semi-tasteful drawing of a couple obviously engaged in foreplay, I dined on house guacamole, veggie taquitos, and a whiskey-based cocktail that tasted of lemon, raspberry, and ginger. Now, however, I wish I hadn't eaten so much.

The night is charmingly brisk, and as I step up to the attendant, I'm glad I've tied my light grey bell-sleeve sweater to the strap of my purse.

"Name?" the teenage boy asks, not quite monotone but clearly bored.

"Laurel Cole."

"Laurel Cole? Capitol Records?" he inquires, running his thumb over a stack of envelopes, "Yeah, you got a plus one here?"

"That's ok. I only need one." He hands me my ticket and wristband. My wish for him to have a nice evening falls on deaf ears as he's already shifted his attention to the patron behind me.

Inside the venue, I head upstairs to the Portrait Bar, where I am set to connect with & Then Some's manager, Michael Malley, in a few minutes. The room is cool toned, with ambient lighting and a crackling fireplace in one of the corners. Centered in the room is an ornate crystal chandelier under which sits the bar itself. The name, and I'm just guessing here, comes from the ten or so famous Hibernian faces that stare back at me from all angles and distinguish this bar from the one on the ground level.

Before I can order, Michael strides into the room. He and I met briefly when the band flew to LA to sign their contract and do a session in our studio. Local Rock legend turned manager, Michael's tall, shaggy-haired, in his late 30s or early 40s, and can switch on the charm in a snap, but my favorite thing about him is that you can tell how much he believes in his band. He's not in it for the potential windfall that could come his way. He's there to facilitate the growth of his artist.

"Laurel! So glad you could make it, love." He says, hugging me and bending down to kiss both my cheeks. "Everyone is so excited to see you again. How's Jenny? The baby? All good, yeah?"

"Yeah. They're both doing fine," I beam. "I'm glad I could be here too. How are things going?"

"Great! Really great. We're all amped up and ready to go backstage. The support is fantastic. Duo called Veras. Really like their stuff," Michael's head bobs as he talks. "Have you got a drink?" I shake my head. "Sir, please get the lady here a–" He looks at me, eyebrow cocked, indicating I should finish his sentence.

"Whiskey & Coke, please." I decide to keep it simple.

"And a Guinness for me, thanks."

When the bartender has collected our drinks, Michael takes them both, having paid by cash despite my polite protests. He leads me back downstairs. My heels click quietly as I attempt to match his pace along the multiple concrete floored hallways to the band's dressing room. After two fast raps on the door, Michael opens it, announcing my presence to the four young adults spread about the room. & Then Some is made up of Colin Byrne- primarily lead vocals/guitar, ready and well suited to be the music industry's next accented heart-throb; Dylan Quinn, secretly my favorite member,- a pretty brunette who somehow perfectly encompasses both the cool girl and the girl next door, manning the drums; Rory Foley-the quiet, curly-haired bass and piano player with his own sect of admirers; and, rounding out the group, the band's resident rocker chick, Stephanie Mulvenig- rhythm guitar and the occasional lead vocal.

"Laurel!" they all say in almost harmonious unison, getting up to greet me.

Colin gets to me first. He's so tall that when he hugs me, pressing me tight against his tattered t-shirt and lifting me off the ground, my head hits somewhere in between his chest and belly button. "So glad you got to come! No offense to Jenny." He winks, causing my stomach to flip.

"Ok, settle down there, Romeo," Stephanie rolls her eyes as she steps in front of Colin to hug me. "We can't bring him anywhere, I swear. How's the baby?"

"She's beautiful," I answer, "I have a couple pictures if you want to see."

Dylan is next in line. "'Course we want to see!" She squeezes me tight. "Hiya, pet. How was your flight?"

"It was really good. I slept almost the whole time." She laughs as I hand her my phone with Juni's pictures already available on the screen.

"Oh my goodness! What an angel."

"Hi, Laurel." Rory runs a hand through his auburn coils and gives me a brief side hug after passing my phone to one of his bandmates.

"So, how long are you here for," Michael asks, sitting down on the couch and starting on his beer. "In and out?"

I can practically feel my eyes gleam as I once again process my reality, "Actually, I don't leave until the fourth. Jenny and Pam, her wife, had planned to stay an extra week and have one last pre-baby vacation. When things happened the way they did, they kind of gifted the trip to me."

"No way!" Stephanie exclaims from where she's perched herself on the makeup counter. "That's class." I smile at her.

Dylan tilts her head inquisitively from the chair next to mine. "Were you able to bring someone with?"

I shake my head. "No, but that's ok. I honestly didn't know I was staying for longer until I was in London."

"What I'm hearing," Colin says as he hands my phone back to me and flops down on the couch between Michael and Rory, "is that your holiday begins after our show, which means–"

"Colin," Michael warns in a low tone.

The musician glances at him for a moment, baby blue eyes shining, "Which means," he states slowly, "unless Michael reveals himself to be a total tool, we should take you out after the gig."

I'm genuinely stunned by this kind offer and try to object, but Dylan puts her hand on my knee and raises her eyebrows. The band is smiling now, all eyes on their manager.

Michael groans but consents. "Fine," he says, "but we're still heading home at 10:00 AM. Don't think I won't leave your hungover arses here." All four members cheer.

Through the conversation that follows and what I already know from work, I am able to piece together the band's upcoming gig schedule. Tonight is a test run of sorts for their upcoming UK and Ireland tour that kicks off in two weeks in their hometown of Kilkenny. It's routed over a month with a week-long break in the middle, ending back here in Dublin with two more sold-out shows at the Olympia in mid-October. They are then set to write and record what will be their debut album locally until early November, when they are booked for two shows in the US (NYC and LA). By then, we hope to have generated enough American interest to moderately fill out both the Bowery Ballroom and The Troubadour, respectively, sitting them up to open on an amphitheater tour next Summer. This could change, of course, but it's the current game plan.

Eventually, the pre-show playlist signals it's time for the main event. Wanting to catch at least some of Veras, I excuse myself and locate my seat in one of the VIP boxes on the second level. The view is phenomenal, not only of the stage but also of the audience. It's exactly what I need. As requested, my wristband also allows me access to the floor. One of the most useful things Jenny has taught me is in between the main set and encore, get down into the crowd, if possible, and simply listen to what people are saying. It's a surefire way to quickly and successfully assess an artist's fans on what they naturally connected with during a live performance. Jenny gets in and out pretty fast, but I like to hover until right after the lights go down for the second time to feel the electricity that shockwaves through the crowd as the screams swell and music cues in again.

♥

As I linger in the back of the standing section, finishing a water bottle, and watching the encore, I know one thing for sure: If we play our cards right, and we usually do, & Then Some is going to be massive. It'll take time, but all the signs are there. From Stephanie's very first note to the current beat of Dylan's drums, the fans have not stopped screaming. It is made up predominantly of young women, which is what we want, as it is young women who carry our industry and ultimately decide who is made for superstardom and who isn't, and has belted every lyric-even to the songs that haven't been recorded yet. There is an instant artist-to-fan connection here we won't have to try to manufacture. In addition, there is also talent. There is no denying the members of & Then Some are talented individually. They have to be. But together, on stage? They are something to behold. I have a few notes about their image and their sound, which I've jotted down in my phone, but for the most part, Capitol's job will be to help them fully realize the aesthetic they've already crafted for themselves.

As the song ends, I spot Michael, and together, we duck past security and into the backstage area.

"What'd you think?" He inquires louder than necessary now that we're behind the sound system.

"They're fantastic, honestly. I'm really, really excited to be working with you." He beams at me. "Hey, listen," I venture, wanting to get something off my chest, "while it was sweet of them to offer, I don't need to be shown around tonight if it messes with your schedule."

He brushes aside my concern as we enter the dressing room. "Nonsense. I was just trying to reign in Colin. The lad can get carried away sometimes. He's quite the hopeless romantic, that one."

"Helps him write a good song, though," I offer, earning another grin from the manager.

"I am absolutely buzzin'," Colin shouts, bursting through the door, drenched in sweat with his bandmates in tow. He gulps down a water from the fridge before putting his arm on Michael's shoulder, "Now, what's that you were saying about me, Mikey?"

12

Laurel

After the band signs autographs for and takes selfies with a small gathering of fans waiting outside the theatre, we wait fifteen minutes, then set out for a pub called The Auld Dubliner. Steph and Rory seem annoyed by this, citing Temple Bar as the over-priced tourist-filled area of the capital, but Colin and Dylan insist on their chosen destination.

"Christ's sake, Steph, would you drop it," Dylan says, whipping around and cutting her off mid-whine, "Colin and I have it all sorted." Stephanie crosses her arms, the leather sleeves of her jean jacket groaning, but remains silent.

When we round the corner, I know exactly where we are. Well, one building, anyway. The Temple Bar, a pub, though not the one we've set out for, is indeed a famous tourist attraction. With its bright red facade, I've seen it in the background of many an Instagram photo. Dylan links her arm with mine as we pass it, her momentum swaying me into her.

"I know it's a touristy area," she states, "but it's worth seeing since you've never been here before. Plus, the pubs shouldn't be *that* packed on a Sunday night." By the time I register the flash of uncertainty in her gaze as she tucks a strand of dark brown hair behind her ear, it's gone.

"No, this is great," I encourage her.

"Just promise me you'll go somewhere more local another night." She squeezes my arm jovially as she talks, "I bet Col' can recommend a spot. He did a year at Trinity." I wasn't aware Colin was ever a university student. I can't really picture the singer doing anything other than music, but, in the end, it seems neither could he.

The aforementioned charismatic reaches the door of The Auld Dubliner first and holds it wide for the rest of us. As I duck under his arm, I see Dylan was right. The pub isn't empty by any means, but most of the Sunday night crowd is gathered around the stage at the front of the room, so we easily make our way around the back. While the girls scout for a table, Colin and Rory secure space at the bar to grab the first round of drinks. From one of the mismatched, over-used pleather upholstered chairs, I study the venue. The place exudes antiquated charm. The olive green walls and yellow support columns give the bar a warm and comfortable feel. The hardwood floor is stained and scuffed but not dirty.

As Rory hands me my Strawberry and Lime cider, the Dua Lipa cover the trio at the front have been playing ends.

"Thanks very much," The man at the mic says, "This next song is dedicated to a girl I met on Grafton Street today. She, uh, she wasn't very impressed then, but now I've got my lads backing me up, so let's see if she changes her mind, yeah?"

For the second time today, I hear *American Girl.* Thankfully, I'm not talking because my drink goes down the wrong side of my throat, rendering me momentarily indisposed and unable to react in any other way than shamelessly stretching in my seat to get a better view of the small raised platform. Sure enough, it's him. I regain my composure and rejoin the conversation but keep checking in on my friend? Colleague? Stalker?—Well, I would technically be the stalker in this scenario, so let's not go with that— at the front of the room. When he reaches the second verse, he shoots me a smile but keeps the original lyrics.

The rest of his set consists of *Fast Car* by Tracy Chapman, a Jonas Brothers/Ariana Grande mix, and *Chasing Rubies* by Irish duo Hudson Taylor. As the final note fades away, the singer addresses the audience one last time.

"Thanks a million again! My name is Nolan O'Kelley. These two lovely fellas helping me out tonight were Gerry and William. It was an absolute pleasure playing for you tonight," he says, standing. The music will be taking a short break, but in about ten minutes, the legendary Max Elliot will be here with more tunes, so be sure to get another drink and stick around!" The last part of his statement is delivered in such a way that a decent amount of people cheer, even though I'm fairly certain they've never heard of Max Elliot prior to this announcement.

I consider walking over and talking to him, but I'm beaten to it by a small but avid mob of enthusiastic audience members. Never one to compete for attention when men are involved, I let the notion go, stealing one more glance at the performer, who is placing his guitar in its case, before focusing on my friends.

Steph declares the next round of drinks on her but refuses to buy me a flavored cider, so I switch back to Coke and whiskey. While we're waiting for her and Rory to return, someone knocks on the photo-clad wall next to me.

"So you're really not going to come say hello?" The query was directed to me, but it's Colin who replies.

"Nolan, mate! Fantastic stuff. Smashed it!" The two men briefly embrace as I stare on, mouth slightly ajar. I hastily close it, hoping no one noticed, and try to keep my shock and awe internal. As I had come to terms with the fact the flirty musician I thought I'd never see again was also the cheeky pub performer I had just heard, I now have to wrap my brain around the concept that he also somehow knows Colin and that they are evidently chummy!

Colin turns to me, a chipped-nail-polish adorned hand still on the newcomer's shoulder, and makes our official introduction. "Nolan, this is Laurel," he gestures to me. "She is part of our A&R team at Capitol Records and has graciously flown in to see our show."

"Hello, Laurel," my new acquaintance says too formally, building upon our past interaction as if it were an inside joke. He offers his hand, eyes glinting mischievously, and I shake it.

"Laurel," Colin continues, "Nolan and I were roommates my year at Trinity. He's got more musical talent in his little finger than I have in my whole body, but unfortunately, he also has an aversion to what he calls "industry shortcuts," so here he sits playing the same pub we played while we were in school."

This last sentence sparks approximately seventeen questions in my brain. First and foremost being, 'What is an industry shortcut?' However, the direction of the conversation changes when the busker jovially shoves his friend.

"Feck off," he exclaims, laughing and sitting down in Stephanie's vacated spot by my side "Howya, Dylan. You well?"

"Pretty well. Wish you'd agreed to write with us, though."

"I think you lot do alright without me." She shrugs sweetly in response and drains the last of her vodka cranberry. "Did you get all of your shopping done earlier?" Nolan asks, attention back on me.

"Oh yeah," I answer, "I just needed a few things I forgot at home, so nothing too hard to find."

"How much did you forget?" he chuckles. "I saw you walk past the pub I was in with a hape of bags." He's very into eye contact, which, on the one hand, makes me feel like I'm the only one in the room, but on the other, doesn't give me a lot of time to decide what information to respond to: that this is the third time he has seen me today—so maybe he is the stalker, after all!— or his judgment of my shopping habits. I narrow my eyes at him, deciding to tell him it's none of his business when Colin butts in.

"Wait, you two know each other?" he questions from across the table, eyes wide.

"Not really." I start to argue as Nolan puts his denim-clad arm around my neck and drowns my claim in his own.

"Oh, you know, Laurel here watched me busk on Grafton Street today and then publicly humiliated me by rejecting the cover I personalized just for her."

I slide into Dylan, gasping, "Do not try and make me the bad guy here. I did not humiliate you or reject the song! I said I didn't really like Tom Petty."

You can practically hear everything click in Colin's brain. "You're the *American Girl,* girl!" He claps and shakes his head. "What are the odds?"

I, however, ignore him, not finished with Nolan yet. "Look me in the eyes and tell me how I reacted didn't get you more money than fawning over you would have."

The Irishman slouches and lowers his head so that his eyes are level with mine. "I definitely got more money your way, but as Colin will tell you, I don't do this for the money." He winks at me and corrects his posture.

My mouth drops open (I really need to work on that)— *the cocky bastard.* I take comfort in the fact I didn't experience that alone. Dylan's honeycomb eyes are as big as saucers, and her hand is covering her smile. Colin, meanwhile, tries unsuccessfully to hide his laughter with a drink from his empty pint glass.

"Geez, what craic did we miss," the rhythm guitarist inquires as she and Rory reappear, drink-laden.

"Oh, just Nolan." Dylan says, accepting her drink from Rory as he reclaims his seat across from her, "he's in rare form tonight."

As she places an extra pint in front of the busker, Steph exclaims, "What? Did you finally become a dick? Praise Jesus!"

"Only to you, my love," he soothes, standing and kissing both her cheeks before directing his attention down the table, "How have you been, Ror?"

Rory blushes as we wait for him to swallow, "Grand. And yourself?"

"Can't complain."

As she slides in between Colin and Rory, Stephanie hands me my glass. "You know, if you're a whiskey girl, you should go to Jameson Distillery on Bow Street. You don't have to do the tour or anything, but, as a water of life connoisseur myself, they do make some grand cocktails."

I nod, "Really? I don't have anything set for tomorrow, and that sounds wonderful. Is it close?"

"Oh yeah," she assures me, "about a mile across the Liffey." I'm checking the distance from my hotel on my phone when Dylan leans around me.

"Nolan," she asks innocently, "are you working tomorrow?"

He shifts forward as well, toned arms propped on the table. "I am not, as luck would have it. And," he pauses here for effect, "I haven't been to Jameson in a very long time." I can feel his eyes on me now. "So if someone wanted to invite me...I mean, I certainly wouldn't want to intrude, Dylan."

I look up from my phone slowly. & Then Some's drummer and frontman are both staring eagerly at me. The matching sparkle in their eyes makes me feel very much like a pawn in their chess game. But, seeing as I don't know anyone else here and that I can't come up with a good reason to turn down the attractive accented singer...

I move to fully face him, permeating my voice with as much saccharinity as possible, "Do you want to come to Jameson Distillery with me tomorrow?"

"Now, what would have possibly given you that idea?" "he answers with a grin.

A couple rounds later, none of which I have been allowed to buy, Rory suggests we call it a night. There is some protestation, namely from the Colin and Stephanie camps. But as my bedtime alert recently announced it was 12:30 AM, I agree with him, and since it's my outing, I have the deciding vote.

Outside in the street, the light breeze parting around us, everyone waits for me to call an Uber. Once it's confirmed,

I thank the band again for the evening and promise to repay the favor when they're back in LA. After we individually run through goodbyes, they all wish me safe travels and head off into the night. The dynamic between them has somewhat changed with the addition of alcohol. Rory leads the way now, with Dylan holding onto his arm. Stephanie has jumped onto Colin's back, and the two of them lag behind, already bickering about something surely inconsequential. I chortle as I watch them go.

"So, I guess I'll see you tomorrow," Nolan suggests, reaching up to rub the back of his neck, surprisingly sheepish now that we are alone. "Four O'clock okay to start drinking? They close pretty early, like six, I think."

"Yeah, four is fine with me," I confirm with a reassuring smile. "Thanks for coming with."

"'Course," he states matter-of-factly, then adds, all bravado, far be it from me to leave a damsel in distress."

I roll my eyes, muttering a secret retort as my car slows in front of us. "You sure you don't want a ride?" I ask as I get in.

The busker smirks to himself and closes the door behind me, continuing to talk through the rolled-down window, "Nah, I'm good to walk, but right quick, give me your phone." I do as I'm told without protest, not sure if it's the liquor in my system or my own curiosity that has gotten the better of me.

Returning it, he offers an explanation, "Text me where you're staying. I'll pick you up around 3:45 PM. It's a tad far for a walk." Without giving me time to respond, Nolan taps on the roof and steps back onto the sidewalk, ducking his head to the driver to thank her for waiting.

As we pull away, she regards me through her review, "Not that it's any of my business, but if that's your other option, what are you doing letting me take you home, pet."

13

Laurel

Back in my hotel room, nestled under the fluffy white comforter and silken sheets, I can't sleep. Ahead of getting in the shower, I'd sent the Irishman The Dean's address. Taking my phone off sleep mode and opening my texts, I see he's responded with minimal effort, 'thumbs up' -ing my message. I sigh. *At least he has an iPhone.*

I put my phone back on the nightstand and pout. I'm not really sure what I had been hoping for or why. I mean, he's attractive, and he's flirty, but in the end, he lives in Ireland, and I live in LA, and I don't do casual flings on principle, so that's not going to happen, and maybe long-distance could work if we had more time to establish the relationship, but we only have eight days, seven really, and I don't actually know if I'd even want to date him at all if we did live in the same city. Maybe he's just attractive and flirty, and I won't enjoy his company one-on-one and… Oh My Gosh, what am I even thinking about right now!

I groan and roll onto my stomach, shoving my face into a pillow. Being a woman is annoying sometimes.

My phone dings, causing me to shoot up like a rocket and snatch it off the table, which makes me hate myself a little more than I currently do, especially when it's not Nolan but Jenny who has contacted me. I click on the text preview.

> Hey, kiddo! Hope this doesn't wake you.
> We finally got Juni down for a nap,
> so I just saw your notes and video
> from the show. Sounds fantastic.
> I'm so excited to work with them.

I type out a reply.

> Just now getting to bed.
> How are you all doing?
> Everyone sends their love, by the way.
> They missed you!

Jenny's response comes with a photo of a bouquet of pink and white carnations, lilies, and daisies. I zoom in to read the card: Congrats on your new baby! See you stateside! - Michael, Colin, Rory, Dylan and Stephanie xx

> I highly doubt that. ☺
> I'm sure you were much more fun.
> We're all good here. Already tired (lol).
> Mick Jagger is obsessed with Juni.

*I'll try to get it on video later.
I should sleep while I can!*

After 'loving' the photo, I send:

Sweet dreams!

Deciding I should get some rest too, I put my phone back to 'Sleep' and slide deeper into the blankets. I can resume overthinking tomorrow.

14

Laurel

I awake the next morning to the sun streaming through my window and promptly yank the comforter up over my face. A dull ache lingers behind my forehead, an unwanted extension of the night before. There's Tylenol in my toiletry bag, but the bathroom seems miles away. I mope in my own self-induced misery for a moment, finding the strength needed for my quest. Eventually, I scrunch my eyes into as small a squint as humanly possible and feel my way to the doorway. The washroom, naturally darker, is easier to navigate. I reach the sink and down two pills, then fill both provided glasses with water and lower myself onto the cool tile floor to pout and reconsider my life choices.

When my pity party decides to vacate the premises, I struggle to my feet and begrudgingly make my way to the coffee machine. Standing over it, wafting the comforting aroma into my nostrils, my stomach grumbles. I look up at the TV. The digital clock in the center reads 9:45 AM. No wonder

I'm hungry. I grab my MacBook off one of the hexagonal tables, along with the coffee creamer from the fridge, and sit down in front of the Nespresso. Opening *Google Maps*, I do my best to retrace yesterday's morning jaunt. I passed a cute breakfast place on my walk. Maybe I can find it again.

I'm about a quarter of the way through my much-needed cappuccino when I click on a place called *KC Peaches* and immediately recognize the teal exterior. Success. I skim through the menu and text myself the address. With a semi-caffeinated brain and a plan, I'm in a much better mood. Taking one more drink of my coffee, so it's less likely to slosh out of my cup, I amble over to the record player and thumb through the selection. Some notable titles include Damien Rice's *O* and *Born in the U.S.A.*, but I settle on Fleetwood Mac's *Rumors*. Ahead of commencing my morning routine, I snatch the half-empty sleeve of *Digestives* from my backpack: something to hold me over 'til breakfast.

The sun is bright in a cloudless sky, meaning the weather today is warmer than I expected. I'm glad I decided to shed the denim jacket I had originally planned to wear back at the hotel. Belly full of avocado toast and a superfruit salad, I decide to follow a more scenic route home. Strolling up Wicklow Street, basking in the simple joy of the brightly colored storefronts, I catch sight of a small black one, only wide enough to cover the doorway underneath it and split between two merchants. Written on the top of the sign, in plain white capitals, is THE SECRET BOOK & RECORD STORE. I don't think twice as I cross the street.

Los Angeles has a good number of record stores. It should, it's Los Angeles. And while I like Amoeba Music fine and frequent the store often for new releases, my favorite shops are the tiny second-hand stores like The Record Parlour and Atomic Records. I have found many a beloved vinyl that way.

I slide my sunglasses onto my head as I pass through the corridor. Ads for gigs long past, old album release posters, and other music memorabilia paper the walls to the store entrance. The musk of the old books greets me before I can see them. At the end of the hall, a step down reveals a single room that makes up the entire reseller. Books are piled high on tables in the center, or rather wood slabs held up by a plethora of card-board boxes, and shelves brimming with volumes run along all the visible walls. I learn the actual name of the establishment is Freebird Records. I applaud their use of intrigue to get people through the door. There's a hidden alcove in the back. Entering it, I'm met with hundreds if not thousands of new and used CDs and case upon case and cart upon cart of used and vintage vinyl.

Aware I do not have all the time or money in the world, I allow myself to flip through the classic rock and R&B filings. There is not a lot of old vinyl I do not have, thanks to my parents' collections and the store, but I keep a running wish list in the back of my mind for occasions such as these.

About to declare the venture a bust, I have to keep myself from shrieking when I land on *Sam Cooke* (1958). There is no way this is an original pressing, but I don't know if the album was ever re-released. I slip the record out of its sleeve and inspect it. It's covered in fingerprint smudges, but those can be wiped away. Other than that, it seems almost pristine. I re-sheath it and tuck it under my arm.

Running on adrenaline now, I sift through the Irish section just in case, pulling out *The Corona*s' most recent album, *Wasteland, Baby!* for Taylor, and even though I already have it, T*he Academic's Acting My Age* EP because they're part of the Capitol family and it's exciting to run across it in this store.

Back out on the brick-lined street, I'm giddy with excitement over the four purchases swinging in the bag hanging off my arm. I've taken less than three steps toward home when I see a young girl placing a double-paneled sign in front of a royal blue doorway: Murphy's Ice Cream. I pause. Why not? I **am** on vacation.

15

Laurel

I don't so much get ready to go to Jameson Distillery as touch up what I already did this morning. I don't change out of my blue polka-dot wrap dress, but I wipe off the outsoles of my Keds. I let down and re-curl a few deflated pieces of my hair, quickly brushing through them with my fingers to blend them in and freshen up my makeup with new coats of concealer, mascara, blush, and highlighter.

The hit Bruce Springsteen album is locked onto the turntable when my phone rings, not my cell phone, my room's phone. I hastily swallow the bite of pre-made pasta salad I picked up at Tesco Express on the way back to The Dean as I answer it.

"Hello?" I say, glancing at my iPhone's screen. It's 3:42 PM. Nolan should be here any minute.

A female voice chirps uncertainly back to me, "Hello, miss, there's someone here who would like to talk to you. He's very insistent. May I put him on?"

Instantly aware of where this is heading, I scoff internally. "Yes. It's no problem."

"Hello, Laurel." The busker's baritone voice comes through the receiver.

"You could have just texted me, you know?" I laugh, "I would have come down."

The Irishman gasps, "What kind of charlatan do you take me for?" Chuckling, he adds, "I tried to come up, but they wouldn't give me your room number."

" I can't say I blame them. I'll be right there." I hang up before he can poke fun at anything else, carefully stop the album, grab my purse and jacket from the back of the couch and head to the elevator.

When I reach the ground floor, Nolan is sitting in one of the plush grey chairs by the lobby windows, scrolling through his phone. He's dressed in a fitted black t-shirt and dark jeans, making me glad I stuck with a casual vibe as well. Glancing up as I walk toward him, he grins (My stomach does the tiniest of somersaults.).

"There you are," he declares, standing, sounding like I had kept him waiting for half an hour instead of a few minutes.

"Hey," I respond, stopping in front of him. "How was the rest of your day?"

"T'was alright," he shrugs. "Nothing special. Yours?"

"Good. It was good," I reply, fidgeting with my fingers until I think to clasp them in front of me. "I went out for breakfast, then explored for a while."

There's a brief lull during which we awkwardly stare at each other, but Nolan breaks it by freeing his keys from his pocket and gesturing toward the door. "Shall we crack on?"

"Sure," I say. He grabs a grey jacket off the arm of his chair, throws it over his shoulder, and makes his way out onto the street, pulling the door ajar with no apparent exertion at all.

Parked a few yards down the road is a matte golden, older-make, boxy, Fiat hatchback we definitely do not have in the States. I stand on the sidewalk, balancing on uneven cement, as Nolan unlocks his car and walks around to the driver's side. I open my door, having heard the lock click. To which, he simply rests his hand on the roof and stares at me.

"Oh, you're driving then?" he asks, eyes alight. I peer into the car to see the steering wheel directly in front of me. Mumbling to myself for my idiotic mistake, I make my way to the other side of the vehicle, trying to hide the blush creeping into my cheeks.

As I slide into the proffered entrance, the local chuckles, "There we go." Closing the door after me, he climbs into the driver's seat. "Play me something," he invites, passing me the AUX cord and gearing up the car.

"What?" I question, caught off guard by his blunt nonchalance.

"Play me something." He repeats himself. I furrow my eyebrows in response, staring at him as he navigates out of his parking spot. "You're the one who works in A&R. Play me something you think I'll like, something new, to me anyway."

"I don't know what specific strangers are going to like," I stammer, "that's not what I do. It's not person-specific."

"Ok, well then, play something you like."

I stare at him for a moment. "Fine," I sigh. I like showing people new music, but I like doing it once I know their tastes. I scroll through my followed artists on Spotify, considering the songs I've heard Nolan cover and the way he plays them, trying to find someone with at least a similar sound. It takes me longer than I'd like.

"Any day now," he prods without removing his eyes from the road.

"Do you want me to hurry, or do you want to hear something you might enjoy," I snap in return. This earns me the slightest smirk as he holds one hand up in mock surrender.

As *Something to Hold on to* by Harry Strange begins to play, I glance over at him, bracing for a teasing retort, but his face is expressionless, eyebrows nearly knitted together as he genuinely listens to the song I've chosen. Much to my regret, I discover this to be an immense turn on. When the song gets to the chorus, his mouth splits into a grin. I have to look away, suddenly very aware of the lyrics. Maybe this wasn't the most prudent song choice. Near the second chorus, the driver inhales sharply, reclaiming my attention, but I find him enthusiastically bobbing his head to the beat.

"That was bang on," he beams at me as I pause the music, "Can you send it to me?" I nod.

"Ok, your go," I say as I text him Harry's artist page link.

"Unfortunately for you," he states, easing his car over to the street's edge, "we're here."

I get out of the vehicle and endeavor to orient myself. I don't see anything identifying Jameson right away, but maybe we're around the back or something.

"You alright?" Nolan inquires, shrugging into his jacket.

"Yeah. This just doesn't seem like where I imagined a distillery to be. In my head, there needs to be more space, I guess."

He laughs. "That's because we're at mine. The distillery is right around the corner, though." He pauses, and I can see the flare of panic in his eyes that's frequent in people I've recently met. "I figured it's best if I drop off my car, but we can get a lift from here." The end of his sentence is asked more than stated.

"Oh no, I'm good to walk." I smile at him reassuringly. It's not lost on me that this means he went out of his way to pick me up. "Thanks for saving me an Uber."

"Don't mention it," he replies easily. "If I hadn't, then I wouldn't have heard that song." He winks at me before spinning on his heel and leading the way down the road.

16

Laurel

Because we aren't doing the tour, I only get to see the lobby of Jameson Distillery, but the longer we sit at the bar, the more enchanting it becomes. This could be attributed to the fact I am evaluating the Irish tourist attraction through American goggles or because I have already had two drinks; the first a classic Whiskey Ginger, the second a specialty cocktail that tastes of butterscotch called a Molly Bán. But, as the shadows on the far wall signal the progression of afternoon into evening, I slowly realize it is because I feel like I'm sitting in the grand foyer of a refurbished castle.

This probably isn't the distillery's intention, but given that the former factory has been here since the late 1700s (according to a plaque I read by the door), I don't think it can be helped. The flooring, some of which has been replaced by glass panes, allowing you to see the tunnels below, is made of large slabs of stone. The walls are mostly exposed grey brick. Part of the back wall is rounded, reminding me of a turret, one side of which houses an obsolete roped-off fireplace. To top it all off, hanging from the ceiling, over the entryway, is a five-tiered Jameson bottle chandelier.

Over the past hour and a half, Nolan and I have wound our way through the usual "you're basically a stranger" topics and other various small-talk. He asked about Los Angeles, how I like it, and how I came to work at Capitol, rounding off with what brought me to Ireland. I, in turn, have learned that he grew up a few hours from the city, moved to the capital for his terms at Trinity, finished his course in Business, Economics and Social Studies, and tried for a year or so to find a job he didn't hate. Eventually, he decided to throw in the towel. After much coaxing from Colin, Nolan had begun busking and working what he calls The Pub Circuit. What began merely as a way to be able to make enough money to stay in the area still pays his bills three years later.

At one point, I tried to extract information about what Colin was like as a first-year college student, but his friend remained tight-lipped.

"Ah, no. Not my place," he had said, eyes swimming with memories, "at least not without him here to defend himself."

All in all, it has been a very pleasant outing. However, and this is barely a con, somewhere in between our first and second cocktails, the staff changed for closing. Our laid-back, tattooed, unobtrusive male bartender was replaced by a vivacious blonde woman whose extreme attentiveness had absolutely nothing to do with me and everything to do with my conversation partner. By the time we ordered our final drinks, it was as if I wasn't even there. For the most part, I found this amusing and her subtle flirting techniques admirable. If he and I knew each other better, I would 100% point out that she is clearly interested, but we don't, so I privately invent a drinking game to play when she stops by. One sip for witty banter. Two sips if she attempts to touch him. One gulp if he actually reciprocates her advances.

Now, with our third drink almost gone and the distillery closing in thirty minutes, I call the mixologist over to settle the tab.

"Just the three cocktails then, ma'am?" she suggests with surface-level congeniality.

"No, no. I'll do all six," I say. The quickly masked flare of annoyance that crosses her face confirming my suspicion that she was hoping to write her number on Nolan's receipt.

"Hey, no. You don't need to do that," he protests, reaching out and putting his hand over mine as if my card is not already with our server.

I insist, holding his gaze, which in my inebriated state is equal parts overwhelming and inviting, and cite last night's bill, "It's to make up for yesterday."

The woman has frozen between us, currently unsure whether or not to run the full amount or my portion.

Eventually, the singer reclines in his chair and places his hands behind his head, stating in a cool, calm voice, "Well, it is the least you can do, considering you didn't tip me."

As the server disappointedly walks away, I gasp and slap my acquaintance in the chest. "I was talking about the pub! And yesterday, you said it didn't matter." I grab my drink off the counter and suck down another mouthful to try to stop my brain from analyzing the tone and density of Nolan's pectoral muscle and how it had felt under my hand, however brief the physical contact was.

He looks at me, eyes gleaming, rubbing the sore spot, "Well yeah, because I knew I was going to try and play off you for a few extra euro."

"I knew it! I knew that was what you were doing," I exclaim, pivoting away and fixating on my cocktail.

The Irishman laughs. I'm only codding you." I stare at him perplexed, causing his laughter to settle deeper in his stomach. When he's recovered, he closes the gap between us and states in an over-exaggerated American accent. "I'm just joking."

"Sure…" I say, half glaring at him as he sips his whiskey.

"I am!" He returns defensively, propping his arm up on the bar. "I really did think you'd like the song. The lyric change was a bit cheesy in hindsight, but it came to me in the moment, and I went with it."

"I did like it," I tell the divot I've found in the wooden bar top.

"Ah, I reckoned." When I raise my eyes back to his, he's beaming as if he's won the lottery. After a beat, he turns away and drains the last of his glass. "How are you feeling?" He inquires as he stands.

" I'm fine," I reply as I collect my card and fold the receipt into my wallet. Nolan holds out a hand to help me off my stool. Even with the assistance, the dismount turns me into a pendulum. "On second thought," I correct, blinking a few times to steady myself, " maybe water and food would be a good idea."

He chuckles and places my hand on the crook of his arm, "Ok, petal. Let's go."

17

Laurel

Out on the street, the subtle chill in the air feels good on my skin. The sound of the evening traffic intermingles with the caws of seagulls gathering to roost.

"So, where to?" I wonder, observing Nolan as we meander over the cobblestones.

He inhales before countering, "Are you craving anything specific?"

I ponder this for a moment. "No, not really. To be honest, I don't feel particularly hungry. But I need water, and food in my stomach would be helpful."

"Hmmm," he muses while considering our surroundings. In the more than brief pause, I take advantage of our close quarters to better examine his features. He has a splatter of light freckles across his nose. The cerulean in his eyes is rimmed with grey. And there's a small scar near the center of his upper lip I hadn't noticed prior. I'm resisting the compulsion to run my thumb over it (okay, maybe food would be more than helpful) when his face splits into what I'm learning is a signature grin. "I have an idea. Can you wait here just quick?" I laser my focus on our location and discern we've made it back to Nolan's car. I let go of his bicep in answer.

"Ok?" I question, but he merely starts walking backward toward what I assume is his apartment.

"Stay by the bonnet. I'll be right back."

He has clearly had some sort of epiphany, so I do as I'm asked and wait. From this side street, I can see the colors of the dwindling sunset mixing in the sky. I watch the pastels fade to deeper hues while I speculate on what he's come up with.

"Right then," Nolan says, bringing an end to my contemplation a few minutes later. When he reaches the curb, he passes me a Hydro Flask. The straw lid already popped and accessible.

"What if," he begins, "since neither one of us is hungry, we head toward your hotel and see if anything looks good on the way? You save on a taxi. I get to see if I missed my calling to be a tour guide. It's a win-win."

I drink from the water bottle. He doesn't need to know I would have agreed to whatever he had suggested, but the fact of the matter is I couldn't have come up with anything better.

There's no point in trying to hide the smile that escapes my lips.

"May I set one condition?" I request. Nolan's only response is a raised eyebrow. "I told Dylan I would avoid Temple Bar."

Transferring a second canteen into his now empty hand, he offers me his arm, "I can work with that."

As it happens, Nolan would have made a decent tour guide. Each landmark, statue, and old building he points out is accompanied by both useful facts and charming anecdotes. Not everything I'm acquainted with has historical significance. I am also gaining knowledge on some of his favorite haunts, pubs he and his friends frequent, and a small park in which Colin got a black eye playing rugby when he was nineteen.

The two of us are so caught up in the scenario we've created that, after an initial few, we completely forget to keep an eye out for enticing eateries. It's only when a new segment is introduced as 'A Brief History of Whelan's' that I grasp how close we are to The Dean. I stop short in the middle of the sidewalk.

"Oh no," I giggle, cutting the monologue off, "my hotel's around the corner. We didn't eat."

"Ah shit." he replies, "Sorry. Let me think." We step out of the middle of the walkway while my guide gets his bearings. I use the interim respite to finish what remains of my water bottle. "Actually, there's a place down the street you may like. I can't exactly remember the menu, but I know it's close, and if the inside is too busy, the beer garden is heated." As if in response, my stomach growls loud enough that a passerby literally turns his head. "Right then," Nolan laughs. "That answers that question."

He grabs my hand and pulls me back into the flow of pedestrians. No more than sixty seconds have passed when I am ushered back off the pavement and through a light green doorway, the top of which is overhung with periwinkle flowers clustered in various color arrangements and magnitudes.

Inside Jimmy Rabbitte's Speakeasy, the dark green walls are covered in eclectic photos of numerous sizes and shapes. Small unframed prints are tacked to a few of the wooden ceiling beams, which match the floor and accent wall behind the bar. The name written on the window in swirling yellow script implies the establishment must somehow get bigger, but I deem its fanciful front room more than suitable. Fortunately, so must Nolan because together, we head to an empty table near a large portrait of a terrier in an 1800s-style suit. With what I'm sure is great poise and elegance, I hoist myself onto the high booth, which runs along the wall. The busker places his jacket on the corresponding stool before venturing to the crowded counter, coming back a few minutes later laden with water and menus.

The fare at Jimmy's is what you would expect at an upscale tavern while keeping with the whimsical theme. In the end, I go for a goat cheese flatbread, Nolan selects a burger, and we decide to split a side of sweet potato fries.

Our order placed, I excuse myself to the restroom. In the short time that has elapsed since our arrival, the restaurant has gotten ever fuller, evening patrons adding to those who remain from the afternoon enticed by ongoing athletic competitions or wrapping up earlier meals. I wind my way through the growing throng, cautious of stray elbows and drink-toting hands, my intuition guiding me through a side door embellished with a four-pane window of textured yellow-tinted glass and down a flight of sturdy stairs. In the slightly graffitied mirror of the washroom, I'm pleased to see the walk and brisk night air have left my reflection's skin perfectly flushed. I reapply my lip gloss and gently run my fingers through my hair to unwind any knots. By the time I'm back, our food is already on the table.

"Oh! That was fast," I say, hopping onto the dark leather seat.

"I know. I was surprised, too," Nolan responds without looking at me. I trace his eyeline to a TV anchored on a half wall to my right. Displayed across it is a soccer match. My conversation partner preoccupied, I people watch as I eat. Most in the congregation are caught up in the game. There are a few groups of friends ignoring it, talking animatedly, content in the entertainment of their present company. A few tables over, two young women sit crammed into the long seat, obviously swooning over whatever has captured their attention. Intrigued, I locate the source. There's another screen on my left, mounted to the wall next to the bar top. It seems to be the sole one in the pub not showing sports but instead playing a movie. When I discern the film is *Leap Year*, I gasp in excitement, much like my counterparts down the booth. However, I unexpectedly take in an inordinate amount of my drink in the process and choke.

"What?!" Nolan startles, tearing his eyes away from the television, distracted by my sudden sputtering.

"Nothing. Nothing. I'm fine," I say, gesturing to the continuing feature behind him and reaching for a napkin. He pivots to see what I'm reacting to but promptly returns to me for an explanation, knit eyebrows forming a trio of wrinkles over the bridge of his nose.

"Big Matthew Goode fan, are you?" He guesses when my coughing renders me unable to answer. "You know he's not Irish?"

I shake my head, "No. I mean, yes, and I know, but," I pause to clear my throat again so that I can properly proceed with my justification, "my friend and I were just talking about *Leap Year*. It's one of my favorites." I feel bad for making a scene over something so trivial, but a smirk appears on Nolan's lips.

"So, you're a fan of the Irish."

I narrow my eyes at him and bite a fry, "I'm a fan of that movie." He chuckles, maintaining eye contact until I quickly lose him once more to RTÉ One.

Since his attention is elsewhere, I withdraw into my phone and text Taylor.

> *They're playing Leap Year in a restaurant I'm at and it reminded me I promised to call you. Can I FaceTime you tonight your time?*

I then add:

> *(would like to FT regardless. I have tea... kind of...maybe...probably not)*

I know she's at work, so I don't wait for a response.

As we sit, with the time that has passed and food in my belly, I begin to feel better. Much closer to sober, I pick up the specialty drink menu and noncommittally peruse it.

"Contemplating a nightcap?" my table mate asks.

"Is it technically a nightcap at this hour?" I reply, glancing at him over the list.

He snorts. "Well, I was going to see if you were game for dessert, but cocktails work too."

"Me getting a drink does not mean I am not game for dessert," I retort.

"Noted," he says, the mirth in his voice abruptly changing into a scowl as he disparages the referee over a call I didn't see.

I lean into his eye-line, wanting to keep up the conversation. "So," I open, playing with the paper straw that has begun deteriorating amongst the ice melting at the bottom of my glass, "where's the rest of it?"

"The rest of what?" Nolan questions, features still trained on the LED display.

"This place." My gesture to the atmosphere of the restaurant is big enough to capture his attention. "The window advertised a 'speakeasy.'"

"Oh, that must be to help with the aesthetic. It's only this room and the back patio." As I mull over this marketing betrayal, the remaining menu is slid into my peripheral, a callused index finger tapping the sweets section. "I'm thinking cheesecake. What sounds good to you?"

When the match reaches half time, Nolan ventures back to the bar to order one Salmon of the Black Water, which I'm hoping tastes like strawberries, one Old Fashioned, one sticky toffee pudding, and one slice of Ferrero Rocher cheesecake.

Cocktails gone and my energy dwindling, we're forced to get a box for what remains of the two desserts and agree to split the tab before wrapping up in our coats and heading out into the ever-darkening night. I'm not treated to any more facts from O'Kelley Tours the short distance back to The Dean, but Nolan fills the silence, chattering on about the kind of season whichever team that was playing on-screen in the bar has been having, mind still on the match. I listen, enjoying the cadence of his accent and responding where needed. I don't dislike sports, so I don't mind the subject, but my lack of all but mild general knowledge, especially when it comes to 'football,' keeps me from truly participating.

As we reach my hotel, he finishes a story about the time his favorite midfielder got injured. We stay close, our combined body heat combating the dropping temperature so that I have to tilt my head back to see his face.

"Thank you for walking me back. I know it wasn't far, but I appreciate it," I say after his tale comes to a close.

"No worries," he replies, sticking his hands in his pockets and stepping onto his own sidewalk square.

I draw my jacket closer together now that he's further away, "Tonight was fun."

"Yeah, it was good craic."

"It was good craic," I repeat, teasing whilst testing out the local jargon. The word sounds strange coming out of my mouth, but Nolan grins at me. In the pride I feel over causing his expression, a thought I'd been mulling over spills from my lips. "I don't know what your plans for tomorrow are," I muse, "but if you're free from two to four-ish, I have an extra ticket for the Guinness Storehouse Tour."

As I've spoken, my confidence has dwindled. Uncertainty and mortification over the possible rejection rapidly replacing it. To save myself, I hurriedly spit out an explanation. "My boss and her wife were going together, so—"

He interrupts me. "I can be free from two to four tomorrow, yeah."

"Ok, cool." I blush, my relief palpable in the silence that follows. *'Ok, cool?!' Am I in middle school?*

"I guess I should let you go in," he says, bringing an end to our brief staring contest. Without warning, he closes the gap he instigated earlier and pulls me snug against his chest. Just as I begin to feel comfortable, he lets go and backpedals long enough to shoot me a wink as he heads back in the direction we'd come.

I frown, calling after him. "Nolan!" At the sound of his name, the busker halts in his tracks, but not before his momentum pivots him again. "Please tell me you're not planning on walking all the way home."

His face splits in the cocky manifestation of mirth I'm coming to know well. "Nah, I'll grab a taxi when I get to Stephen's Green." From this distance, I can't see his eyes, so I can't tell if he's joking or not.

"You swear?"

"Goodnight, Laurel," is the only response I get as he once again turns away.

18

Laurel

At 3:15 AM the next morning, Nightly's *summer* blares from my phone, swiftly accompanied by an incessant beeping from my bedside table. When I got back to my room a brief four or five hours ago, I checked my phone to see if Taylor had responded to my text. She had – nine times. The first several messages were sent one after the other, a barrage of life updates and explanation demands.

> *YES! I have big news. Like major.*

> *Plus I'm in need of your expert advice.*

> *There's construction on Coldwater this week, so traffic has been Hell.*

Which is kind of your fault because
I can't use the carpool lane in this
time of actual need.

But, I love you anyway
and I should be home by 7.

TEA?!? OMG what is it?

Is it a guy?!?

The next arrived 15 minutes later.

You're not responding. It's totally a guy.

And then 10 minutes after that.

Laurel, I checked and it is only 9PM
in Dublin. I know you're not asleep.
I swear, if it's not a man and
you're ignoring me...

All I had responded was:

Great! I'll call you around 7:30PM
to be safe! Miss you!

before putting my phone on 'Do Not Disturb' and going
to sleep.

I've set two alarms this morning in an effort to ensure I actually make it out of bed. I groan, despite the fact I can't wait to talk to my friend and begin incoherently smacking the alarm clock, as ceasing the more unpleasant noise is my first priority. It takes enough time for Jonathan Capeci to get half-way through the first chorus for me to successfully turn it off. I grab my phone and flop back onto my pillows. After hitting the stop button, I allow myself one deep breath, then sit up and tug on the pair of cream heathered socks I had the presence of mind to lay out ahead of crashing.

Dragging myself to the coffee maker, I do some light stretching as it steeps. Hot drink in hand, I retreat back to the bedroom, intent upon snuggling back under the covers and FaceTiming Taylor from a comforter cocoon.

But simply ogling the inviting mess of pillows and sheets in front of me summons a yawn. So, instead, I grab my computer from the end of the bed and head to the bathroom. Sitting my mug on the table, I placed inside a few days earlier, I jolt myself awake with a few splashes of cold water from the sink, then climb into the tub and press the call button by Taylor's contact. She picks up at the last second, nose and mouth filling the screen, hair dripping.

"Sorry. Sorry. Sorry." She says, "I lost track of time. I got to go home a little early today, so I went ahead and jumped in the shower. Give me one second."

I sip my coffee and stare at our bathroom ceiling as I wait for Taylor to clothe herself. A few minutes later, my view whirls and blurs as my roommate carries her phone into her bedroom. When she's situated on her bed, she lifts the screen to eye level.

"HI!"

"How are you? / How's Ireland?"

We say at the same time, practically screaming at each other. The unintentional overlap sends each us into a fit of giggles. If anyone else was there to see our beaming faces, they would think we hadn't seen each other for months, not just two, almost three days.

"Ireland's good," I answer when we've calmed down. "You'd love it. It's been a nice break. One I didn't know I needed, honestly."

"Aw, I love that for you." I recognize Taylor's impish smirk and know what's coming, "And now you've met a hot Irishman, so we'll absolutely be going back."

I push down all telling emotions and roll my eyes. "Ok, one: As Taylor Swift champions: you need to calm down. Two: I never said anything about there being any man, hot, Irish or otherwise. You came up with that on your own and three: I want to know what this major news is?"

"Nah, it's ok. You go first."

"Do you know what time it is where I am?" I tease, "If you want to sit here and talk about me, I'm heading back to bed, and you call me on your morning commute."

Well, in that case," Taylor's nonchalant disposition alters when a wide grin breaks across her countenance barely foreshadowing her squeal, "JEREMY ASKED ME ON A DATE!"

"WHAT!?" I scream, jolting upright, "When? How? Saturday?"

"Yes! And Laurel, he like, properly asked me." She's nodding her head as she speaks. "Look." She gets up from her bed and races down the hall toward the entryway, flipping my view to her back camera as she goes. "He had flowers when he showed up at the store."

"Oh My Gosh, Taylor!" I cry as a gorgeous bouquet of Summer blooms comes into view.

"I didn't notice until I was cutting the stems that a note was tucked inside." She angles her phone so that I can see the small piece of paper next to the vase: 'Are you free Tuesday night? Around 7? - Jeremy.'

"Dude." I'm smiling too hard to be more eloquent.

"I. Know." she declares, switching the camera back to her face. "I always assumed I would find this kind of thing completely nauseating, but it's sort of nice."

"Tuesday is in 24 hours for you. I cannot believe you waited this long to tell me."

She dismisses my incredulity, positively glowing, "I figured you were busy."

I lovingly sigh and shake my head. "What are you wearing?"

"That's what I wanted your help with. I can't decide." Taylor says as she returns to her room and props me up on her bedside table. I can see several items of clothing have been draped on her desk chair, one over the other.

She runs me through three options while I nurse my drink: a green rayon midi-dress with little white flowers and a square neckline, a white floor-length dress featuring a large pink floral pattern and a slit to her upper thigh, or a black Lady Gaga *Chromatica* tee tied into a crop top with high-waisted hot pink pants."

"Taylor," I question, shocked by the variants in dress code, "what are you guys doing?"

"I don't know!" she whines, the delivery indicating she's been dying to vent her frustration. "He won't tell me."

"No way!" I exclaim.

"Yes!" She dramatically bellyflops onto her mattress and picks her phone back up. "I even FaceTimed him to be like, 'You can't *not* tell me. I need to know what to wear.' And all he said was, 'Don't wear heels and bring a jacket.'"

I chortle at her annoyed Jeremy impression, pondering the outfits before I respond. "I think the best bet would be the first option, the green dress, with a jean jacket and some sandals."

"But what if I'm cold and wish I'd worn pants?"

"The Lady Gaga outfit may be too casual if you can't wear heels to dress it up."

Taylor's eyes go wide.

"I have no idea what he has planned! I didn't even know this was happening." I stammer, shutting down her upcoming accusation, "Even though we've known him like a year, this is still a first date."

"Yeah, that's true," she says with a shrug. I can visibly see anxiety tensing her shoulders.

"If you're really worried you'll be cold, put a pair of sheer tights in your purse. If you end up wishing you had worn pants, you can put them on in the bathroom. I bet he won't even notice." Once again, Taylor and I both burst out laughing.

"What would I do without you?" she eventually asks, propping her chin on the knuckles of her free hand in mock consideration.

"End up wearing the equivalent of a bridesmaid dress to a first date," I answer sincerely.

Taylor gasps. "That white dress is not a bridesmaid dress!"

"Taylor, if I google that dress, I bet every photo result is either of someone at a formal attire wedding or from the marketing shoot. Come to think of it, I'm almost certain you bought it for Crystal's wedding in Napa."

"Ok, fine," Taylor concedes. "It's maybe not the best idea for a first date outfit, but I was panicking."

"The green dress will be perfect," I say, sensing, even from thousands of miles away, she is still somewhat unnerved.

Taylor simpers as she sits up straighter and declares a subject change, "Ok, that's me done. Now what's the tea?"

"The & Then Some show was *so good.* I'm super excited to work with them. I really think they could be huge." I pause and gleefully watch Taylor's face fall.

"That's it?" she deadpans, not even trying to keep the disappointment from her voice. "Your tea is that this band I already know you like and work with is 'really good'?"

"Yeah?" It takes all my concentration to swallow the giveaway rising in my throat. I let her frustration ferment a fraction of a second too long before I add, "Oh! After the show, they introduced me to Colin's old roommate and–"

"I KNEW THERE WAS A GUY!" Taylor erupts, "YES! I KNEW IT. I KNEW IT."

I laugh, basking in her immense satisfaction, allowing the moment to linger until I'm ready to recount the last two days in as much detail as I can remember.

19

Laurel

"So, I'm seeing him again later today," I finish.

By the time Taylor is up to date, I have replenished my coffee and relocated to a chair on the balcony.

"You like him,"my friend states, a smug smile playing at the corner of her lips. "One might even say you have a crush."

I groan, burying my face in my knees, which I've tucked into my chest. "Stop. I mean, yes, I may have an unwanted, illogical and recurring fantasy this lasts beyond next week, if it even is anything–"

"It's something," Taylor purrs.

"Whatever." My retelling ended up being a humbling experience. The optimism that led me to alert my friend of Nolan's existence dimming to plausible rationality in the light of a new day. "Crush or no crush, I feel stupid. There's no point to it when all is said and done."

"Laurel, babe," she begins, "I love you to pieces, but would you please look at the situation? You have a— and, unfortunately, I'm forced to guess here, but would like this confirmed with a photo as soon as possible—hot, accented musician literally panting over you."

"I do not." I can already feel myself getting flustered. "I told you we're just hanging out. He's keeping me company because I literally don't know anyone else. It can't really be more than that."

Taylor purses her lips. I can tell she's pondering her next words because I watch her eyes become more somber than they have during the entire phone call, and when she speaks, her tone has grown sincere. "When it comes to anyone else, you are one of the biggest romantics I know. But when it's your turn to get swept off your feet, you're as levelheaded and reasonable as they come."

"Falling for him would be setting myself up for heart-break," I retort.

She presses gently, "You don't know that for sure."

"Yes, I do. We're already on borrowed time." I can feel tears gathering at the corner of my eyes, so I close them and force down a few settling breaths.

"I wish I could hug you right now," Taylor sighs. "Don't cry. Please know I am not judging you or trying to psycho-analyze your reasons for thinking this. You know your heart and its limits better than anybody else. You do not have to take my advice. But I need to say this: you're in Ireland. Maybe Nolan will only be a ten-day fling. Maybe he'll be the love of your life." I release a strangled chuckle at her jump from temporary affair to soulmate. "You don't know. Live a little and stop making excuses."

There's so much affection permeating her words I can't help but offer a soft grin in return. But it's too early for this kind of conversation, so I gesture noncommittally, transitioning her to my back camera to show off the first rays of the sun peeking over the buildings that make up my view.

"Text me and let me know how the date goes," I tell her.

"You too!" she replies, eyes twinkling again.

I laugh, for real this time, "Shut up! You're going to make me regret telling you."

"Love you!"

"Love you too! Bye!"

I slouch down in my chair, my cheeks sore from the last two and a half hours of smiling and laughter and my heart a little tender at Taylor's parting appraisal. She isn't wrong, but practicality has gotten me this far sans broken heart. Not that I've given it much opportunity to break. Absentmindedly, I reach for my cup. Instead of grabbing it, my fingers send it teetering toward the edge of the table, the spike in my anxiety derailing my train of thought. Once the mug is safely in my lap, I contemplate getting back in bed for a few hours but conclude that would do more harm than good to my already tragic sleep schedule. I'll just have to make it an early night. When I've summoned the willpower, I retreat to the den, grab the book I bought at London Heathrow and snuggle up on the couch.

♥

My phone's clock reads 1:45 PM as my Uber pulls up outside the entrance of the massive structure that is the Guinness Storehouse. Both sides of the street are lined by multi-story brick buildings connected at various points and levels by skyway bridges. As I exit the car, to my right are three enormous metal cylinders, which I presume are vats full of in-process beer. This is the level of antiquated grandeur I was expecting from Jameson Distillery. Nolan had offered to pick me up, but I'd declined, mostly due to the brewery's close proximity to Jameson but also because I'd planned to spend the first part of my day educating myself in Irish History and didn't want to feel rushed.

This was supposed to mean going to EPIC: The Irish Emigration Museum, but after becoming engrossed in my reading and losing track of time, I had re-routed to The Little

Museum of Dublin, a smaller establishment—as the name suggests—with a charming feel, promising 'not to sell an ideology but simply to remember the past.' There, I had spent the early afternoon wandering from room to room, soaking in the different exhibits and all the things they had to tell me. So far, it has been a very charming Tuesday. However, when I see Nolan walking toward me, his Henley shirt sleeves rolled past the elbows, I can't help but believe, even if it is against my better judgment, that my day may be about to get even better.

As soon as he reaches me, he wraps me in a quick hug. Telling myself I'm purely doing it per Taylor's request, I take a mental note of what he smells like. A detail I was unable to properly provide when we texted mere minutes after our phone call, a fact she found utterly appalling.

You haven't checked for his socials, and you don't know what he smells like! Honestly, Laurel, he could be absolutely grotesque for all I know.

I had assured her she would judge his appearance acceptable if not more than so, and swore to do some online stalking eventually, but so far, this trip has felt so 'go, go, go' that I haven't found the time.

If she must know, the Irishman smells good and not like 'oh, that smells good' good, but like, GOOD. I'm not a cologne aficionado, so I can't say what the fragrance's notes are per se, but the scent conjures up images of rainy days and warm blankets, wool sweaters, and fireplaces. It's consoling and warm. *Did he smell like this last night? Maybe? No. He couldn't have. I would have noticed, I think? It's probably for the best that I didn't.* I move away, allowing the space between us to dilute the aroma and clear my head.

"How's she cuttin'?" he inquires, withdrawing his arm from around my shoulders.

I look up at him, shading my eyes from the sun. "I'm sorry. How's what?"

"She cuttin'," he beams, "How are you?"

"Oh," I blush. "Good. You?"

"Pretty sound, actually," Nolan says as he holds open the visitors' entrance door.

Directly in front of us is a small flight of stairs, which means this place is even bigger than one would guess. At the bottom, we turn the corner and emerge into a concrete room. The walls are papered with black and white images of Guinness days gone by that contrast nicely with the red columns and revealed steel framework reinforcing the ceiling. The bold print signage above us directs patrons who have purchased via the website to a short line against the back wall that leads to a number of self-service kiosks.

"So," I begin when we are properly queued in the line, the overlapping conversations surrounding us illustrating that it consists mostly of tourists, "did you actually get a cab home last night?"

Nolan's eyes glint mischievously. "I meant to. I really did, but it was such a beautiful evening that I couldn't waste it, you know?" I fight the urge to hit him, opting instead to narrow my eyes. He snorts, bemused, as we're carried forward, "So what did you do with the rest of your evening, then?"

"I…" I ponder the previous evening, post-Jimmy Rabbitte's, searching for something witty to fill the blank, "slept," I finish lamely, shrugging because it's the truth. The rest of my night was uneventful.

"You must have done something? Watch telly? Eat a midnight snack? Anything?" Nolan pauses, awaiting an answer. His insistence on the subject throws me. I bring my gaze to his. His eyes read as jovial as ever, but there's a hint of apology in them as well. There's a chance he may have taken what I wanted to be a playful, flirty continuation of the evening prior as me being miffed he walked all the way home. I add this occurrence to my list of instances that prove I should never be blatantly coy. Some people are blessed with that superpower. Others, like me, are not.

"No, seriously," I emphasize, reaching out and putting my hand on his arm as a gesture of good faith. The family in front of us finishes with the machine, so the rest of my recap is fragmented as I tap the screen to retrieve our tickets. "I went to bed pretty much right away. I had plans to call my roommate at 7:30 PM Los Angeles time, which meant I had to get up around 3:00 AM."

"Christ." Nolan exclaims, " She," "he/they," he tacks on as an afterthought, "must be some roommate."

"She," I start, but then pause to hand our passes to an usher.

The young bespectacled man chats amicably with his co-worker as he grants us admission. "All set then, ma'am. If you follow the arrows on the ground, they'll guide you upstairs to the tour.

"Thank you," I respond cheerfully.

"Thanks a million," the attendant says, waving us through and making me smile.

"She," I resume as we mount more steps, this time heading back to ground level, my companion slowing his pace to stay next to me, "is my best friend. Before everything with Jenny, my boss, and this trip happened, I had agreed to be her wingwoman at a party. That party became a date, and I wanted to be able to talk through everything with her ahead of it. With the time difference and both our schedules, there really wasn't any other option besides that, so I did what had to be done." Willing to risk tripping on a stair, I glance over at Nolan only to encounter his full-faced grin. "What now?" I question.

"Nothing," he replies, "I just hope you got some sleep after."

I shrug, "Not really, but I'll be alright." He chuckles and shakes his head.

The first floor is exponentially larger than the one below. On this level, the steel beams have been painted baby blue, and the wallpaper has been exchanged for the aesthetically pleasing feature of exposed brick. When we reach the landing, we're ushered to the left of two glass elevators whose shafts climb up through a substantial hole in the center of the room. This route forces us to walk past what huge white LED letters claim to be 'THE STORE' à la the exit of almost every major theme park attraction.

As neither of us feels the need to buy anything at the moment, we stick to the edge. Rounding the elevators, we join a small cluster of people gathered near a passage in the back wall, once again LED labeled, but this time with the word 'START' and a glowing downward-facing arrow. Nolan and I join the quieting crowd a few seconds before the Guinness employee at its center begins to speak in a well-practiced, even tone.

"I'm going to give you a very brief introduction to set you off on your self-led tour, which you can access at any time through the doorway behind me." He says, gesturing to the signage, "Arthur Guinness, our founder, began his journey back in 1759 by signing this lease right here on the ground for a period of nine thousand years." Peeking at the concrete floor through the legs of those in front of me, I can barely make out a glass-covered piece of paper at the guide's feet. The staff member pauses a few beats to let the burst of bewildered banter to die down, "And, as a fun fact, if you'll look up through this opening here," he gestures over his head, "you will see we are standing at the bottom of the world's largest pint glass. If this massive cup was filled, it would hold 14.3 million pints of Guinness." This is met with a second shower of oohs and aahs which dissipate as I gawk at the ceiling stories above. "As part of your tour today, you do receive one such pint, keep that in mind as you learn more about the ingredients, history, and culture that tell the Guinness story."

"Have you done this before?" I ask as the group disperses, soundtracked by a light round of applause.

"Yeah, actually," the local replies, "but not in donkey's years. I think it was with Colin right after orientation."

"Well then," I say, pressing forward, "lead the way."

20

Laurel

"I'll have the char-grilled vegetable toastie, please," I tell the middle-aged woman behind the counter. A clip holds her hair in a messy bun, the pieces falling into her face streaked with grey.

"Alright there, darling," she says, clicking my order into the tablet in front of her. "Would you like to add the Guinness crisps for an additional two euros?"

I nod, "Yes, please."

"If you'd like to redeem your complimentary pint now, we recommend the Guinness Extra Stout with this order," she advises, indicating the various spouts behind her, "but a lot of customers like to save it for the Gravity Bar."

Prior to this, we had endeavored to cash in our drinks at Guinness Storehouse's top-floor attraction. But, upon discovering the overwhelming number of people also hoping to enjoy their beer with a view, I had made it known that my hotel had a suitably delightful rooftop restaurant of its own, so for my sake, the experience wasn't necessary. The two of us had instead retreated down two floors to Arthur's Bar, a contemporary eatery at which Irene had made Jenny late lunch reservations.

"That's OK, thanks. I'll use it now." I pass her my paper token as I continue, "but I'll just have a draught."

She smirks knowingly, "Not a fan of carbonation?"

"Not in beer." I shake my head.

"That'll be €10.20, love," she reads out the total. I hand her my card. "We'll bring the food over to you when it's ready.

Nolan, having ordered ahead of me, grabs both our professionally prepared pints off the bar. I lead the way back to our appointed table, a round, two-person high top tucked away in a corner alcove that has been staged like a vintage pub. A snug hideaway in the otherwise industrial restaurant. We sit down across from a replica bar fully stocked with Guinness relics and decorated with antique posters, signage, and old sports memorabilia. Mounted in the corner, an old television set showcases a black-and-white soccer match.

"Cheers," the musician says, clinking his glass with mine.

"Cheers," I reply as I bring the cup to my lips. I grimace as I swallow. When Nolan sets his ale down a few moments later, it's about a fourth of the way empty.

"I'm sorry," he blinks, genuine befuddlement crossing his features, "but what on God's green earth was that?" He's gesturing to my pint, of which only a small amount is gone.

"I took a drink?" I respond, utterly baffled myself.

"No, petal," his furrowed brow inclines toward me, "what you've done is make a haymes of draining a Guinness."

"I'm sorry. I– I just–," I stutter the first part of my response, exhaustion giving rise to frustration, "I don't like beer anyway, ok? This stuff is heavy and thick, and if I wanted to consume fermented carbs, I could eat moldy bread!"

Nolan, not expecting this outburst, chokes on the second sip he was consuming. It takes longer than usual for the fluid to leave his lungs as it's impeded by laughter. Coughing subsided, he clears his throat with another tug from his mug before responding.

"You simply haven't been taught how to do it," he says, eyes back to their usual jolly state.

"Ok, teach me then" I challenge, lifting my cup back up and staring at him over the rim.

"Oh no," he chides, "you've already gone and ruined that one for yourself." Confiscating my pint from my palm, he swigs down a considerable portion and sits it on his side of the table. "We'll have to get you another." Giving me no time to protest, Nolan stands and walks back to the bar.

"Ok," my torturer prompts, eyeing me over his third beer. Our food has come, and with it, his secret request. "Now you've learned. This is the test."

Already overwhelmed by the feeling of the first pint sloshing heavily in my belly, I pout, "Nolan, I'm going to be full."

"You can drink this one slower," he promises. "Just get it started."

I sigh and raise my glass. "Cheers, I guess," I glower, bracing myself to endure two big gulps, making sure I get through the foam and to the liquid below.

"Brilliantly done!" the Irishman proclaims, clapping and ignoring the expression of disgust on my face. He may have taught me how to stomach the stout, but he did not succeed in making me like it. "So," he proceeds, cutting into his Beef and Guinness pie, "was this morning as 'epic' as you hoped it would be?" I'm pleased he remembered what my plans were.

"Yes and no," I explain. "I got caught up in my book and left later than I wanted, so I ended up at The Little Museum of Dublin instead."

His eyebrows raise in recognition as he swallows. "Ah, sick. I haven't actually been in there yet, but I've heard good things. How was it?"

"Really well done. I learned a lot. One of the temporary exhibits is about U2, so that was a fun surprise." I answer, popping a few crisps in my mouth.

"You know, I can't vouch for its educational appeal, as I've never been," Nolan adds after a moment of thought, "but there is a Rock N Roll Museum here.

"Really?!" I exclaim. A music museum is somewhere I would very much like to visit.

Seeing the light flare in my eyes, he backtracks, holding up his hands, "Now, I don't know if it's any good or if it's a standard Temple Bar tourist attraction, but it might be worth looking into."

"I definitely will. Thank you." After attending to my sandwich and its quickly cooling contents, I glance up to find the busker smiling to himself. "What is it?" I inquire.

"Nothing important," he replies, shaking himself back to reality, "I was remembering one night when Colin and I were walking back to our dorm after going out. We passed the Rock N Roll Museum. Colin, completely buckled, stops, points at the building and says, 'I'll be in there, Nol.' Just wait and see.'"

I chortle at the shared memory, "That sounds like him."

There's a lull in the conversation for a moment or two as we eat. Strangers' chatter becoming the white noise in our setting.

"Did the guys tell you," Nolan breaks the silence by asking, "I was in & Then Some?"

It's my turn to choke on the mouthful I've taken.

"What?!" I stammer in between coughs, "No?" I gesture for him to expound while I compose myself.

"Yeah, I was a founding member. That's how I know everyone. Colin and my hometowns are not far from each other, so during the summer, I'd go visit, and we'd all write and play and what have you." He declares this as a simple matter of fact, but I'm still having trouble comprehending this news.

"What? What happened?" I impose. "Obviously, you're all still friends."

Nolan laughs, "Nothing horrible or anything. The band began to get local traction ahead of our second year. They all wanted to push into it, and I wasn't comfortable leaving school, so I essentially quit."

"I'm sorry," I say, not knowing how else to respond.

"It's nothing to apologize for," he states after another drink of his beer. "It was my call. Would I go back and undo it if I could? 'Course, but I still write, and I still play, so I'm doing okay." I hum assuredly, trying not to feel sorry for him.

"This is completely not my place," I speak slowly, searching for his permission to continue. He regards me genially, so I go on, "But have you asked to re-join? I can't see them not letting you, not after seeing you all together."

He scowls more at the idea than at me and crosses his arms. "No. They've done so much work over the last few years. It wouldn't be right for me to come in to reap the benefits now."

"Yeah. I can understand that." I pick at the crumbs on my plate as I process this new information, the feeling I'm treading on eggshells weighing down on me. "Wait..." I begin, recalling Dylan telling me two of the songs on the debut EP were part of their original setlist, "you said you wrote with them. Did any of those songs make it to the EP?"

A proud grin blooms on Nolan's face, "Yeah, two."

"Which two?" I request eagerly, almost positive I know the answers.

"All I Could Do & B-sides"

"*B-sides* is my favorite." I confide, Nolan's countenance brightens further. "You said you still write. Have you recorded anything?"

"I have a few songs on streaming, but nothing's really taken off." He shrugs, then eats the last piece of his pie as if to solidify the information's insignificance.

I stare at him, combatting the impulse to slide into the Artist Development side of my brain. Unfortunately, I lose. "Do you promote it?" I then remind myself not every musician wants to be "famous," so I add, "Or is it a just-for-you kind of thing?"

"I'll slip some original stuff in between covers when I busk, but that usually doesn't draw as big of a crowd, so I don't do it a lot. Plus, endorsing yourself on Instagram and Twitter can only be done so many times before you realize you're reaching the same people."

"Have Colin or the other guys ever pushed the songs?" It seems like an innocent enough question, especially now that I know he used to be part of the band, but I don't receive a reply. In fact, I'm left to wonder if the inquiry went unheard when he pulls out his phone.

"Speaking of covers," he says, "I'm really sorry, but I need to get going, or I'll be late to my first stop on the pub circuit. I'd invite you along, but you'd be sitting alone all evening. Plus, there's your whole 3:00 AM issue.

"No, I'd love to come, for a while anyway. I can always leave early," I offer. Not wanting to leave him—*On such an odd note!* Not wanting to leave him on such an odd note is what I meant to think.

Nolan leans across the table, "Laurel," he presses in a calm, gentle tone, "I mean this in the nicest way possible, and you look absolutely lovely, but." I frown. "I can tell you're dead knackered."

"I'm fine," I retort, hoping the words stifle the most inconvenient yawn of my life.

Their apparent failure earns a chuckle. "What about this? I'm busking on Grafton again tomorrow afternoon. You can go get some sleep now and come by and listen for a bit then."

"I guess that could work," I concede, feeling my eyelids grow heavy now that my energy level has been brought to my attention.

"Okay then," my escort says, standing, "finish your pint, and we'll get you to bed and me to work." I stare at him. The whole debacle over the beer has me worried he's serious, but then he winks and helps me off my chair.

21

Laurel

Back at The Dean, I have a significant problem. While physically, I feel exhausted, mentally, I am wide awake. Based upon the amount of fatigue I was feeling in Nolan's car—he insisted on dropping me off, claiming my hotel was on the way to his first gig—I was expecting to be out as soon as my head hit the pillow. Instead, all I've been doing for the last hour is trying to fall asleep. I have laid on the bed, the couch, even the floor at one point out of sheer desperation. The curtains are drawn tight in an attempt to trick my brain into functioning like it's nightfall, but alas, here I lay, feet near the headboard, one pillow under and one pillow over my head, the new owner of 742 noisy sheep, no closer to respite than when I had only one. I throw the cushion, covering my face back to its original place.

Swinging my feet over the edge of the bed, I sigh and rub my tired eyes. The nightstand clock mocks me with its burnt orange: 6:06 PM. I do the math in my head. *If it's 6:00*

PM here, then it's 10:00 AM in LA. Taylor's date isn't even close to happening yet, let alone over. I tilt forward until my head is in my hands and groan. Sitting up again, my focus lingers on the LUSH products splayed on the vanity top.

"Well," I vocalize to no one in particular, "might as well take a bath."

♥

I've been submerged long enough to need to replenish the hot water and have Little Mix's *LM5* jump over to their artist radio. When my stomach finally gurgles in protest, I open my eyes to see that my toes, which are peeking out from underneath the waning bubbles, have transformed into prunes. I shift slowly, trying not to displace too much water, and reach for my phone. I've been soaking for a good 90 minutes. I gasp, then chuckle. That's a record even for me. While I never dozed (this would obviously be less than desirable given my location), I did succeed in momentarily quieting my brain, so I'm not feeling as drained. My next unplanned item of business? Dinner.

I yank on the stopper chord, breaking the suction, and stand, letting the water on my body add to the slowly receding pool as I climb out and wrap myself in a heated towel. I hum the Nina Nesbitt tune coming from my speaker until I discern it doesn't fit my mood and click through the station, finally settling on one of the girl group's newer songs. With a few taps, that album is positioned next in my queue.

As I dab my body dry, I get an idea. I grab the robe from its hook near the door and shrug it over my shoulders. Collecting my pajamas from where they have been discarded on the floor, I drape each piece over the towel heater. They'll need time to warm, so I pad into the den, riding high on my own ingenuity. I could have sworn I saw something about room service by the snack tray. Sure enough, balanced against the wall, tucked into a clipboard, is a menu: Two pages single-sided, one food, the other desserts, and drinks. I run my finger over the listings. Carrying my options with me to the desk, I follow the instructions in the center of the black rotary phone and dial 1 for room service. While it rings, a deep reverent tremble, I doodle mediocre flowers on the branded notepad nearby.

"Room service." A soprano voice trills, "What can I get you?"

"Oh. Hi," I respond, transitioning from budding fauna artist to hungry hotel guest. "May I please have the Wild Mushroom Risotto and a Vanilla Gelato, please?"

"Sure thing, love." There is a pause while the hotel employee jots down my order. Once they finish and dictate it back to me, they ask, "Do you want this charged to the card provided to the front desk at check-in, or would you like to be charged separately now?"

"The card on file works for me," I confirm, conscious I had it switched to my personal debit.

"Brilliant. That'll be a €22. 27 change on the card, yeah?"

I answer while fixing the stem on one of my flowers, "Mmhm. That's fine."

"Alright then, we'll get that ready for you. A runner will be up in twenty to thirty minutes with your plates. Have a nice night, ma'am."

"Thanks. You too," I offer before restoring the handset to its bracket.

22

Laurel

Sitting on the couch, burrowed in my favorite oversized cardigan, I nibble on what's left of the risotto, staving off my desire to lick the plate…even though I am alone and no one would see me do it…still, I shouldn't. I set the dish back on the table and stand, not only to get away from it but also to retrieve the gelato from the fridge. It's a tad melted, as my room does not have an actual freezer, but I figured the SMEG, in conjunction with a partially filled ice bucket, was better than nothing. While I'm up, I run a cycle of water through the coffee machine, cleaning it out for the chamomile tea I've planned to have following dessert.

I plop back down on the sofa and pour the supplied pecans and hot fudge over the ice cream. As I take my first bite, the show I've been watching, *Gogglebox*, a local, non-American reality series in which regular people from across the UK react to various television programs and news segments, comes to an end. (Yes, I have spent the last hour watching people watch TV.) As the credits roll, a British-accented female voice sounds through my speakers.

"Finding love isn't easy. Up next on E4, the *First Dates* restaurant is open for business."

Intrigued, I keep the channel playing, marveling at the difference between the advertisements that run here and those in The States. When I'm a few more spoonfuls into my dessert, the scheduled entertainment returns, and I settle back in, pleased to learn *First Dates* is another reality broadcast about just that: single people meeting for the first time after being set up on a blind date.

When it comes to romance, Taylor may think I make excuses to keep myself from getting attached, but that's not because of a lack of effort or desire for connection on my part. For instance, within moments, I'm rooting for certain restaurant patrons: a young woman who was broken up with out of the blue and a senior gentleman whose wife passed away four years prior. By the time I'm scrapping the base of my sundae cup, corners of my mouth adorned with chocolate, I've devolved into a blushing, giggly mess. My laughter gives way to stunned exclamations about twenty minutes in when the show reveals a minor twist: after their date, sitting in the same room, post individual interviews, the couple has to share whether or not they would like to continue seeing each other. In the span of an hour, I experience hope, heartbreak, joy, sorrow, and everything in between. I'm delighted a second episode is to follow. I brew my tea during the intermission, not wanting to miss anything.

I'm enjoying my evening in more than I had anticipated. Of course, I anticipated I would be long asleep by now. Yet, the night is not lost. As b-roll footage from the episode they're about to air is overlaid by the narrator explaining how the program works, I blow on my newly made drink, helping it reach a consumable temperature.

Halfway through the consecutive installment, I'm astounded—I'm not really sure why, but I am—one of the newly introduced participants is a busker. It's a perfectly normal profession, but it reminds me of mine (I'm using the possessive term lightly). I keep the TV on but pull my laptop toward me. Instagram seems like a reasonable enough place to start. Typing Nolan O'Kelley in the search bar brings up a few users, but none of the last names are spelled correctly. As this simple task of social stalking may become a full-fledged sleuthing job, I sit up straight and place the computer on my legs. I backspace and replace my search with 'Colin Byrne.' There are several, but the first result is the only user I follow: @colinpbyrne. (The P is for Peter.) I click it and head straight to the people he's following, groaning when I realize I can't search by typing in a name.

During the next commercial break, I retrieve my phone from the bedroom and repeat the process. Lucky for me, Colin follows less than 1000 people. As soon as I type 'Nolan,' I've narrowed my results down to three, one of which is @_nolanokelley_. Why it didn't come up on my web search, I'll never understand. Nonetheless, I type the username into my MacBook's search bar, wanting a bigger viewing area than one I can fit in my pocket, and sure enough...success. I have acquired my target.

Most of the photos are candids of him both around the city and in the countryside. There are some staged portraits that, I'm happy have been used as the artwork for his three singles. *Two or three more, and he could have a full EP.* There is also a handful of group shots, mementos of celebrations and outings with friends. As a precautionary measure, I skim the profiles of the women who make multiple appearances. Nolan hasn't mentioned any significant others, past or present, and he's been spending a lot of time with me to be someone with a noteworthy crush, but that doesn't necessarily mean he's single. Coming to, I put an abrupt and violent end to this thought process by slamming my computer closed. Once again, I'm getting ahead of myself. Not that there is even anything to get ahead of. I remind myself this trip has an end. By this time next week, I will be back in Los Angeles, miles upon miles away.

When *First Dates* comes to an end, with a third and final segment slated to follow, I recommence my cyber session. Tapping the browser's back button to reload the musician's page. Interspersed between the pictures are videos of him busking and singing in what must be his bedroom. I click on a few, grinning when one is a recording of the Adore You /Cruel Summer mashup he was performing when I met him. I stop myself before I go too deep and scroll back to the top of the page. Never one for games, and because I'd officially call us friends, I go ahead and hit the follow button.

On a new tab, I navigate to Twitter and follow similar steps. His username is the same. *Good for branding purposes.* Nolan doesn't tweet much. His pinned tweet contains the Linktree for his newest single. The ones below incorporate the media I found on Instagram, with some humorous and informational retweets in between. I toggle to the 'Replies' tab and notice he's pretty decent about responding to messages he's been tagged in. Out of curiosity, I check his follower count: 2,113. He follows 529 accounts, so the number isn't awful. I note his Instagram statistics as well. He has slightly over 5,000 followers on the platform. I'm not surprised at the higher total. It's not set in stone; nothing in the music industry really is, but of late, I have found more people prefer images over words when it comes to content. Lastly, I use the photo-sharing application's website to DM the profile to Taylor, accompanied by a message.

> *Twitter is the same.*
> *Taylor, do not, I repeat,*
> *DO NOT, like anything.*

Twitter front and center again, I follow the link in Nolan's pinned tweet to his Spotify page, letting it load in my desktop app. Not willing to miss the first fifteen minutes of my newest obsession and wanting to give the artist profile my full attention, I set my laptop aside, letting the request process.

After the introductions for the newest batch of romantic contenders come to a close, my phone chimes, announcing an Instagram notification. Taylor has responded to the forwarded account. She must be at lunch. I slide it open.

OH. HE IS CUTE.

Then another is delivered.

Can I follow him, or would that be weird?

I laugh as I type back, knowing she's joking.

> *Right?! Maybe not yet.*

She replies immediately.

Boo! You're no fun!

I won't.

Have you listened to the songs yet? 🖤
Are they good?

I answer with:

I was about to! I have them queued and ready,
but I was waiting for this show I found to finish.
It's called First Dates. I don't think we can get
it in the States, but it's really cute. You basically watch people go on blind dates. Lol

He told me he wrote B-sides
and All I Could Do, though.

Her messages pop into the thread in rapid succession.

Oh, fun!! I'll see if it's on one
of those niche streaming services. Lol.

Like the & Then Some songs?!?
Dang!!

I'd listen now, too, but I should
probably get back to work so
I can leave early. 😊
Let me know how they are!!

I shoot back, smiling.

> *I will!! Have the best time ever!!*
> *Let me know how it goes,*
> *even if it's some ungodly hour here.*

I can see she's no longer active, so I close the software and lock my phone.

When the episode draws to a close, the broadcast's hopeful melody playing over updates of the lasting couples' relationships, I switch off the television, lay down and situate my computer onto the cushion next to me.

"Ok, Nolan," I challenge aloud, "let's see what you got."

I was correct. He has three original songs: *Monday Morning*, *Walk Away,* and the latest release, *Butterflies*. I hover over his debut, planning to listen from oldest to new, but first decide to check his metrics. I wish I didn't have to, but I do.

Nolan currently has 6,963 monthly listeners. His top song, *Monday Morning,* which also happens to be the oldest, has 465,000 plays. Not bad, considering it was released a little over a year ago. I return to my internet browser and search for his name. There are five videos uploaded to his YouTube channel. Three are lyric videos for each of his songs. One is him singing *Butterflies* live from his couch. The last is a video of Colin and him sitting on a park bench singing *High Hopes* by Kodaline. They had longer hair and noticeably fuller faces during the time they shared at Trinity. The rest of the search results are as I expected: Nolan's social media links are listed, as well as a half dozen videos other people have uploaded of him playing to Grafton Street. There are no interviews with smaller music publications or local news outlets; nothing listed proves his songs have been publicized anywhere but his own pages. If this really is the case, his stats aren't terrible. I mean, they aren't the figures we'd want for an up-and-coming artist, but at this point, I'm not sure he wants that. His answers to my career questions back at Guinness Storehouse bordered on vague.

Reminding myself he is not an artist I have been hired to evaluate but someone whose music I'm simply trying to enjoy, I close Chrome and, back on Spotify, press play. The songs remind me of & Then Some, but more acoustic. This isn't a criticism, especially once I realize there may be one person playing everything I hear. I wonder how he envisions his sound and make a mental note to ask him if it comes up. The lyrics and melodies seem directed at me, the recipient. *Monday Morning* makes me feel content and happy. *Walk Away* in tone is harder and more upbeat but is lyrically solemn, if not sad. *Butterflies* is hopeful and, to be honest, makes me a little giddy. When I'm done, I genuinely have no notes. Nolan makes good music. I wouldn't be shocked if he turns out to be one of those artists whose careers feel like lighting in a bottle. Once the spark catches, it swells to a wildfire without much assistance. However, unless he's simply hoping to get lucky, which is extremely rare but not unheard of, this would require outside promotion, which he doesn't seem to have or want, for that matter. But again, not my client.

I let the songs start again on a loop while I explore the artists his "fans also like," one of my favorite features on this streaming platform. Three I'm familiar with, & Then Some, Dermot Kennedy, and Keywest, and three I'm not, Ryan McMullan, The Riptide Movement, and Little Hours. I peruse the profiles of the artists I don't know out of habit, jotting their names down on the iCloud note I keep available on my desktop for this specific purpose.

When the newest song, which was released two months ago, fades out, I yawn. It's a few minutes after 10:00 PM, and my brain seems to have finally decided it's ready to sleep. I place my MacBook on the table, leaving it to charge next to the dregs in my teacup, and stretch as I rise, psyching myself up to drag my body down the hall. Eyelids already drooping, anticipating sleep, I crawl into bed, pushing my phone safely onto the bedside table with my fingertips. Before it's out of my reach completely, however, I inch it back toward me. Maybe I should listen to *Butterflies* one more time, just to make sure it's my favorite.

23

Laurel

With my alarm off and the curtains drawn, I'm not awed that I slept until 10:00 AM. Well, 9:30 AM, but I had laid in bed, ruminating over the past few days, feigning repose, until my need for caffeine drew me out from under the covers. As I wait for the Nespresso to brew the concoction to which I have become hopelessly addicted, I resort to another vice. Unlocking my phone for the first time this morning, I'm astonished to see I have notifications from almost every social platform, not to mention multiple texts and two missed calls. Unless it's my birthday, I never wake to this level of notoriety.

As I make my way around my room, opening blinds and unlatching windows, bathing the furniture in Gaelic sunshine and beckoning in the sounds of urban living, I check the calls, both of which are from Taylor, but she hasn't left a voicemail. Taking this as a positive sign, I move on to the texts, confident they will contain what she was calling about. My assumption is correct. Six of the seven messages are from my roommate. The first two are voice notes.

"Hey, Girl! It's me. I don't really know why I'm talking like this is a voicemail. Anyway, you have been up since 3:00 AM, so I don't really blame you for sleeping through my calls. I just got back from my date, and it was fantastic, fan-tas-tic. I want to be able to tell you about it in real-time, so I won't give too much away now, but since you weren't here, he came in–what am I saying, he would have come in even if you were here. You guys are friends–but he came in and–we didn't do anything, by the way. I want to take it slow– he still came in, though for like a nightcap, I guess, and he can make cocktails. Not mixed drinks. *Cocktail* cocktails. I can't remember what the one he made was called, but we had all the stuff in our kitchen, and it was delicious."

I save the first message as the next one begins.

"OH! We went to Melrose Rooftop Theatre at E.P & L.P! I couldn't wear heels because they set up turf on some parts of the roof. I mean, I could have worn heels, but...you know."

The four texts that followed half an hour later cover a different subject.

BTW, I listened to Nolan's
music while I was getting ready.

He has no business being that good.

Can't wait for him to write a song about you.

I roll my eyes and check the time in Los Angeles via my clock app, not wanting to attempt even simple math decaffeinated: 2:00 AM. I shouldn't call her back now. I respond to her messages in spite of the chastising purple typeface at the bottom of the chain proclaiming her notifications' silenced status.

OMG. Stop!!!!

I can't wait to hear all about it!!!
Melrose Rooftop! SO. FUN.

I'll call you tonight (my time) sometime.
When are you planning on eating lunch?

The final text is from my mom.

Hey, baby girl! Just checking in

to see how things are going.
What have you been up to?

I reply with a general account of the *& Then Some* show, including some caveats about Rory, knowing he's her favorite, and my various Irish outings that have followed. I don't mention the busker. Not because I want to keep him from her, but because I don't want her to read into me hanging out with him. (AKA: I don't need to deal with innocently probing questions that make it necessary for me to vocalize what I'm thinking, feeling and maybe even, although I'm loath to act on it, hoping for.)

I view the singular Facebook prompt, wanting to clear it from my screen. It's the usual 'Someone you haven't thought about in years' has a birthday today. Help them celebrate!' I squint hard at the profile picture. I'm not even sure who this is. The woman must have gotten married cause the name doesn't ring a bell either. I can't recall the last time I posted, so I'm not sure why I still have my account. I sigh, telling myself I should delete the app while fully acknowledging I won't.

My TikTok alerts are all DM's from Taylor. I'll watch those later as I'm finally feeling brave enough to tackle the more urgent issue: the twelve Instagram notifications that populated overnight. When the home page loads, I can see its seven direct messages, two follows, and three likes. I tap the heart at the top right of the screen to see all but one of them have come from @_nolanokelley_. He not only followed me back, but he must have done some light cyber-stalking of his own because one of the photos he liked was from February. I don't post very often, but you still have to scroll for a minute to get to pictures from six months ago. The other follow is from @monmornbutterflies. I chuckle to myself, presuming Nolan hadn't attained this level of dedication from anyone yet, but sure enough, a quick scan of the account confirms he has at least one superfan. If we were a team trying to grow his fanbase, this would be a point for the good guys. *But we aren't, so I really need to stop doing that.* I go back to my homepage and touch the message icon in the corner. Most recently, I have received five DMs from Taylor. However, my eyes catch on the user listed below her. Nolan has interacted with my profile twice. The latest activity was 9h ago. From the preview, I can see he's replied to my story, but I have no clue which one. Vacations tend to make me a little trigger-happy when it comes to posting "live" updates. My mind races as I struggle to swallow, pressing the text in my inbox, irrationally panicking over the possibility I uploaded something I wouldn't want him to see. A half laugh/half snort escapes me when I discover he's reacted to a clip from *First Dates*, over which I've placed the text: *NEW OBSESSION.*

How are you not sleeping? Haha

It's not particularly funny, but I had managed to stress myself out enough in the moments preceding reading it that the noise was born from sheer relief. His message prior is another story response, this time to a video he'd filmed of me "properly" drinking a Guinness, but it's merely the 'clapping' instant emoji. Since he can now tell I've seen his message, I feel pressured to converse within a suitable time frame. As I am not naturally witty, I like to have a friend provide the assist, but at 2:00-5:00 AM on a Wednesday morning, literally every person on my roster is asleep or perhaps, for those with non-traditional work schedules, too intoxicated to provide any decent suggestions. Or maybe I shouldn't respond at all!! I groan, take a deep breath, and then type the solitary reply that comes to mind because the patriarchy has conditioned me into believing not saying anything makes me cold-hearted and cruel.

Trust me, I was thinking the same thing.

As soon I hit send, a wave of nausea and regret washes over me. Was that the dumbest possible response? I could unsend. I know that's an option now. But resorting to the measure would feel like a new low. Plus, it may still notify him the way iMessage does. I idiotically have never tested it. So, instead, I let out an irritated huff, toss my phone onto the couch and make my coffee. I drink half the cup, pretending to be chill while actually hyper-aware of the device's presence and any noise it is or isn't making.

Knowing I will feel this way until he either responds or I see him again, I stand and head for the shower. Maybe the rainforest waterfall will help me clear my head. As I pass the balcony doors, a flock of pigeons flies by, the increase in their song reminding me I had a Twitter notification as well. In a split second, I've used the wall to propel myself into a U-turn. Unfairly annoyed by the current state of my emotions, I over-aggressively handle my phone, sliding up the lock screen, hitting the bird app, and then, once it loads, the bell icon in the lower banner.

Nolan O'Kelley *followed you*

I smile. I hate admitting it, but now I do feel a little better. Crushes really are the most inconvenient.

24

Laurel

Since I'm not meeting up with Nolan until around 2:00 PM, I leisurely get ready for the day, pausing between styling my hair and doing my makeup to have brunch at Sophie's. Fresh-faced and donning a simple Rolling Stones tee dress, I browse the menu. Though I'm alone, I've managed to snag one of the plush red and white booths by the window, allowing me a pristine view of the city skyline while I ponder my options and sip a Bellini. If I had to describe The Dean's rooftop restaurant, I would define it as rustic, art deco chic. In the last hours of morning, the main room, with its walls made entirely of glass, except for a small section of exposed brick, captures the natural light wonderfully. At this time of day, there's no need for the tiny spotlights scattered around the wood paneling above my head. Under my feet, my semi-slip-on sandals graze the matching floorboards. However, the large black and white diagonal stripes tiled in the corner of the eatery closest to the entrance, the rounded orange and gold pizza oven next to them, and the center bar's red and white slate exterior make everything feel a little less like a see-through barn loft. When my waitress returns, I settle on the Blueberry Pancake Stack with Orange Butter and Maple Syrup (Mostly because, now that I know it exists, I have to find out what 'orange butter' is.) and, for health reasons, a Carrot, Ginger, Apple and Kale juice to drink.

I'm feeling much more relaxed than I was an hour or so ago. The shower and subsequent pep talk I gave myself while in it definitely helped. As I was drying off, fluffy towel encasing my body like a security blanket, I had followed the Irishman back on Twitter and left it at that. No DM-ing, no liking anything to show I scrolled. Nothing. A vibration from under the arm I've rested on the table interrupts my reflections. Glancing down, I see light peeking out from the edges of my overturned phone, teasing me with the promise of a notification. Serotonin and endorphins flood my system in a Pavlovian response. *There's really only one person this could be.* I mentally consider other options as I reach for it. *Actually, that's wrong. Maybe Jenny is up with Juni, or someone on the & Then Some team has a question.* I flip the device over and hold it up to my face. My intuition was correct. *Always trust your gut, ladies and gentlemen.* Nolan's sent me a location pin. Before I have time to inquire into what it marks, another adrenaline rush hits as the thread continues.

This is where I'm planning on setting up. If the street's busy, I usually play from like 1:00 - 4:30.

I 'thumbs up' the message, but still reply.

Sounds good!

He responds right away, and for the next few minutes, we exchange a series of texts—all of a strictly platonic nature.

You don't have to come the whole time by the way.

I repeat songs sometimes, so it could get pure boring.

Just duck in whenever you want.

I'll probably be ready to leave my hotel around 2, so I'll make my way over then.

Alright, I'll keep an eye out for you.

My mate is backing me with his Cajon.
His girlfriend is coming.

She's bringing a chair and is going to sit
off to the Side and watch.
Do you want me to ask if she can bring two?

If she doesn't mind, that'd be great. Thanks!

This time, it's Nolan who uses the 'thumbs up' reaction.

I'm putting my phone back down when my food arrives. Perfect timing. I cut into the pancakes and sigh.

They're delicious. (Orange butter, it turns out, is simply butter with an added hit of orange flavor. It's butter, but better...on blueberry pancakes, at least.)

25

Laurel

Deciding what to wear, I told myself not to. Doing my makeup, I told myself not to. Getting dressed, I told myself not to. But, now, on my way to Grafton Street, enveloped in other pedestrians waiting at a crosswalk near St. Stephen's Green, I check Nolan's social media. About an hour ago, he posted a video on his Instagram story of him and his friend setting up, telling people where he was and how long he'd be playing. The same information was also shared via Twitter. This pleases me as it is exactly what I would have advised him to do. I add this shard of knowledge to my growing pile of puzzle pieces I hope will eventually form how my friend sees himself as an artist.

Satisfied, I tuck my phone back into my purse. As much as I've enjoyed how walkable the Irish capital is thus far, the frequent choice of cobblestone and brick pavement does keep catching on the toe of my shoes. For this particular outing, I have chosen to wear my magenta suede ankle boots. Not the most practical choice, I will admit, but they match the little pink flowers featured among various other colored flora on my muted gold bell-bottom pants almost perfectly. I've simplified the outfit by tying a plain white tee a half an inch or so above the high waistband and thrown on my jean jacket in case the temperature drops.

Reminiscent of the day I met him, I hear Nolan before I see him. My interest is piqued when I get close enough to register the cover as *Boo'd Up* by Ella Mai. The busker's version is acoustic, obviously, and he's set it to a slightly slower tempo. The rhythm beat on the box drum pairs nicely with the guitar. When I match with the edge of the crowd, the object of their attention sees me, smirks, and inclines his head toward a pretty redhead seated off to the side behind the two men. I walk over and greet her with a small wave and a hushed, "Hi." She beams warmly back at me and pats the empty chair next to her. The song reaches the final chorus then. Goosebumps shoot up my arms despite my jacket as Nolan's friend, whose name I realize I do not know, joins him in well-practiced and gorgeously blended harmony. As nonchalantly as I can, I readjust in my chair, trying to shake off the chills.

As the last few notes fade out, my neighbor leans over and whispers, "I know. It used to get me too, but then the eejits started rehearsing in our apartment, and it kind of lost its magic." I focus on her. She has a thick accent, which coincides pleasantly with her soft figure and kind green eyes, which are currently flecked with teasing. "I'm Roisin. The grizzly-looking fella on the drum is Eoghan. Doubt Nol' will have time to introduce you 'til they're done." Regarding Eoghan, I agree that 'grizzly' is a very apt description. The percussionist is burly, tattooed, and wildly bearded with hair to match that is currently twisted into a bun at the back of his head.

"I'm Laurel," I allow in an equally hushed tone, extending my hand.

Her eyes twinkle as she shakes it, "Oh, we know, love."

That, I will be sure to discuss with Taylor later, but to the stranger, all I say is, "Thank you for bringing an extra chair."

"Ah, don't mention it." Roisin waves me away. "You never know how long these things can go for. Crisp?" She offers me the bag that had been sitting next to her. I select a few as Nolan calls on a young teenage girl near the front of the gathering. He must be taking requests.

"Do you know *Moral of the Story* by Ashe and Niall Horan?" she questions sheepishly. He encourages her with a sure smile.

"To be clear, you'd like me to specifically sing his lyrics, yeah?"

She simmers. "Yes, please."

"We can do that for you." He winks as he counts off to Eoghan, flustering the preteen enough to warm her face to a mortified bright red and sending her friends into fits of giggles.

♥

About an hour goes by like this, the street performers accepting suggestions or playing songs they've rehearsed while Roisin and I talk softly in between. Truth be told, I've already grown quite fond of the girl sitting next to me. Quick-witted, sarcastic, and brutally honest in the most endearing way, she's in the middle of giving me the low down on the busking session regulars, our heads bent low in the thrill of quietly delivered gossip when a sharp whistle catches our attention. Our faces pivot toward the sound.

"Oi, Ladies!" Eoghan raises his voice, and the audience laughs. My eyes swivel to Nolan in search of an explanation, but the only hint I receive is the oft-used cheeky expression plastered across his face.

"I was just telling our friends here that, if they didn't mind, I was going to play one of my own songs, and then I asked you, Laurel,"he lingers here for the briefest of seconds, bringing forth another round of mirth from the assemblage, "if you had any preference."

"Oh, um, sorry," I answer, clearing my throat. I sit up straighter and make my face a parody of chagrin to match his mockingly admonishing tone. "Let's see, why don't you do…" I trail off as if I need to think it over, but I know which one I want to hear. The crowd, however, does not, and 99% of them are locked onto me, waiting to see what I'll choose. The more anticipation I can build, the better. Nolan just has to be able to live up to it. I give it one more moment, staring at the ground as if I'm in deep contemplation before I find his eyes, "hmmm, *Butterflies*," I finish.

"*Butterflies* it is then," the singer verifies, grin refreshed as he turns back to his eagerly awaiting public.

26

Laurel

The band closes their set around 5:00 PM with a *The Galway Girl/Galway Girl* mashup, which I thought blended both songs rather beautifully. As the final collection of listeners thins, Roisin stands and stretches. I watch the boys begin to divvy up their earnings. Sensing this means they will be heading our way shortly, I get up as well, helping her fold our chairs and stuff them into their carriers.

Suddenly, Eoghan has added to our company, having snuck up from behind and wrapped his arms around his girlfriend's waist, "So, my darling," he says in a deep, husky vocal that matches his unkempt exterior, "which song did you like best?"

Roisin attempts to wriggle out of his grasp, but she is not successful until he bends significantly to plant a sloppy kiss on her cheek. "Feck off, Eoghan," she huffs, wiping her face. She whirls to resume packing but responds to him. "In my opinion, the new Holly Humberstone was the best bit, but that may be because I haven't had to hear it upward of a thousand times."

I can't help but smile when her accent adapts 'thousand' to sound like 'tousand.' Eoghan happily shakes his head. The two of us make eye contact when she crouches to grab the empty chip bag, and the percussionist steps toward me.

"Howya?" he inquires, offering me his hand, "I'm Eoghan."

"Nice to meet you, Eoghan. I'm Laurel," I inform him as I complete the handshake.

"She knows we already know who she is!" Roisin calls from a nearby trash can, "You don't have to pretend." I can practically taste my ensuing blush.

"Sorry about her," Eoghan chuckles before alluding to something behind me.

I twist in the direction to catch Nolan, guitar cased and swung onto his back, walking toward us. "Not even paying attention," he chastens, clicking his tongue to embellish the feigned disappointment displayed in his features.

"I should take the blame there," Roisin states plainly as she joins the circle.

The Irishman deadpans. "Oh. Well, I'll be sure to add it to the list then." Aside from a brief narrowing of her eyes, Roisin ultimately ignores this, as if it is nothing more than what she expects.

"Besides, you could not have asked for a better recovery," she continues, nudging me with her elbow, "quick on her feet, this one is."

Knowing this isn't always the case and subconsciously wanting to downplay the compliment, I suggest a quantifier. "Depends on the moment," I amend genially. My response isn't quite heard over Nolan's, as we've spoken at the same time.

"Yeah, I'm learning that," he says. When I look at him, he's already staring at me.

Eoghan breaks the brief silence which follows. "So, anybody down for a bite and pint?"

"Please. I'm fecking starving," Roisin moans.

"Sure, yeah," Nolan agrees, then addresses me, "Laurel," he queries, "you okay staying with this lot, or do you have other plans for dinner?

"No, this lot's great," I echo, earning another O'Kelley grin.

Eoghan moves across our posse and places both his hands on my shoulders, squatting down so his eyes are level with mine. "Alright then, Laurel," he declares, "as our official guest of honor this evening, I'm about to give you a very important job." I inhale deeply, steeling myself to the oncoming responsibility, confused but not concerned. "Now, I need you to really try not to make bags of it, as the success or failure of the night rests on your decision."

"Eoghan, leave her alone," Roisin cuts in, but her boyfriend only holds up his hand.

"Have a little faith in the American, will you," he scolds, focus still on me. When her retaliation is a simple exasperated roll of her eyes, he proceeds. "We," he gestures to the three Irish people in our circle, "eat around here once a month, if not more, and we each have a spot we like best. So, in order to keep the usual ructions from occurring, we will each describe our favorite local pub. You, my dear, will simply pick the one we go to, yeah?"

I nod in response, "OK, I can do that."

"Quality," Eoghan beams, reinstating himself between his friends. "Before we begin, I just want to say, since you have known our Nolan here," he points accusatorially at the busker, "for three days longer than you have us, you may not want to pick his choice as it would seem like collusion." The entire group erupts with laughter.

"You don't have to do this, you know?" my so-called partner conditions, sliding closer to me once everyone has caught their breath.

"No, I want to. It seems fun." I smile at him. He winks in return.

"Okay then," Eoghan becomes the practicing emcee. "Roisin, ladies first." She sighs but commences her pitch.

"P. Macs is my favorite place close by. It's cozy and eclectic," she starts. "It's about a five-minute walk away, toward Stephen's Green, if you know where that is."

"I passed the closest part of the park coming from my hotel."

"Fabulous. The food's typical pub fare with a few vegan and veggie things. Craft beer is its specialty when it comes to drinks." She backpedals when I wrinkle my nose. "But, as that doesn't appear to be your thing, they also have ciders. My favorite part, the real selling point, in my opinion, is they have hapes of board games." Up to this point, I like to believe I have remained mostly, if not totally impartial, in terms of my facial cues, but at the mention of board games, my eyes go wide. I grab Roisin's arm.

"I know!" she exclaims, placing her hand over mine.

This scene causes Eoghan's jaw to drop and Nolan to double over once more. When he's rallied, the drummer indicates for him to go next.

"Lad," Nolan assuages, still chortling, "it's not even worth it. Look at them." He gestures at Roisin and me, still standing with our hands clasped. "Mine is a place that pours a nice pint of Guinness. Yours is a sports-themed establishment. P. Mac's will have some craic. We can play games." He leaves my side to comfort his dejected friend, patting him encouragingly on the back, "Solid idea, mate, really, but you need to let this one go."

"Sorry, baby," Roisin says, smirking at her boyfriend. "You and Nol go put the things in the car and meet us there." She throws him their keys and links arms with me. "Laurel and I can go get a table."

"Women," Eoghan mutters as he's led away.

27

Laurel

"They've gone and bonded," Eoghan shouts, exasperated by the boys' lack of luck during the first game of the evening. "I tried to tell you letting them be on partners was like signing our death warrants, but did you listen to me? No!"

"Oh, don't be such a sore loser," Roisin reprimands as she stacks our fifteen winning Taboo cards against Nolan and Eoghan's seven. "Fancy another round, boys? We can shake up the teams if it'd help your egos." I chuckle as I clink glasses with her.

P. Mac's proved to be exactly what I hoped it would. Located on the bottom floor of the Drury Court Hotel, in a space at the corner of Stephen Street Lower and Digges Lane, the bar is exactly as Roisin described it. The used furniture and antique wood ground the room and its warm, comfortable aura, while the various lamps, red melted candles stuck in everything from candelabras to old cider bottles, and the use of neon signage bathe the space in a more liberal glow.

Roisin and I had sat next to each other at the table we'd secured upon our arrival, leaving the men to slide in opposite, with Eoghan seated in front of me and Nolan diagonal. When they took longer to show up than expected, Roisin had lost patience and purchased the first round, anticipating what her friends would order. We waited until they were settled to select our meals and get the first game underway.

"I'd say yes," Nolan professes in rejoinder to Roisin's proposal, "but I believe our food is here." He bows his head subtly in our direction. Our interest piqued, we turn to see our server, a boy in his late teens, coming toward us slowly, arms laden with plates and an anxious expression on his face. After he had taken our order, we'd easily come to the conclusion this was his first shift. He was well-meaning and attentive but nervous and not very familiar with the menu. "Need some help, mate?" The boy doesn't comment but instead regards our party with pleading eyes. The busker stands and bridges the few feet between them, carefully commandeering the two plates resting above the waiter's wrists.

"Thanks a mill," he shares as if Nolan has hung the moon, his enamored countenance mirroring my own.

With a reasonable amount of assistance, everything is eventually placed in front of the proper patron—a Veggie

Sloppy Joe for me, Double Decker Beef Burger for the moment's savior, Fresh Fish Tacos passed to Roisin and a P. Mac's Ruben to Eoghan. "Sorry about that," the boy apologizes, "It's my first day." We all smile at him encouragingly and promise he's doing just fine. "Can I get you anything else to drink," he asks. We gratefully accept the offer, passing him our empty pints and bottles. "Same thing all around, yeah?"

Dinner plates stacked neatly at the end of our table, Nolan and I have almost beat Eoghan and Roisin at a game of *Dirty Minds*. Essentially, a guessing game in which a player chooses a word or riddle from their booklet, depending on what has been rolled, and reads one of the facts about the term or the entire puzzle to the other person on their team, who then attempts to infer what is being described. The twist is that all of the sentences read are overtly sexual, even though the answers themselves are innocent. Hoping to enliven the atmosphere, Eoghan picked the game for our dessert course entertainment. Everyone had agreed to play, coalescing over the possibility we'd soon match the surrounding sconces, especially when Roisin and I were broken up, her and my new partner switching seats in the re-coupling. When eye contact was submitted as an additional requirement, I was sure my naturally awkward demeanor would seal our fate. While there have been a few uncomfortable moments, surprisingly, I have fared better than expected. In fact, if Nolan gets this word right, we win the game.

"No pressure," I say, reading the first statement to myself, practicing mentally ahead of voicing it out loud, "Ready?"

"Shoot," the Irishman confirms, taking a drink of his beer.

I toss my hair over my shoulder to shake off any lingering discomfort. "I discharge loads from my shaft." The sentence brings forth a millisecond-length smirk as Nolan searches my eyes for any leads, but I haven't known him long enough to figure out a way to give one.

As if reading our minds, Eoghan leans forward and warns, "No cheating."

"Hmmm," my teammate muses without disrupting our connection, "what has a shaft?" I can't help but snort. He smiles, "Golf club?"

I shake my head, "Men and women go down on me." A wide grin spreads across Nolan's face, and he sits up straighter.

"A lift," he states confidently. I cheer and put my booklet down in between us, revealing the solution. Eoghan slams his hand into the wooden surface, sending a round of laughter through the group.

"Damn it," he interjects, "Laurel's with me if we do teams again, jammy lass."

I chortle, "works for me."

"Phew," Roisin exhales, fanning herself, "I don't know about anybody else, but I could use a smoke after that." She stands, and her boyfriend follows suit.

"I'm all good," I admit, staying seated, "but I'll go order another round."

"Class! We'll have the same," Eoghan requisitions, shrugging into his jacket. "Nol', next match is on you. Try and keep the vibe up, will you now." He winks as he and Roisin head toward the door.

Nolan chuckles after his friends, "He's going to feel like pure shite tomorrow if he carries on like this. Roisin will kill him."

I smile as I drain the last of the liquid left in my cup and stand. "I like them."

"Yeah, they're good people," he concurs, passing his empty ale bottle to me and using both hands to cradle *Dirty Minds'* decomposing packaging. "I'm going to grab a new game, but then I'll come help you carry everything." I look down at my already full hands.

"Yeah, I think I'll need it," I simper.

At the bar, I set everyone's empty containers in front of me and order a fresh one of each.

"Let me guess. You ordered a Guinness," Nolan postulates, materializing by my side right as the my cider is being slid over. I laugh as he takes it, along with the accompanying glass, situating the items so that there is room for more.

"I have had enough Guinness to last me my whole trip. Thank you very much." I avow, rotating toward him.

He places his empty hand over his heart, face twisted in a mimicry of pain. "And here I was assuming I'd converted you."

"Sorry," I respond with a pitying grimace, "I don't think you can change my taste buds."

"Ah," he ruminates, "I still have a little time." I hold his gaze, tipsy butterflies attempting flight in my belly. Nolan breaks it with a wink and heads back to the table. Maybe *Dirty Minds* affected me more than I originally presumed because, as he walks away, I'm left feeling more breathless than usual.

28

Laurel

Five cards to win *Red Flags,* a game a lot like *Cards Against Humanity,* but instead of filling in the blank, you build a date for whoever is "single" each round, a fictional suitor which the other players then get to add a flaw or "red flag" to, turned into ten, which became fifteen. Before we knew it, we were two rounds deeper in our alcohol consumption, seats pushed closer together as the pub crowded around us. When Roisin and I had made our most recent trip to the bathroom, a perilous journey we each accomplished solo only once (and not to perpetuate the stereotype that women always go to the restroom together, but because P. Mac's toilets lay hostage at the end in a red-walled hallway; the gothic lighting and black and white flooring of which make it feel like Satan himself is waiting for you in the stalls), I had checked my phone and learned two things. The first was the shocking truth that it was 9:00 PM. The second was I had four texts from Taylor, the most recent of which was delivered about thirty minutes prior.

Hi! This is me checking in to see
if you knew about when you'll be calling.
I can chat whenever. I don't have any
meetings and can close my office door anytime,
so no worries. Just curious.

I checked your location and you're not at your hotel,
so I'm assuming you're with Nolan. I want to reiterate:

I am not busy today. I am free all day.
Do not leave the attractive
Irish singer because of me.

Love you.

The third text was sent with iMessage's echo animation. I giggle as it plays, maybe a touch more than usual on account of the number of ciders I've consumed, and reply while I wait for my new friend.

I'll call you soon! Promise!!

Back in the land of the living, seemingly safe from our immediate untimely demise, I apologize to everyone and explain I've got a call at 10:00 PM. My table, now cognizant of the fact we have commandeered our spot for almost four hours, agrees the beverages we are currently drinking will be our last.

Fifteen minutes later, if that, all our tabs are closed, and a few hurried waters have been consumed. As we emerge from the restaurant, the shadows cast by the overhead street-light mime our farewells.

"Well, Laurel, love," Eoghan slurs, having exchanged his ale for liquor considerably more times than the rest of us, "it was lovely to meet you. I hope the rest of your stay is just as favorable." I laugh more at the exasperated scowl on Roisin's face as her boyfriend begins to use her as a personal crutch, than at the bearded man's words.

"Thank you, Eoghan," I say, "it was nice to meet you as well. And you, Roisin," I add, smiling at her. "Thanks again for the chair earlier."

She shifts her boyfriend's weight around her neck and off her shoulder, "Any time. Do you have anything else planned for while you're here?"

"I've got a bus tour tomorrow, actually. I'm not sure where I'm headed because I didn't book it, but it leaves from the Molly Malone statue at 8:00 AM."

Roisin winces, "Ah. You better get to the scratcher then," she admits. From context, I'm guessing she means bed, so I endorse the statement with a grin and quick hug.

"Can you manage him, ok?" Nolan inquires of her. She shrugs good-naturedly in response, Eoghan's body bobbing with the gesture.

Her eyes sparkle as she intones, "Ain't my first rodeo" in her best American country twang. I chuckle. "I called a cab while we were inside," she finishes in her mother tongue. Unbidden, Nolan fishes his keys from his pocket and tosses them to her. She catches the jingling missile easily in her free hand.

"I'm going to walk Laurel to her hotel, but Eoghan and I dropped your car at mine earlier," he clarifies. "The sofa bed is made. There's room for you both on it." She beams at him.

"You're a topper, Nolan O'Kelley," she says.

"I know," he agrees, winking at her. With the slip back into his usual charming confidence, I feel my insides liqui-fy. Knowing there's a good chance my unabashed gawking is revealing the sentiment, I quickly endeavor to rearrange my features as he turns the two of us down the road. The action makes me realize I was already holding onto his arm.

"I changed my mind," Roisin yells after us, " You're still an eejit, even if you're a nice one."

We chortle at this, and I use it to cover for the light pink glow blooming over my skin, onset by the discovery of my new habit.

The wind has gathered strength in the late evening hours, rendering it necessary for me to fully utilize the support the Irishman's closeness allows. For most of our stroll, we talk about the night we've just had, Roisin and Eoghan, and what my highlights were from the busking session, but as we near The Dean, Nolan quiets. It's not until it comes into view, the rhythmic beats of the nearby burgeoning nightlife washing over us, that he speaks, "So a bus tour, huh."

"Yeah," I assent as I endeavor to keep upright, "I'm excited."

"It's good you're getting out of the city," he remarks without looking at me. But as we walk a few steps further, I can sense he is. "It'll be good to have some time to yourself too. You can contemplate life as you're carted through the Irish countryside." I stop a few feet shy of the lobby door, which brings him to a halt as well.

"Nolan," I question, letting go of his arm so I can fully face him, "would you like to come with me tomorrow?" This insecure fishing technique doesn't strike me as one he employs often. I search his widening eyes for any justification for this tactic, wondering what I could have said in the last few minutes to put him on edge. Unfortunately, his bewilderment at my suggestion has me second-guessing my interpretation of events. A fresh flush coloring my face and neck as I open my mouth to recant the invitation.

As I blubber, the shock on his face ebbs as his lips begin to curve, splitting his face in two. "I mean, have I not proven myself as a tour guide? Don't you want me to come?" My embarrassment is reborn as indignation. Without a reply, I smack him in the chest and walk away, leaving him laughing behind me.

"I thought I had done something to make you uncomfortable!" I call back.

Within seconds, he's in front of me again, hulling me into his chest, clutching me there to inhibit any further movement while he catches his breath.

"Stop, Stop. I'm sorry." He pants between chuckles. "Do you mind if I join you, honestly? I'll understand if this has ruined my chances." He loosens his grip slightly as he ceases, giving me room to escape the sound of his heartbeat. When I peer up at him, he cocks his head apologetically. *I do have two tickets.*

"Fine," I resolve reticently, trying to make it seem as if my brain is not already psychoanalyzing why he wants to come, "but you're now in charge of breakfast."

"Bang on," he says, letting me go enough to kiss my forehead. "I'll meet you here at 7:45 AM, alright?" To stunned to speak, I merely nod as he backs away, hands in his pockets, exultation a practically tangible halo.

When he's a decent distance away, I finally recognize I have not reached my intended destination. I travel the remaining feet in a daze. Mumbling a response when the porter welcomes me back at the door. I'm unsure how I heard him, given that every voice in my head is still screaming high alert over the fact Nolan's mouth touched my skin. My brain must be on autopilot because I've pressed the phone icon next to Taylor's contact before I even reach the elevator.

29

Laurel

I stayed on the phone with Taylor for much longer than I had anticipated. Yes, we talked about her date with Jeremy as intended (It was the definition of perfect and not in a 'cheesy' sense, but in a 'yes, this is realistic enough for me to believe it happened, and yet it's still inconceivable' way), but the majority of our conversation had occurred after. Not able to hold it in any longer, I had begun my side of the retellings with the part I most needed to discuss.

"Well, Nolan kissed me," I announced as casually as possible, hoping to keep Taylor's transatlantic emotions at bay from the other end of the line. To no one's surprise, I was unsuccessful.

"WHAT?" she screamed. I cringed as I yanked the phone away from my ear, doubling down on the gesture as I pictured her unsuspecting co-workers staring apprehensively at her sealed-off but not soundproofed office. A string of interrogatives followed her exclamation, but I didn't catch what they were as I was furiously trying to add details to my announcement.

I repeated the same quantifier over and over until I was sure she'd heard me, "On the forehead! On the forehead! On the forehead!" Finally, Taylor was quiet, likely waiting for me to shut up, "and we were pretty intoxicated," I concluded.

"Ok, but still. I need context. Start from the beginning."

Tale spent, and goodbyes said, I had crawled into bed around 1:00 AM after forcing myself to shower and blow dry my hair. It may have begrudged the tasks then, but I knew there was even less of a chance they would happen if I put them off until morning.

Those are the reasons why I am now standing at the Nespresso machine, narrowly less than six hours later, begging it to steep faster and bemoaning my past volitions. It may be the hangover, but I feel like the brewing system listens. In record time, I am back in the bedroom, steaming coffee in hand, weighing my options. I don't really have time to do anything but get ready ahead of Nolan's arrival, but every fiber in and all the aching bones of my body are begging me to climb under the unmade sheets. However, the Laurel of last night (overaggressive Type A busybody that she is) had accounted for this because right as I've reached the point of considering whether or not a messy bun or un-styled high pony would suffice as a hairstyle for this outing, a second alarm blares out from the nightstand. I groan as I shut it off and fling the comforter so it once again rests uninvitingly over the pillows.

Thirty minutes later, skincare complete and an outfit chosen, I'm feeling much more like myself. I'm in the middle of changing into my favorite denim romper when someone knocks on the door.

"One minute!" I squeak, startled, and hastily endeavor to re-button my tie-dyed PJ top while also trying to shimmy the matching shorts from their tangle at my ankles as fast as I can manage. In my tizzy, I free the door without checking the peephole.

"Top of the–" The busker materializes on my threshold, exaggerating his accent and doffing an imaginary cap. Mid-sentence, his joke gets the better of him. "I'm sorry," he chuckles, "I can't say it with a straight face."

There's a pause in which I just stare at him, blinking repeatedly and waiting for my brain to register his presence. In a way, it has, but instead of focusing on words and appropriate greetings, it's devoted its limited early morning energy to two things: cursing him but somehow still admiring him. The breakdown seems to be 25% / 75%, with the lesser portion of my cogitations running to some semblance of *Oh, he's a morning person, fantastic* while the majority hones in on what he's chosen to wear, *Laurel, he's wearing a John Mayer T-shirt. You went to that tour! Oh, and cuffed jeans, you like cuffed jeans. The grey Converse are a nice touch, too, don't you think.*

When fifteen seconds pass without me articulating a single sound, Nolan, blue eyes already bright with mischief, prompts politely, "May I come in?"

"Is it 7:45 AM already?" I finally submit into the dialogue, stepping aside and self-consciously holding the sides of my miss-fastened shirt closer together. My guest deposits the coffee and donut box he was holding on the hexagon-shaped table nearest him.

Surveying the den, he discloses calmly, "No, I'm early."

"Ok?" I trail off, more than marginally annoyed at his unexpected presence and subsequent lack of explanation. If I'd had my way, he wouldn't have seen me in this state until we knew each other a little better. "I'm going to go finish getting ready," I gripe, snatching a sugar-coated pastry from among the display. As I head down the hall, I relax enough to extend a hospitable olive branch, "Feel free to turn on the TV or use the record player."

Once I feel properly dressed, I send a text to Taylor in invisible ink.

> *It's ten there, so you're awake.*
> *I can't really discuss it right now, but guess*
> *who showed up 30 MINUTES EARLY!*

I expound via the slam effect:

> *Not to my hotel in general, to MY ROOM.*

As I send off the second message, an enigma presses on my frontal lobe, demanding attention.

"Nolan," I demand from in front of the bathroom mirror, "how'd you know which room I was in?" As I wait for a response, I can hear he's chosen to play the Sam Cooke vinyl I purchased and smile at the choice. My residing irritation wanes by the smallest fraction.

"Oh, that's kind of your doing, to be honest," he replies from the den.

"My doing?" I wonder, more to myself than to him, as I define the top layer of my waves with my curling iron.

"Yeah, the receptionist on duty usually works nights, so she's seen me drop you off a few times. It was easier to persuade her you were expecting me."

I'm straining to hear him over the music, so after a quick glance to make sure no spare undergarments or the like are strewn about the two back rooms, I interrupt.

"Can you bring me my coffee?" I shout.

"Are you decent?" he calls back. I roll my eyes before coating my upper lashes in a thin layer of liner, rounding out my usual natural look.

Maintaining our current volume, I return. "I wouldn't ask you if I wasn't."

"You never know. It could be a ploy," Nolan says at a normal speaking audible. I jerk my head up from inserting my earrings and am confronted by his reflection leaning on the main doorframe, one ankle tucked behind the other.

I move to pluck my drink from his outstretched hand, "You came anyway, I see."

"I did," he affirms without breaking his stare. (I would like to revise my statement from earlier—Dirty Minds has definitely affected our relationship.)

A volcano erupts in my brain, lava flowing over my body in waves. The sip I was consuming catches in my throat as I momentarily lose my ability to breathe. Taking the excuse to recover, I cough a few times, pivoting back to the mirror to tie my hair into a loose ponytail.

"I fail to see how that's my fault," I tell the glass, picking up our previous conversation.

Nolan's eyes flick to mine in the mirror, and I expect the cocky comment right away. "If you didn't need walking home every night–"

"Nope." I state plainly, cutting him off, "I never request it. You always offer." Unfortunately, he doesn't play off my retort but simply smirks as he raises one arm to toy with the top jamb of the entryway.

He stays silent as he watches me tie a brightly colored scarf around my updo's elastic band. His scrutiny is trying upon my required concentration. When I've achieved the desired result, he inquires, "Where's the tour to anyway? Did you check?"

"Oh, sorry! I meant to text you. Cliffs of Moher."

"It's alright. I figured it was either the cliffs or Giant's Causeway." Nolan pushes himself off the door as I head into the bedroom to put on my Keds. He follows via the hall. "The cliffs are better, in my opinion, and not just because now Eoghan owes me a fiver."

"You took bets on where we were going?" I ask as I sit in one of the chairs, amused.

He politely explores the bedroom as he answers, "Well, Roisin didn't, but that's to be expected."

Shoes suitably laced, I sit up to find the Irishman beaming at me, so I grin back. I withdraw my phone from its new home in the pocket of my white cardigan. It's barely 7:30 AM.

"Well," I proffer, standing, "I guess we can head over. I'm ready if you are."

"You aren't bringing a bag?" he questions, face a mixture of distress and confusion.

Baffled, I pull my purse away from my hip and raise my eyebrows. When he only elevates his own, I decode the pantomime, "It's not overnight. I don't need more than my purse… do I?"

Nolan shrugs as he swallows more coffee. "I mean, technically, no, but we are heading all the way across the country. I brought one to be safe. What if the bus ends up banjaxed on the side of the road, and no one can fix it until morning?"

I eye him suspiciously, but he doesn't give, inclining his brow toward my nearby backpack as if its very existence proves his point. "You would know," I concede.

30

Laurel

As early as I felt I had to get up, the rendezvous at the Molly Malone statue was not our bus's first of the morning. When we board the coach, many of the plush seats are already occupied by passengers, some bleary-eyed and clutching insulated cups while others appear eager and at home in their claimed area. None of them seem to have Nolan's recommended "emergency bags," but then maybe none of them are, or know, locals.

The survivalist and I spot an empty row near the middle of the vehicle and settle in. I claim the oft-coveted window seat, but he doesn't seem to mind. I watch as he stows our bags in the overhead storage. Doing so causes his T-shirt to ride up, revealing a sliver of chiseled torso, the muscles in his abdomen stretching taunt as he makes space for our luggage in the overhead storage. I ogle them for a beat longer than I probably should before forcing myself to fixate on the flock of pigeons gathered on the tram wire outside the window.

I wouldn't have minded a solo trip, but getting to spend time with Nolan every day has made my time in Ireland truly something I wasn't expecting. I had pictured myself wandering and relaxing, content in my own company as I took a hiatus from the responsibilities and routine of my everyday. But instead, each passing adventure has been more enjoyable than the last as I have gotten to sample what a life here could be. My pleasant musings are tinged with melancholy when I remember for the umpteenth time since Sunday night that even if there is more than just friendship between the two of us— and it's becoming more and more apparent this is the case— my trip has an end date. In four days, I won't be in Ireland anymore. Yes, we could still talk—on calls, FaceTime, social media, what have you—but it wouldn't be the same as it is now. There wouldn't even be a waning period where we could go from seeing each other every day to every other to once a week and so on. Long distance with no clear endpoint is not something I want to put myself through emotionally, physically, or mentally. It works for some people. Distance may make the heart grow fonder, but the inverse is "out of sight, out of mind." With something this new, those aren't odds I'm willing to gamble my heart on. (If you're on the fence, watch *Like Crazy*. I know it's a movie, but you'll see what I mean.) I struggle to inhale over my increasing pulse and berate myself for letting my feelings get this far out of hand.

I've drawn even closer to the verge of a minor hysterical break over my future predicament when Nolan plops down next to me, drawing my attention and chasing away any anxiety and indecision.

"Not bad," he says, looking around. "I was picturing our drive in something much less luxurious.

I laugh, "What were you picturing that people would pay to spend six hours in?"

"Honestly? One of those hop-on-hop-off buses you see around all the tourism locations with the hard plastic seats and the open tops."

"And you still wanted to come?" I inquire, genuinely astonished by the level of discomfort he was anticipating.

His reply comes in a tone both playful and sarcastic as he bumps my elbow with his own, "Yes, Laurel. I still wanted to come."

I am about to respond when the bus doors close, and our driver, now seated in his place of honor, begins to speak.

"Good morning, ladies and gentlemen," he greets us, accent strong but part of an even-paced and careful diction that denotes the time he has spent in his chosen profession. "Welcome to *Paddywagon's* day trip to the Cliffs of Moher from the wonderful Dublin City. My name is James Flannigan. I know, nice traditional Irish name there, James. I am delira and excira to be taking you all the way to your destination and back today."

"Delighted and excited," Nolan whispers, slouching to translate the local slang.

"Thanks, but I'm pretty sure I got that one." I don't dare turn my head, but I can see him grinning in my peripheral when he sits tall.

"So if you need any help or have any queries for me at all, don't hesitate to ask," James continues. "As we make our way out of the capital, I will point out a few landmarks as we pass them, but as we seem to be stuck in traffic at the moment, let's use this time to go over today's itinerary. In about thirty to forty-five minutes, we will be making a quick stop at a petrol station for coffee and snacks, should you desire them. After that…"

Closer to forty-five than thirty minutes later, I'm back on the coach with a gas station cappuccino in my hand, a water bottle and snacks shoved into the provided pouch in front of me, and Nolan next to me trying, and so far failing, to connect to the on-road Wi-Fi. On the way to this first stop, we, among other things, were educated on the tour rules. There are three big ones:

1) No hot or smelly food on the bus

2) No smoking or alcohol on the bus

3) If you are more than five minutes late for the bus's set departure time, you will be left to arrange your own way home

As the Paddywagon navigates back into traffic, James comments on the weather, "I have to tell you, you're in luck. It's a good day for drying, which is just a bit of Irish slang for 'it's sunny."

Nolan whistles at me quietly. I pry my focus from the driver and take in the flask tapping against my knee. I feel my lips part. Once my eyes track the path to his face, he mouths 'Bailey's.'

"Rule breaker," I chide in a hush, delivery bordering on teasing.

He bends down, and I'm once again painfully aware of how close his lips are to mine, "Do you want some or not?" he hedges, non-verbally daring me to say yes.

In answer, I pop the lid off my wax-lined paper cup and hand it over.

"Rule Breaker," he copies, as my mug is filled to the brim.

31

Laurel

As the cityscape changes to suburbs and then green pastures, Nolan and I decide to play a drinking game with the contraband liquor we added to our morning beverages. For the next thirty minutes, we entertain ourselves by coming up with and following ten simple rules. I finish my cappuccino before he finishes his tea.

"I'm out," I announce, shaking my cup. "Does that mean I win or I lose?" My head is splashing in and out of a kiddie pool, and my skin feels hot. I know our alcohol-to-mixer ratio was relatively low, but my lack of proper food and water consumption has made it feel higher.

Nolan, cheeks a light rosy hue, ponders this conundrum for less than a second. "It definitely means you lose." I scowl at the sanguinity that settles over his face and haughtily reach across our space to dispose of my trash in his seat-back pocket-made waste receptacle. I hear his breath catch. *No. I definitely imagined that, right?*

"Well, I think it means I win," I contest, moving back into my assigned area and crossing my arms.

My competition opens his cup. "Honestly, I've only got about half a drink left." He tilts his head back, draining the rest of the contents, Adam's Apple tracking the action. "Why don't we call it a draw?" he suggests with a semi-smug smile.

I'm hoping he can't tell, but the Baileys in my system is working in Nolan's favor in more ways than one. I find this borderline drunk version of myself does not mind ending our game in a tie. In fact, she's kind over it and in favor of something that gives her an excuse to be ever so slightly closer to him.

"Fine," I sigh, uncrossing my arms, "I guess that's fair, considering you were the one who made it possible in the first place." The Irishman seems pleased.

"Glad I'm good for something." He winks. It's body language he's used over a handful of times in the few days I've known him, but this iteration sends the butterflies that seem to have taken up permanent residence in my stomach soaring up into my throat. *Ok, maybe we used more liquor than I realized.*

I decide, much to the intoxicated part of my brain's horror, that I need a tiny detox. I can't summon the willpower to get up and get away from him completely (even if I could, there's nowhere I can make an excuse to go), so instead, I transition into a forward-facing position and simulate the action of daydreaming out the window. I'm congratulating myself on what I'd consider a fully sober response to the situation when Nolan undoes all my efforts.

"I don't know about you," he confides, "but I need some food in my system." As we've put all the snacks in front of my chair, he scoots over to see what his options are. When he angles forward to grab a packet of salt and vinegar crisps, I feel his arm slide around my shoulders. I don't register my reaction as a conscious choice, maybe because, for a half-second, my brain freezes like a deer in headlights, but I adjust my posture marginally to more comfortably fill the new space that's been created. Once a few breath cycles have gotten me used to our current proximity, I rotate away from the double-panned glass to read his face.

"Want one?" Nolan offers, his head inclined and eyebrows raised. Other than that, he's wearing the same expression as always. The chips held aloft between us.

"That's probably a good idea," I agree, popping one into my mouth. He smirks at me.

Over the speakers, James' voice picks back up as he goes over the history of whatever town we are passing through. As the musician's thumb metronomes between two freckles on my upper arm, we both seize the opportunity to concentrate on something besides the other person—or, in my case, at least pretend to.

I'm not saying we're a couple now or anything (I'm not entirely unhinged), but our relationship has changed. After the past 12 hours, the voice in my head is no longer asking *if* he likes me but knows he does. In the end, the final step over the friendship line was simple. It wasn't a cinematic event. It wasn't a shocking declaration. It was him making the overt choice to put his arm around me and me intuitively deciding to lean into it. It feels like it did before, but easier somehow. It feels like a weight has been lifted off my chest, and I can breathe. I know there won't be any more back and forth. There's no room left to gaslight myself into running away. In spite of my misgivings and my better judgment, for the time being, I want this. I'm choosing this. Taylor is right. I might be leaving in a few days, but currently, I'm in Ireland. I should live a little while I'm here.

32

Laurel

After a few anecdotes, James announces that until we reach our first stop, we will have to entertain ourselves, as he has run out of things to tell us about the passing greenery. Not wanting to leave those in his charge completely unattended, he swaps his voice over the speaker system for music. Traditional Irish melodies float through the bus and mingle with the tourists' prattle, not quite loud enough to hear and not exactly quiet enough to truly ignore. I'm content humming along softly until teasing laughter sounds in my ear.

"You and the bus are playing two different songs, petal," he says. I blush.

"Really?" I counter, angling my head in an effort to hear better.

"Completely. I'm afraid." Sure enough, what I recognized as The Pogues' *Dirty Old Town* is something I had never heard at all. "Here," he proceeds, fishing his phone out of his jacket pocket and offering an earbud, "I'll play it so you can hear it better."

When *A Pair of Brown Eyes* by The Pogues finishes (at least I had the band right), Nolan hands the device to me. I glance up at him in question. "Your go," he remarks.

I slide back into my seat, holding the iPhone with both hands and tapping the surface with my thumbs. "Can I have a guideline or something?" I request.

My neighbor chuckles, "You can't just play a song?" I worry my bottom lip. My mind has drawn a complete blank.

Nolan's eyes grow bright and mischievous, "Okay, I'll bite." He slouches so he can see the phone's screen. "Category is...Guilty Pleasure songs." My nose scrunches involuntarily.

Typically, I don't like people calling any music their guilty pleasure. I feel like it demeans the artist. If someone wants to listen to a certain song, they shouldn't feel the need to hide it. However, he's accommodating me, so…

"I don't really know if I'd call them a 'guilty pleasure' per se," I clarify as I type, "but they're different from the things I typically listen to." I click on BROCKHAMPTON'S artist icon, causing *SUGAR* to play. "It's either them or Post Malone."

"I know about BROCKHAMPTON," Nolan states. "One of the members is Irish, I believe."

I nod and hand him his phone. "You choose. Same topic."

"Guilty Pleasure? Oh, BTS for sure," he declares without changing the song.

I snort. "Sorry. BTS isn't allowed to be classified as a guilty pleasure. They are one of the biggest music groups in history. There should be no shame in listening to BTS." *See this. This is what I mean. Because BTS's fanbase is primarily young women, Nolan thinks it's odd for him to like them as well. Ok, mental rant done.* "Sorry. Sorry." He apologizes, hands up in mock surrender. "I didn't know there was an artist impact threshold. Let me see." I watch him while he scrolls through his music library.

I advocated for this musical get-to-know-you game as a way to hit the hormone breaks, but, much like when I introduced him to Harry Strange on our ride to Jameson Distillery, the fact he's taking it so seriously is becoming an emotional turn-on. "Ok, what about this?" he asks cautiously. "I really like this one song by a local band called Wild Youth. Their stuff is more electronic pop than I typically enjoy..." Nolan pauses, waiting for my approval. I smile, signaling his reasoning is valid, "...but I always end up unconsciously singing it in the shower."

As the song begins, mental images of the scenario he's described flood my brain. I swallow to regain my bearings and moisten my throat. "I'll accept it," I say as the phone is returned to my hands with a new category in mind. *Yeah, I definitely played myself.*

33

Laurel

Three and a half hours later, the Paddywagon pulls off the highway and into a small town. We'd stopped and stretched our legs for a minute in a place called Kinvara, roaming around the colorful sea port village and its stonework castle's grounds, but besides that, we'd been bus bound, happily en route to our main destination.

Nolan yawns. "Perfect timing," he commends. "I'm starting to get hungry."

"Me too," I concur, shaking off my own drowsiness.

The two of us had spent the last hour talking quietly, pointing out things we saw as we traversed the 'Wild Atlantic Way.' Our guide wasn't lying when he promised breathtaking views on this stretch of the trip. Occasionally, I snapped a photo of a cliffside sheep pasture or crumbling manor home, but mostly, I contentedly watched the world go by, using Nolan's body for support as I stared out the window.

"Ladies and gents," James calls from the front. "Welcome to Doolin. This is intended to be our lunch stop, but as the fare is not included in your ticket, feel free to do anything you'd like. If you are needing to have a meal, however, may I recommend either FitzPatrick's, McGann's, or Gus O'Connor's pubs. O'Connors is near where I'm hoping to land us. But, if you would rather go for a bit of a dander around the town, I'd be happy to set you off toward one of the other two." When the coach comes to a complete stop, our driver adds, "We're a bit ahead of schedule, so let's say be back in your seats in an hour and fifteen. I'll see you by 13:45, ok?"

We join the line inching toward the door, eventually emerging into the Irish sunshine.

Doolin unfolds exactly as I expect a town in the Gaelic countryside to. We debus across from a light pink house with green windows and a thatched roof. When I round the transport, I can see *The Sweater Shop*, the pink building, is the last in the row of small mismatched stores—I assume they're stores, although they look like houses—which line the street. It isn't until Nolan and I have rounded the vehicle, however, that I let out a sound that can only be described as a cross between a gasp and a hum. Across the roadway, parallel to the row of shops and restaurants, is a small stone wall. At various points, couples and small groups rest on or against it, chatting happily, completely used to what I'm seeing. On the other side of the wall lay rolling green hills dotted with telephone poles and horses. I spot the beginnings of a neighborhood off to one side of the slopes, but the true recipient of my adoration is the lone home in my primary field of vision: a medium-sized yellow house with a grey roof and children playing in the yard.

"What?" Nolan inquires, nudging my arm.

"It's just very…" I struggle to conjure the exact word, "…quaint, I guess," I finish, even though it's not quite what I mean.

He shrugs fondly, "That's the majority of Ireland then. Come on, let's sort something to eat." We follow most of our tour group down the street and into the championed Gus O'Connor's. The slate and black wood storefront advertises seafood and an 1832 establishment date in fresh gold paint.

Despite the good weather outside, the pub is dressed in a comforting, snug manner, most befitting to the small open space. There's a fire burning in the basalt fireplace which matches the granite tile on the floor. The walls, a mix of white-painted cement, brick, and stained wood, are covered with images of an Ireland, and specifically Doolin, of yore.

"Dining in or simply here for a pint," a pale-eyed stewardess with a short blond updo requests when we reach her station.

"Dining in," I reply. She leads us and a few other famished travelers deeper into the area with the hearth, seating our party at a small square table next to the wall prior to placing the rest but promising to return. I slide into the booth.

Nolan shakes off his jacket and drapes the outerwear over the back of his chair. "Thanks a million," he credits the woman as she passes back by to deliver our menus.

"Oh! You're Irish," she gasps, polite shock etched across her features.

"Last time I checked," he jests, putting a hand to his chest and thigh and then exchanging them for his arm and head as if unsure.

The hostess heats to a bright shade of red, toying with the end of her ponytail as she consults me for assistance.

"Ignore him," I suggest with a pitying grimace.

This seems to console her, but she still makes a plea for vindication, "I'm not really sure why," she explains to the busker, "but I presumed you were a tourist. I guess all those people were tourists, and then she was American, so... my apologies."

"Sure look," Nolan addresses her affably. "I'm not offended. I was just codding you."

"Someone will be with you shortly, she curtsies minutely in acquiescence, her skin slowly returning to normal tone as she heads back to her post.

We giggle quietly to ourselves, emotionally defusing the situation.

"And here I thought I was doing a decent job teaching you the basics of being Irish," he shares once we're through.

I shed my cardigan as I prod, "Is that what you've been doing?"

"Well, yeah. Is it not true in the last few days, you've learned about Irish whiskey, Dublin City, drinking Guinness, pubs, Irish music, and presently the Irish countryside?" He's been counting the lessons off on his fingers and concludes by shaking his right hand and thumb at me for emphasis. I can't help but grin.

"Should I be preparing for a test?" I challenge, placing my forearms on the table and pushing into them.

Nolan replicates the posture as a cocksure smirk crosses his face. "Why else would I be spending so much time with you?" My jaw unhinges. *The open gall of this man sometimes. I swear.* He winks as he stands, not giving me time to respond. "I need to run to the jacks. If someone comes by, can you get me a pint?"

I use my first moment of solitude since this morning to check my text messages. I have six, all from Taylor, delivered hours ago.

OMG. What?? (sent with echo)

No way.

Are you mad? I'd be kind of mad.

*Wait, were you dressed,
or were you like morning you?*

*Not that morning you isn't
indisputably incredible.*

*Please call me tonight when
you get back from your trip.
I'm dying over here, and
I need to know everything.*

Can I get you anything to drink?" Our waiter proffers after clearing his throat to get my attention. He's middle-aged, balding and less than enthusiastic about his current predicament. "Pint of Guinness, perhaps?" He proposes, clicking his pen.

"Oh, sorry!" I say, stowing my phone. Snickering as an idea roots in my brain, "Actually, can I get a Bulmers Red Berries and Lime and a bottle of Budweiser if you have it?"

Luckily, Nolan gets back from the restroom before our drinks are brought to the table.

"What looks good to you?" he asks, perusing the menu. "I'm leaning toward either the fish and chips or the," he breaks off when the Budweiser is placed in front of him.

"Thank you." My smile is dripping honey as I'm handed my cider, the server pledging to collect our order shortly.

The butt of my joke waits to speak until the man has walked away. I can tell by the way he's chewing his cheek the retreat is not happening fast enough. "Laurel, love," he finally questions pleasantly, "care to explain?"

"I just figured since you were spending all this time teaching me the basics of being Irish," I convey as I concentrate on pouring my cider into the accompanying glass, "I might as well teach you the basics of being American." When I swallow my first sip, I meet his eyes.

"Fair play," Nolan laughs, the sound resinating through the tavern. "Fair play."

34

Laurel

Unbeknownst to me, our bill had been paid while I ran to the restroom. Since he was no longer at our table, as I expected him to be, I meandered toward the door, peering into the different areas as I passed them, hoping to spot the Irishman. I was about to give up and exit the establishment when a hand grabbed mine as I weaved my way through the crowd near the bar.

"Sorry. I didn't expect another bus load to traipse in here," Nolan states, tucking between my body and the gentleman next to him and leading me out the door.

We stayed connected as we strolled down Fisher Street and re-entered the bus. It's also how we exited the coach fifteen minutes later after being handed our Cliffs of Moher admission tickets and agreeing to meet back at the entrance by 3:30 PM.

As many in our group commence the upward climb to the cliffs, Nolan and I stop at the Visitor Centre to see if we can procure a map. Not only are we successful, but we are also granted access to a small shortcut. Directed by staff toward an elevator and advised to go up a floor and through the Cliff's View Cafe, we exit the building through different doors, following a path that joins the main trail a few feet above the lowest viewing platform. From there, the real work begins. Although the central walkway is paved, the slight incline and sporadic gale force winds (I am somewhat exaggerating, but balance issues aside, for a person my size, a strong gust can feel like a gale, ok?) leave me practically clinging to Nolan's bicep. He bears my weight easily as we ascend. Overall, I'm pleased with the accessibility accommodations worked into the natural attraction. Although the two of us choose to stick to the stairs, where we can pause and shelter near the walled edge if need be, there are ramps that track a path beside us and conjoin to ours at each landing point.

Given the wind's angle is more against than for us, it takes us around fifteen minutes to reach the pinnacle of the cliffs, O'Brien's Tower. The structure, which looks like a turret from a small fortress, sits atop a wide, flat flagstone. Given false confidence by the momentary and current lack of wind, I release my friend's arm and go forth alone in pursuit of an informational placard or panel. As I imagine the possible histories: a monk living in solitude or a prisoner banished to a lonely existence, I find what I'm searching for and bend to read:

'Cornelius O'Brien (1782–1857) a descendant of the first High King of Ireland, Brian Boru, was landlord of the locality. He became MP for Clare in 1832, and held the office or 20 years. He built this tower in 1835, now referred to as O'Brien's Tower, as an observation point for hundreds of tourists that began to come to the area traveling along the country's Wild Atlantic Way.'

Oh, so it's merely a really, really old viewing pedestal. Still cool from an antiquity perspective. However, far less romantic.

As I stand, the wind picks up again, catching me at the perfect moment. I feel myself knocked off-kilter and, falling backward, brace myself for impact. It never comes. I hadn't heard him walk up behind me, but instead of hard stone, my body weight is simply transferred into Nolan's chest.

"Woah. Careful there." The musician says, setting me back on my feet. "The winds a right melter today, yeah?"

35

Nolan

As I pull Laurel into me, the gust that threatened to toss her blows the scent of her shampoo into my face, or maybe it's her perfume. Whichever it is, it reminds me of the flowers my sister is obsessed with. I believe they're called peonies, but I could be wrong. "The winds a right melter today, yeah?" I advise, gently propping her upright again.

When we'd reached the apex of the paved pathway, I could tell by the sparkling curiosity embedded in her expression, Laurel wanted the observation tower to be more than it was. She'd unwound her arm from mine and wandered toward the structure. I let her go as the wind had died down, and I didn't want to seem overbearing. However, I also knew this present calm was merely Eurus' swift inhale, so I kept a few paces behind.

"Thanks. That was a close one," the American says, dusting herself off. She peaks up at me, cheeks lightly flushed and a shy smirk gracing her lips before she turns back to the Atlantic Ocean view.

"You know, there's a myth about the winds up here," I contemplate aloud, making a bid for her attention. "Well, the myth partly has to do with the winds. They're more a featured extra than a character."

"Oh, yeah?" Her head tilts as she glances over her shoulder, and I know she's been ensnared.

I simper, pressing my back against the tower wall and continuing. "Legend has it," I start, waiting a beat to make sure I've really piqued Laurel's interest. When her focus doesn't falter, I begin. "A long, long time ago, there was a witch named Mal who fell deeply in love with Cú Chulainn, a legendary Irish warrior. Unfortunately for the witch, her love was unrequited. Mal, however, not wanting to count her losses, decided she would not be denied and began chasing the gallant man all around Ireland. They ended up near these cliffs." As I'm milking my retelling for all it's worth, complete with exaggerated gestures and dramatized voices, I'm not astounded when Laurel giggles and backtracks a step to rest next to me. Her brown eyes now eager to know the rest of the tale. *Nolan - 1. Atlantic Ocean - 0*

"With no other escape, Cú Chulainn vaulted to the island known as Diarmuid. Mal, believing she could also make the jump, followed. As she leapt for the island, a gust of wind arose and assisted her. Cú Chulainn, seeing she was going to make it, quickly hurtled back. The witch, with the false confidence from her last jump, did the same. But without the wind, she fell short and crashed into the rocks below. Some people say Miltown Malbay, a town about an hour south from where we are now, is named in her memory." By the end of my tale, Laurel's visage of bemused intrigue has shifted into sheer shock.

"Are you serious?" she interjects. "What kind of story is that?"

"Apologies," I offer, linking our arms again so we can safely resume our walk around the structure. "It's the way it goes." She breaks eye contact, shaking her head incredulously but still smiling.

"With how stunning this place is, I expected something a little more …"

Laurel trails off as her lips part, leaving her thought unsaid. I trace her widening gaze and inwardly groan. This is the one thing I was hoping to avoid.

"Oh my gosh, you can keep going!" she exclaims, pointing to the place where the pavement devolves into gravel, and those with a death wish can continue walking along the top of the cliffs.

Truth be pressured from of me, I do not love heights. Indoor heights or rooftop bars, I'm fine with. But natural heights, as they rarely have barriers, tend to make me —rightfully— uneasy. I force a chuckle, trying to keep my actions light. "Petal, you almost got blown over in the safe zone. I'm not really sure the coastal hike is for you."

"I promise not to let go of you," she immediately volunteers, peeking at me through her lashes. It's a cruel tactic, but I resist.

"What if I refuse to go," I opine.

She wasn't anticipating this possible ultimatum, so more than a second passes before she responds. "Then I'll go alone, for just a second and not that far." She grins. Without giving me a chance for rebuttal, she's set off toward the gap in the fencing.

Now, as that wasn't what I was expecting, I freeze. Laurel hasn't looked back once. When she's actually taken a few steps outside the stone enclosure, I come to my senses and jog to catch up to her. Once we're in step again, she slides her hand around my arm. "Change your mind?" she inquires, smug eyes twinkling and eyebrows raised. She's teasing me. I have half a mind to pick her up and carry her back to safer soil. She's a very small person. I have no doubt I could do it. My internal calculations must have shown on my face because her eyes narrow like it's the scenario she's waiting for, so I shrug.

"I don't think I could face Roisin, let alone Colin and Dylan if something happened to you." She snorts and tightens her grip, forcing me a little closer. The subtle downward tug of her presence is both exhilarating and grounding.

We travel the pebble-made path in contented silence, the wild air howling as it collides with its obstacles and whips our hair into our faces. Laurel seems contentedly silent. However, my own outward solemnity is a result of the incessant Hail Marys I'm reciting in my head. I'm on upwards of fifty when my anchor stops. "Want to sit?" she indicates with her free hand to the ten or so people spotting the cliff's edge. I can feel the blood drain from my face at the very proposition. Like Hell, do I want to do that.

"We don't have to." Laurel, sensing my hesitation, proceeds along our current route, yanking on my arm in an attempt to spur me into motion.

"No. Let's," I answer suddenly. I'm not sure how the stilted words found their way out of my mouth. My subconscious seems to have decided being still nearer to the certain death is better than being in motion further away.

"Are you sure?" Laurel verifies, puzzled. I don't blame her. My decision and my appearance must be at odds.

I somehow manage to wink. "Only if you promise not to let go of me." Laurel blushes, increasing my confidence by one percent.

To access the outcropping of grass-covered rock on which most people are sitting, we have to step over a ledge that hits between my ankles and knees. Laurel studies it for a moment.

"What I'm thinking will be easiest," she says, "is if you go first and then help me from the other side."

"Ok, sound," I nod, stepping over and reaching for her hand.

As we head nearer to the cliff's edge. I feel a familiar knot form in my stomach. I'm 99% sure Laurel has cerebral palsy. One of my mam's friends has it, and Laurel's disability is definitely similar. But, the query has never really come up, and, even if it had, how does one make that type of inquiry without seeming like a right git, especially after not mentioning it for four days? Frankly, it's a moot point, so I was good at leaving it at my probable diagnosis, but Roisin then pointed out that incorrectly assuming might make me a prick.

"What if you're wrong, Nol'," she had said, "and it's something else entirely?"

There are pros and cons to both sides, I have to admit, but what it all comes down to is what I want is to know Laurel, and I want my facts to be correct. Once we're seated, I give myself a minute to work up some nerve—and acclimate to my impending doom—before I clear my throat. "Can I ask you a question?" I pose.

She considers me inquisitively, "Yes?"

"I hope this doesn't come across as rude." My opening doesn't land as confidently as I'd hoped, but Laurel doesn't seem offended, so I press on, "do you have cerebral palsy?"

For a millisecond, she goes somewhere else. The light in her eyes fades to the dimmest flicker. I'm worried I've sent everything arseways when she smiles. It's subtle, a hint of what I've become accustomed to, but it's there.

"Yeah. Yeah, I do," she affirms. "How did you–"

I interrupt her as relief pours over me, explanation rushing out faster than my tongue can manage. "My mam's friend has it too. It's not a big deal or anything. I was just curious." As I breathe away any remaining discomfort, the knot in my stomach gets a little tighter. Not because I'm still anxious but because of the way Laurel is looking at me.

36

Laurel

Rarely, in my almost twenty-seven years on this planet, has someone outside the disabled community really known what cerebral palsy is. Never has this happened with a man around my age. Not only does Nolan already know someone with the diagnosis, but he's familiar enough to recognize it in others.

I'm confident enough in myself that I don't mind explaining, and I don't get offended when people inquire after the physical manifestations with good intentions. But, having someone already understand felt like a first breath after nearly drowning. I didn't know how bad I wanted it to happen, maybe even needed it to. Now that it has, all I can do is smile as unforeseen alleviation rushes through me.

"It's not a big deal or anything. I was just curious," The Irishman finishes with a lopsided grin. It's an undersized, embarrassed version of his usual face-spitting show. As I watch it grow, I know beyond a shadow of a doubt this is it. This is the moment Nolan O'Kelley won me over hook, line, and sinker.

37

Laurel

"Laurel, wake up. We're stopping." A pleasant accent rouses me gently. Sunlight is still streaming in through the window when I open my eyes, causing me to squint and pivot into his chest. I blink a few times to adjust to the glare.

After our penultimate stop in Bunratty, it was all I could do to keep my fatigue at bay. We had re-boarded the bus at barely past 5:15 PM, but the Guinness I had been annoyed into drinking was sloshing heavily around my stomach, feigning the feeling of having eaten a three-course meal. When the perpetrator of my apparent exhaustion had relaxed around me, tendered an earbud, and played me the EP of an artist named LYRA, I didn't have much of a choice but to let her cool, haunting voice guide me into a dream.

"I'm sorry," I say, sitting up and resisting the urge to rub my face. "I didn't mean to fall asleep."

Nolan tucks a strand of hair that has escaped my pony-tail behind my ear as I stretch. "It's. ok. I dozed for a minute myself, if I'm being honest." I don't know if this is true or not, but it makes me feel better, regardless.

Over the intercom, James reminds his passengers this quick gas station pit stop will be the last until we reach the city. While Nolan is busy collecting our trash and storing his iPhone, I check my reflection in my cell's camera to ensure nothing embarrassing, like dried drool or smudged mascara, has taken up residence on my face. Thankfully, for once in my life, I seem to have slept semi-angelically. Aside from my slightly unkempt hair, I don't immediately notice anything which needs to be wiped or covered. I eased the scarf and rubber band loose, running my hands along my temples to lessen my updo's crease, and deposit both into my cardigan pocket, adding my phone as we stand to vacate our row.

"Here," Nolan says, handing me my backpack. I watch him get his own, figuring he needs to grab something out of it. Instead, he throws one strap over his shoulder and uses his head to indicate the exit bay.

"What are we doing?" I ask as he shuffles me through the doors.

Out from under the cover of the coach, I notice the sky has begun to gray. "Best be quick if you can," James counsels the group. "We can stay for about fifteen minutes, but we might try to make it a smidge quicker. I'd like to stay ahead of the weather."

The busker grabs my hand and hurries me around the back of the bus. "Nolan, what are we doing?" I repeat.

"There's something here I think you'll want to see," he states by way of explanation, hauling me forward so we can walk side by side. "We're close, but I want us to have these just in case."

I'm in two minds regarding this personal detour. Firstly, I'd like to take part in this additional excursion and be fun and spontaneous. Secondly, I will feel terrible if we miss, or worse delay, the bus. I hastily craft an appropriate response. "I'm sure whatever you wanted me to see is great, and I appreciate the thought. Really, I do. But, I don't want to ditch James, you know?" Nolan halts in front of me and adamantly cocks and eyebrow. "What?" I question.

"I'm shocked, honestly," he discloses. My forehead furrows as I wait for him to continue. "Do you really think that I, founder and CEO of O'Kelley Tours, would not alert another tour company of a possible excursion? I can't believe you consider me that disrespectful."

"Wait. What?" I reiterate, hoping my lack of under-standing does not have to do with my mental acuity but with the fact I have only recently woken up.

A grin blossoms across my friend's face. "When we were in Bunratty, I told him you and I might bunk off if the petrol station stop was where I anticipated it would be." Instantly, I feel my face change to match his.

My singular worry evaporated, I squeeze Nolan's hand. "So, where are we going?"

"That, Laurel, love, is a surprise," he says with a trade-mark wink.

38

Nolan

To put it poetically, I have royally fucked up.

39

Laurel

You know the one thing people always say about assuming. Well, it's true.

Given Nolan had said bringing our emergency bags was only a precautionary measure, I was assuming our destination was five minutes away, seven max. I assumed we were headed for something intended to be simply seen, a view or a landmark, something we'd appreciate for a minute and then return to the gas station from whence we'd came.

We've been walking for about forty-five minutes now, the terrain below us changing from cement to sod to asphalt and back to grass, and I have no idea when we're going to stop. The first ten or so of these were enjoyable enough, filled with mystery and intrigue and flirtatious banter. Then, we ran out of sidewalk. It was my decision whether or not we proceeded with our journey. With no chance of making it back to the Paddywagon gang in time, I elected to see it through.

There were fields on either side of the street where we could walk, and Nolan seemed sure we weren't far from wherever it was we were heading. After what I estimated to be close to half a mile, we crossed over a highway and passed a few supply warehouses, but then the scenery became nothing but trees and brush on all sides. It was at this point I first felt my guide's surety start to give way. In the last fifteen minutes, he hasn't said anything to me other than a quick physicality check-in, which I appreciate.

I'm certain we're lost, but as there's nothing I can do to help rectify this, I give Nolan space—emotionally, in reality, I'm still holding his arm—and let my mind wander. In the grand scheme of things, I'm fine. In a real emergency, we could call for assistance. I don't want to throw a wrench in this plan, especially when it's clearly not running smoothly, and I am sure we'll get back on track eventually. We probably still have a good thirty minutes of daylight left. Of course, there is the small possibility Nolan could be luring me out into the woods to kill me. (What a way to go, though. Right?) Inwardly, I chortle at my own dark humor.

Finally, unexpectedly, I'm tugged to the left, which veers us off the main road and onto a residential street. I'm hoping the transition means Nolan's found what he's looking for.

Did we just walk through a sprinkler? I glance around, my gaze roaming over idyllic countryside houses and white picket fences, searching for the offending landscaping device only to eventually and reluctantly raise skyward in search of the source of the moisture. Alas, what I felt was rain and not a lone drop. We've been caught in a light misting. I wouldn't even classify it as a sprinkle. But it might be what brings an end to our escapade.

"Nolan," I press, breaking the silence and sliding my hand down his arm to intertwine our fingers, "Are we close?" I do my best to ignore the micro-droplets falling into my eyes as I blink up at him. The busker sighs before facing me. His expression isn't angry. The tension in his jaw reads as annoyed, the furrow of his brow disappointment.

"I swear it's right up here," he says apologetically, "but now it's spitting, so I understand if you–"

The street we've been tracing has curved wide, creating a gap in the surrounding foliage. The scene that emerges from between the trees elicits a gasp from my lips, cutting off the singer's statement. Silhouetted against the dimming sky is a massive fortress. Actually, it's better than a fortress. It's crumbling from centuries in the elements. But even at this distance, I can tell Nolan has brought me to the castle ruins from *Leap Year*.

40

Nolan

I watch Laurel's face. She has mist clinging to her eyelashes and hair. Her smile grows ever wider as she comprehends what she's seeing. The last hour: the long walk, the rain, and my frustration at my miscalculation of the distance is suddenly worth it. Laurel lets go of my hand and uses both of hers to cover her mouth.

"Is that?" she asks, stare locked on to ancient remains, palms hardly hiding her grin. I can't help but beam at her unabashed reaction.

"It is," I state confidently, before effecting a teasing tone. "But if you want to go, I completely understand. I mean, it's probably going to rain soon, and it's getting dark–"

"Oh! Shut up!" She laughs and walks back toward me, grabbing my hand and practically dragging me down the road. When we reach the street corner, Laurel bounces up the small set of steps that serve as the park entrance, fraying my nerves and readying my reflexes as I watch the soles of her sneakers find purchase on the slick stone. The effect worsens when I notice the drizzle has made the base gravel path, which leads up to Rock of Dunamase, into the beginnings of a mudslide. I stop short, jerking Laurel backward and into me.

"What?" she implores, dumbfounded. "Are we not allowed to get any closer?"

"No," I reply, unable to keep myself from chuckling at her lack of observation and wanting very badly to kiss her forehead again. "Look at the ground."

She does and frowns. "Oh."

I think for a minute, debating all the various ascents and options. "Here," I decide, removing my backpack and squatting as deep as I can manage on the softening terrain, "hop on."

"How is this going to be helpful?" she doubts, momentarily debating the choice, but caving and jumping onto my back.

"Will you just trust me?" Once she's settled, I pluck my bag off the turf and pass it over. "Can you hold on to this?" Hands resting on my collarbones, Laurel effortlessly grips the pack. Not having to worry about scout footing for us both, I can more easily navigate the pathway. Our inevitable descent may be a different story, but in no time at all, we make it to the crest of the hill. "See," I boast, "I'd think you'd have accepted my constant ingenuity by now, but maybe it's hard to comprehend." Laurel digs her heels into my thighs in way of a response, but it doesn't do much damage.

When we're safely "inside," I set my cargo down on the remnants of a staircase and survey the rest of the architecture, shelving our luggage in a mostly dry crevice. "I've actually never been here," I say. "But when the film came out, everyone was talking about it. Obviously, it was a tad more intact then, or maybe they used CGI, but here you are."

'It's perfect." Laurel jumps off the final step and sets about exploring, her head an awe-filled pendulum, "Thank you.

Don't thank me; thank Roisin. She's the one who knew where it was." As the words leave my lips, I'm not sure why I'm sharing them. Why would I not want full credit for this grand adventure? After all, I am the one who remembered Laurel saying it was one of her favorite movies. That was me.

"Hmm," Laurel muses as she inspects an almost intact doorway. "Come here. I need a hand."

I'm beginning to believe this woman may have the world's worst survival instincts because she has found the one section of remains that I would guess were once a second story and is trying to reach them. I reluctantly give her a boost. She hauls me up behind. Thankfully, I am incorrect. We're less on an upper level and more in a new area of the castle. There's a partially eroded wall in front of us permitting us to see out over Dunamaise.

"The view's different," Laurel voices openly. She doesn't sound disappointed or upset. She's purely sharing a thought. The sun is sinking below the horizon, bathing the town in its golden glow as we admire the pink, purple and orange-strewn sky, the light fall of water soundtracking the scene in its soothing pitter-patter. In time, my focus wanders back to the American. When she finishes beholding her back-drop, she twists toward me. Her face is flushed from the wind and the climb and simple, undiluted happiness. "What?" she asks, in question to my prolonged stare.

I've known Laurel Cole for a total of five days, four realistically, so I don't really know how to articulate what I'm feeling without sounding like I've lost the plot. But, the reason I've wanted to spend so much time with her—aside from the fact she's exceedingly interesting and quite pret-ty—is being with her is easy. It doesn't feel like a choice in a good way. It feels more like...breathing. You don't make a conscious decision to breathe. It just happens. It's natural. You go from inhaling to exhaling. We go from standing here to my hand gently cupping the side of her face, brushing a wayward strand of hair behind her ear, and guiding her lips to mine.

41

Laurel

My body realizes what is happening about a millisecond ahead of my brain. Feeling Nolan's eyes on me, I broke away from the cinematic setting, only for him to continue studying me, mute. "What?' I demanded when my skin began to heat, the word almost lost in the giggle that bubbled up with the use of my vocal cords.

The wind had picked up as I'd spoken, propelling me a breath nearer. Without a word, he reaches out and touches my chin, delicately caressing my jaw with his thumb as he tilts it up. His other hand slowly comes to rest on my opposite cheek, having first swept an unruly lock of hair from my view. The busker's eyes trace a path between the triangle of my face: Right eye. Lips. Left eye. Right eye. Lips. Left eye. Each rotation moving our mouths ever so slightly closer together.

"Is this–" he tries, his nose grazing mine. The rest of his inquiry is dropped on a shaky inhale as my premature nod causes our lips to catch. (I'd filled in the blanks. Is this *ok?* Is this *what you want?* Is this *what you've been thinking about since I sang American Girl?* Yes to all of the above.) It's there and gone, the barest hint of a kiss, but it's enough. We come together again. And then break apart. Then, together for a few seconds more before we part for a few seconds less. And again. And again. The cycle continuing until the small moan of his name absconds with my exhale.

Nolan's mouth crashes into mine. What was sweet and gentle and searching, becomes hungry and consuming all at once. The constant mist has dampened his T-shirt enough for droplets to slide through my fingers as I knot my hands into the fabric at his chest. The hand that was on my cheek is now sliding into my hair. I'm pushing up on my tiptoes in an effort to reach more of him, feel more of him, taste more of him, eager to close the non-existent space between us.

Sensing my rampant desire, Nolan steps forward, using the momentum to easily pivot our bodies. Another step, and I'm flush with a taller section of the slate wall. When his knuckles take the brunt of the impact, he fractures the kiss, staying close enough that all I can really see are his lips. Instantaneously, the corners begin to slant upwards, causing the scar I'd noticed at Jameson Distillery to pale. The illusion of the familiar expression has me pulling his mouth back to mine. My hands dig into his shoulders, immediately wrapping around his neck as he shifts closer, his body pressing into my own.

You'd hope—in the spirit of Irish Romance Adventures and all—the universe would do me a solid and let me kiss Nolan in the middle of castle ruins uninterrupted, but no. Mother Nature keeps a very watchful eye. After a time frame, I personally would define as much too short, what had been called "a spitting" becomes a downpour. I can't help but laugh when neither of us reacts to our new predicament, the sound dancing onto the Irishman's tongue. The chill of the raindrops sliding down my skin becomes a pleasant contrast to the intensity building in all the right places. Sure hands knead my hips as Nolan bends to pick me up. As my feet leave the ground, the sky illuminates to a blaring white before thunder crashes above our heads.

"Holy shite," he says as we tear away from one another. He's face is pointed into the deluge, so he's definitely commenting on the weather, but when I tell Taylor about this, he'll be talking about me. When he looks back down, he's smiling, chest still rising and falling at a rapid pace. My focus snags there for a moment despite the monsoon. "We should get inside." I catch his eyes and wordlessly agree, my mind still preoccupied with issues besides my own safety. If it wasn't for the lightning, there wouldn't be much of a point. We're already soaked.

Huddled under one of the more intact archways, Nolan eventually gets through to a local taxi service.

"A car will be here in about ten minutes," he informs, a crack in the stone on my left. The sentence is delivered in a calm, almost serious tone. Silence echos around the cavernous keep fragments, the rain becoming white noise until laughter overcomes us both. Emotionally and physically, I'm exhausted. The fact we could have driven here in a mere ten minutes or less versus our hour-long walk sends us over the edge. When we're both just giggling, he tucks me against his body and kisses the top of my head, my skin squelching against his drenched cotton covering.

"We should probably start back," he murmurs into my hair.

♥

I'm sitting by the fireplace in yet another quirky pub, nursing a hot buttered rum and waiting for Nolan to come back. Our taxi had dropped us at Sally Gardens roughly ten minutes ago. Even with the kind driver blasting the heat, we had still walked through the door practically dripping. I'd ordered us both warm drinks and found a seat by the flames while he ducked into a quiet hallway and tried to get us home.

"So, do you want the good news or the bad news?" he inquires, appearing from amongst a crowd of pitying gawkers who part around him.

I pass him the other mug. "Should I be worried there is bad news?"

"It's not really bad news, but we've missed the last train of the evening, and there wasn't a single taxi service willing to make the one way." He pauses, letting me process the information.

I watch a drop of water fall from one of his curls and follow a worn path over his eyebrow. Once it rounds his cheekbone, Nolan sits next to me, careful not to bump my drying clothes with his sodden ones. "I see."

I enjoy another sip of my drink while he continues.

"So I called Eoghan and Roisin. I reckoned if anyone was willing to be our knights in shining armor, it would be them, even if they'll be complete eejits about it for months on. They're happy to do it and promised to leave first thing in the morning. But Eoghan's got a pretty big gig tonight... Roisin herself doesn't have a license...I don't think we can get home until morning." The Irishman takes in a mouthful of creamy liquor and swallows. His eyes, currently fixed on an overturned bottle cap camouflaged into the floor, haven't found mine in almost a full minute. He's not teasing me. He's not trying to be cheeky or flirty. This isn't 'a move.' In fact, he seems stressed again.

"Nolan." At the sound of his name, the musician finally swings his head in my direction and raises his eyebrows over the top of the cooling cocktail. "I'm not upset. If I wanted to be at my hotel tonight, I would have made us stay on the bus. I have my backpack, remember? I have pajamas and clean clothes and toiletries. If Roisin and Eoghan can't come until morning, they can't come until morning." I put my hand on his knee. "It's fine." The creases troubling the bridge of his nose and corners of his mouth fade once he searches my features for any sign of discomfort or deceit.

"Are you sure?" he questions, voice still strained with anxiety.

"One hundred percent. Drink your drink. I'll find us a place to stay." I excuse myself to a forgotten corner. From afar, I watch Nolan's shoulder muscles relax as he adapts to our situation, sheepishly rubbing out a knot at the back of his neck. I'm not lying. I really am feeling incredibly at ease. I'm sure the rum is helping a little, but right now, the only thing I really want is to change my clothes and, if possible, take a warm shower. I unlock my phone, which miraculously survived its impromptu waterboarding, and, since it seems appropriate, google the phrase 'nearby B&Bs.'

42

Laurel

I do my best to shake the puddles off my shoes before parading into the carpeted foyer of our acquired lodgings.

"Coming! Coming! Coming!" A disembodied voice trills over the jingling of the entrance bell, which announces our arrival. As we reach the welcome desk, a small elderly woman skids into the room, her gray corkscrew curls bouncing every which way from within their twisted bun, a few escapee ringlets falling around the edges of her coke-bottle glasses. "Good evening. How can I help you?

"Reservation under Cole. I just made it," I say as she whips her mouse back and forth, resuscitating the monitor of her computer.

"Oh yes! You poor dears!" she exclaims, finally realizing the sopping state of Nolan and me. "Yes. Yes. Yes. I'm Aiofe. I spoke to you on the phone. Let's get you two taken care of right away." She yanks a large antique key from one of the six hooks behind her and motions for us to follow. Padding down the hallway at the pace of a professional speed walker.

I'm relieved when she ushers us into a charming, bright yellow room with dark oak furniture and an already lit wood-burning fireplace. I had done minimal research online, hastily searching for places that fit my two main criteria: close and vacant. A brief two-minute walk from our tavern, Ivyleigh House, an antique luxury guest house, was both those things. It also happened to boast a five-star rating. Still, in spite of the ivy-covered, cobbled exterior, I was nervous.

This wasn't about the bed. I knew our room would have one queen bed. With four of the six rooms housing a solo mattress, it was the only option on such short notice. And, as I was not actually living in a rom-com, I was prepared to be an adult about it. My anxiety stemmed from which room we would be given. Based on what I had seen on the website, each lodging seemed to follow a color-scheme. All were vintage, cozy, and perfectly suitable havens from the chills I was worried had permanently seized control of my body, but there was a dark red room I felt might seem an overt come-on on my part. Thankfully, that is not a bridge I have to cross today.

"I had my husband get a fire going as soon as I knew you were on the way," Aoife prattles. "The kitchen really solely serves breakfast, but if you'd like, I can have some vegetable stew up here in a dash."

"Oh, that'd be grand. Thanks," Nolan admits, smiling at her. I'm not shocked to see a light pink hue color her cheeks. I've yet to see someone be immune to his charms.

"I'll leave you to it then." She claps, leaving her hands clasped in front of her, "Once you've changed, come and drop your wet things at the front. I'll stick them in the dryer free of charge and have them back to you by morning." This time, I offer gratitude for her additional kindness. She waves me off. Her high energy and laissez-faire attitude giving her the nerve to wink as she closes the door.

Feeling truly settled for the first time since leaving The Dean this morning, I steal a minute to just breathe. I watch as the busker nestles our bags in a white wingback chair patterned with grey feathers before checking on the fire. I know for a fact that in the tatters of my current ensemble, I am not at my most attractive. If I'm lucky, I might be presenting as a 'chic drowned rat.' I'm certain there's makeup residue under my eyes, even though I've done my best to wipe it away, and my hair is more than likely adorned with a crown of frizz. Nolan, on the other hand, looks like he's stepped straight out of that one scene in *The Notebook.* (You know, the iconic one. *I wrote you every day for a year!*) He's discarded his jacket, which did nothing to protect his T-shirt from the rain. Everywhere there's not writing or graphics, the white fabric is cling-ing to his skin. I have visible proof I was correct to presume he frequents a gym, maybe not every day, but often enough to have something to show for it.

The moment I'm feeling safe in my shameless goggling, he whirls around, an insolent smirk sliding onto his face as he accesses the scene, hands he was warming in the flames coming to rest on his hips. "I can go downstairs for a bit if you want the room for–"

"No, it's fine. You're fine. I mean–I need to take a quick shower," I spout, already feeling the blood rushing to my temples. Mortified I'd been caught, I haul my bag from its resting place and escape to the bathroom.

Running my fingers through my hair as it air dries in the heat from the fireplace, I wonder for the umpteenth time where my companion has gone. Freshly showered, I had reen-tered the main room to discover it was empty. I considered using this time to update Taylor, but I want to talk to her, and not knowing where Nolan is means not having an estimate of when he's going to be back. I've started to contemplate texting him when there is a light rap at the door.

As I'm standing to answer, Aiofe opens it and steps through, followed by the missing person, now clad in sweatpants and a blue hoodie, holding two giant bowls of steaming soup. "Thought I could grab your things while I was here, wee love," she relays, holding out the laundry sack she had folded over her arm.

I accept it and place my neatly folded pile of damp clothes inside. "Thank you again," I offer.

"Ah. Don't be worrying about it, dear. Especially after the day you two have had. My goodness." The hostess is already withdrawing from the room as she speaks. "Have the loveliest night. Breakfast is served until 11:00 AM."

When the lock clicks behind her, Nolan steps farther into our space, easing one dish and then the other onto the mantel and then, in lieu of a table, the floor.

"Aoife, let me shower in the other vacant room," he says, explaining his absence as he passes me a spoon."

"I think she has a crush on you," I tease as we sit down in front of the hearth, backs pressed to the foot of the bed.

He shoots me a well-knowing grin, "That checks out. Lots of people do."

I snort. "That one's on me. I set it up too well."

We let the conversation ebb, settling into silence as we eat. I didn't realize how hungry I was. Much too soon, I've reached the bottom of my bowl.

Nolan clears his throat as he sits his equally empty dish aside. "I wasn't making a joke earlier. Lots of people do have a crush on me. Off the top of my head, there's Aiofe, this girl Molly who has followed me on Instagram forever, Roisin for like two weeks until she met Eoghan, you–"

I narrow my eyes and glance in his direction. "I never said I had a crush on you," I clarify, returning my attention to scraping together one final spoonful of broth.

"You kissed me earlier," he declares concisely as if that clears everything up.

I scoff, setting my inedible dregs out of the way and twisting toward him. "Ok, one, people kiss people they don't have crushes on all the time, and two, for the record, you kissed me."

"Arguable," Nolan inches closer as he rebuttals. "For the record," he mimics, "people don't kiss people they don't have feelings for the way we kissed AND–" My breathing involuntarily quickens as the distance between our bodies shrinks "–if it really was one-sided, if I kiss you again right now, are you not going to kiss me back?"

I want to say something witty. I don't want him to have the last word. But his face is so close to mine that I can make out the different shades of blue in his eyes. I can smell his cologne, and see a few water droplets still caught in his hair. He's warm and safe, and he's just waiting. Then he smiles. All I can do is lean in.

This kiss is different from the one at Dunamaise. There's no hesitation. No question of consent. And, for a solid few seconds, no participation from my partner. When I notice what he's doing, I pull away. "Now you've definitely kissed me," he gloats.

"Asshole," I giggle, shoving his chest.

I haven't finished chortling when Nolan leads my chin back toward his. His mouth meeting mine in a confident rhythm. From his position on his knees, he slides forward and guides me into his lap, shifting our weight to a more comfortable placement. The movement rumples his hoodie enough for my hands to find their own way underneath it, roving over the muscles I had outlined with my eyes an hour earlier.

I recoil at the sound of a sharp hiss. "Your hands are cold."

"Oh, sorry," I mumble, automatically endeavoring to vacate the fabric barrier. The singer tenderly grabs hold of my wrists, stilling the retreat.

"I don't want you to stop. I just said your hands were cold," he chuckles. "I'll survive." My face warms for a reason beyond the fact I am facing the fire. "Here," Nolan continues gently, skirting one hand along and then under the hem of my top. I suck in a breath when his skin meets mine, although the fingers on my stomach are a standard temperature. Slowly, he explores up my abdomen, hooking his hand around my ribcage and stoping mere millimeters from my chest. "See? You'd live." The challenge is issued as he brushes the tip of a calloused thumb along the skin still dimpled by the wiring in my bra, raising goosebumps along the sensitive area.

I swallow, desperately trying to coat my suddenly parched throat. The struggle is noted with a grin and wink combo that cements the moment. My mind utilizes the minute pause to sprint toward the decision of more. However, as I'm leaping toward the banner, the choice is made for me. Before his smile even has time to fade, the Irishman places small chaste kisses on my lips and forehead, followed by the unknotting of our tangled body parts and a finalizing fall back onto his palms. "We should probably get some sleep. It's been a long day, and who knows what 'first thing in the morning' means to our friends."

♥

Nestled under the sheets, with my head resting on Nolan's bare chest, I struggle to stay awake. I wasn't tired an hour ago when we decided to go to bed. My heart was hammering against my rib cage, and the forced proximity of the lone mattress was doing nothing to slow it. In an effort to remedy this, my bed mate began educating me on local folklore and singing traditional songs. After a few cycles, the reverberations of his voice and cadenced breathing had eventually accomplished their goal. But, now, in my state of near stupor, I discern that if I do sleep, the serenading ends. As this isn't at all what I want, I blink my eyes a few times, hoping to hide how I had begun to doze.

"Laurel, are you still awake?" Nolan audibly reaches in a hushed tone, pausing the steady rotation of circles he's been drawing on my back, his other hand lazily playing with my hair.

"I am." My response is barely above a whisper, but he hears me.

He's quiet for a moment. I assume he's trying to recollect another lullaby. Instead, he shifts underneath me, snuggling closer, "Are you free Saturday night?"

Befuddled, I wriggle out of his grasp and prop myself up on one hand, hoping I'll be able to decipher his expression well enough in the dark.

"Yes?" I proffer.

"Will you go on a date with me?" He sits up slightly, bracing himself on his forearms, the moonlight outlining his flexed muscles in her champagne glow.

I feel my forehead crease as I fight a smile, "I would love to, but what do you think the past few days have been?"

"Those weren't dates, not officially," Nolan claims, relaxing and coaxing me back into the crook of his neck. "I mean a real date."

"I'm very curious to see how Saturday will be different from today or yesterday or–"

"Stop that," he interrupts, referencing the air I'm directing toward the base of his neck, "It tickles." I tilt my head and catch the tail end of his contented scowl.

After a few silent minutes, I sense myself losing consciousness once more. "Hey Nolan," I summon the energy to ask, "Will you do me a favor?"

"Hmm?" he hums into my hair.

Can you tell Eoghan and Roisin to not get here too early? Maybe see if they want to come in for breakfast?" The end of my request morphs into a yawn.

After a sleepy sigh, he assents. "Yes, petal. I can do that."

43

Laurel

The clock on Eoghan's sedan's dash ticks over to 11:17 AM as we all pile into the vehicle, three members of our party exhibiting telltale signs of the euphoric buzz that is only derived from consuming any amount of alcohol in the morning. The burly, and currently surly, drummer is the odd man out. As our designated driver, his girlfriend refused to even let him taste her cocktail. (Word to the wise: add a splash of watermelon juice to your typical orange next time you make mimosas). As we lounged across the carpeted seats, digesting baked eggs, porridge, granola, and fresh house-made bread with fruit compote, I was touched to learn they had both taken off work to rescue us.

"And miss taking the piss out of this boyo for an hour and a half? I don't think so!" Eoghan hoots, merging onto the main thoroughfare. "So, did you two lob the gob yet?" Roisin reaches up from her place beside me and smacks her boyfriend in the arm.

"I told you to leave them alone, Eoghan," she grumbles.

"Oh, come on! They've one hundred percent been shifting. It's all over their faces!"

I feel mine pink. "Ignore him," Roisin directs me. Nolan, beaming proudly, winks at me from the passenger seat.

♥

The hour's drive back to Dublin is one of the most entertaining and boisterous travel experiences I have been part of. Though Nolan and I don't talk much—as most of my mental function is engaged attempting to process the last twenty-four hours, I imagine his is similarly occupied—our chauffeur bounces from 'I Spy' to the radio to 'Twenty Questions' to Apple Music and back again. We've entered the outskirts of the capital when Eoghan throws both hands in the air.

"OH, FECK!" he exclaims loudly.

At the same time, Roisin yells, "EOGHAN!" while his neighbor dives for the wheel.

"I have just realized I have done us all a complete disservice," the percussionist resumes, back in control of both his emotions and the automobile. Alongside his vocal, I can hear Roisin mumbling a string of curses in a hushed register. "I have not played one Nolan O'Kelley song during our entire journey."

The aforementioned artist humorously accepts the unspoken apology. "That's OK, mate. It's really not necessary."

"Not necessary?" Eoghan gasps before switching to a faux-whisper. "Did you forget you have a potential mot in the backseat? I'm trying to make you look good, sham." Nolan snorts, shaking his head.

Within seconds, *Walk Away* is turned up loud enough for me to feel the bass reverb in my chest. The car, already shaking with exertion, creaks as the body is tossed to and fro by our driver's intense jiving. By the time the music fades and the volume is decreased, we're all cackling, red-faced and struggling to catch our breath.

"Eoghan, love, let the other two play," Roisin requests in between wheezes, "I don't want *Monday Morning* to feel neglected."

Her boyfriend groans. "Yeah. Yeah. Settle down. We all know it's your favorite." His eyes gleam as he teases her through the rearview mirror. "*Walk Away* is the tune, though! Isn't it a right banger, Laurel?"

"It's interesting we all have different favorites," I beam. "Your music really has the potential to amass a large fanbase." It's obviously a compliment, and the comment earns me a shy smirk, but the subject shifts uncomfortably in his chair. The motion casts a shroud over the sedan. As I labor in the strained atmosphere, I'm left with the same feeling I had at Guinness Storehouse: like I've forgotten the chorus of a popular song.

When I've gathered the stamina to gently inquire as to why this might be, the car lurches to a halt in front of my hotel. "First stop: The Dean. If you are traveling to The Dean, please exit the vehicle now," Eoghan announces, using his best conductor impression to lighten the mood. Nolan unbuckles, rounding the car to retrieve my bag from the trunk as I hug Roisin goodbye.

Feet planted on the sidewalk, I squeeze through the driver's side window to once again thank the boisterous Celt. He kisses both my cheeks in farewell. "Any time, Laurel, love."

By the time I finish my farewells, the singer is halfway to the hotel entrance. I meet him at the door. "Are we still on for tomorrow?" I probe, accepting my backpack.

"'Course," he answers simply, brows knitting together. "Unless you changed your mind."

I shrug, simpering. "No. But I wanted to check."

"Pick you up at seven?"

"How about six?" I contest.

The cockiest rendition of his grin resurfaces. "You'll miss me that bad?"

"Something like that."

"Six it is, then." With a quick kiss to my forehead, Nolan jogs back to the car.

All I can think about is how we only have two more days.

44

Laurel

When asked my personality type, I usually call myself an extrovert. I enjoy conversing, engaging with and feeding off the energy of people in my surroundings. However, as the recent happenings of my life have made these factors a constant since yesterday, I allocate the remainder of the afternoon to some much-needed me time. Knowing the sun has not even begun to peek over the Los Angeles mountains, I draw a bath, my non-Taylor-related failsafe for all situations and emotions, thankful I still have half a bubble bar and two bath bombs left. My final bath oil, I set aside for tomorrow.

After applying a charcoal clay face mask for the second time this week, I soak in silence, allowing blackberry-scented bubbles to sink into my skin. Once I feel at ease, I give myself five more minutes before opening the drain. I rinse off in the shower, throw on a rack-warmed robe, and snuggle into my freshly made bed to finish my novel.

♥

Hours later, I wake to a slowly darkening sky, unable to differentiate which of my recent memories are excerpts from my book and which were dreams. I don't remember the ending, but I'm almost positive the page it's splayed to on the mattress beside me is one I've already read. With a yawn, I give up on trying to locate my place, using a wide stretch to set the story back on the nightstand. I round out the effort with a twist, uncoiling the muscles in my back as I check the time. It's 3:52 PM, meaning my roommate should be commencing her commute soon.

I stall the impending call, giving her time to get situated and on the way before I disrupt her routine. As my backpack is closer than the dresser, I change into the PJs I wore last night. There are traces of Ivyleigh House caught between the threads. Hints of smoke and vegetable soup and Nolan. I fight the tension pooling in my belly at the memory, pretending it's a hunger I can stave with a simple phone call. I retreat to the den to dial room service.

By the time I'm comfortable on the couch with another order of Wild Mushroom Risotto and vanilla gelato on the way, it's 4:10 PM. Finally, I navigate to my most recent text conversation, tapping on Taylor's face and then the phone icon under her name. She picks up on the first ring.

"Lord have mercy. I was worried you were dead," my friend criticizes, stealing the greeting from the tip of my tongue. "Hold on, let me FaceTime you."

I adjust my position, bringing the phone away from my ear as I hear the familiar ringtone. When Taylor's camera establishes its feed, I'm surprised our small backyard fills in her background. "Are you outside?" I question. "Shouldn't you be driving?"

"Oh. I'm sick today," she informs me nonchalantly.

Creases form over my nose. Her makeup is done, and her hair is straightened. "Are you ok? You look like you got ready?"

A devious smile lifts the corners of her lips as she sips on her steaming coffee. "Oh. I did, but then you still hadn't called, so...desperate times."

"Oh my gosh! Are you serious?" I say, bolting upright.

"Obviously! I had the time, and I know you literally spent the night at a B&B with a hot Irishman, so needs must."

I beam. "You're insane."

"You love it. Don't deny it," she insists. "Now, before we get to all the juicy details, please tell me you lived 'only one bed.'

45

Laurel

"No!" I exclaim at my television. The interjection was brought forth as the final *First Dates'* credit-roll update notified me that my favorite couple, a heterosexual pairing in their early thirties' did not last past their second meeting. I wipe the peri-salt—lingering from what had been a very pleasant Saturday lunch—off my fingers before taking another bite of my Nando's pita.

I've spent most of the morning getting ready for this evening's date. So far, it hasn't been anything too intensive, just your typical preemptive preparations, which will allow me to start my official regimen at a more reasonable time. To kick off the festivities, my beloved coffee cup and I had gone back and forth between the four outfits Taylor had created toward the end of our gabfest. After much deliberation and a refill, we had finally selected a high-waisted grey linen pant and white puffed-long-sleeved crop ensemble.

Now, fingers and toes both painted Bubble Bath by a mild-mannered tech at a nearby nail salon, I've paused for a midday meal. As another episode begins, I groan and check the time. It's after 1:00 PM, meaning I have roughly five hours until Nolan *should* get here. I definitely have the time for one more, and getting entertainment from other people's love lives does wonders for keeping my mind off my own.

Overall, Taylor was proud of me for agreeing to this outing, delighted I had decided to see where things could go and honored to have influenced the outcome, but her praise had inadvertently knocked me off course. Without the busker directly in front of me, I had begun to doubt the wisdom of my choices and dread the possible unfortunate futures to which they could lead. I beat down my intrusive thoughts and bring my attention up to the television screen on which a 22-year-old is about to meet their paired suitor.

As I switch off my curling iron, my hair now in perfectly disheveled combed-out ringlets, The Party Playlist ™ toggles from Freya Ridings to Dove Cameron. I've cast the music around the hotel room, having hooked up my phone to the Bluetooth speaker system.

"Well, as always, this is as good as it's going to get," I address the mirror as I apply a dab of clear gloss over my mauve lipstick. My oft-quoted *The Princess Diaries'* reference is not delivered in the same tone as Anne Hathaway's Mia Thermopolis. I paraphrase the sentence cheerfully, pleased with my reflection. Grabbing the quarter glass of white wine I have left—the last from the bottle I purchased Sunday—from the sink, I float into the bedroom and slide into the black wedges I've placed by one of the chairs. Sitting the drink down on the accompanying table, I use the seat for support as I stand on one foot to guide the back of each shoe over my heel.

I'm ready early. I had planned to be. Nolan's punctuality two mornings ago had me apprehensive over what time he would show. But it's 5:30 PM on the dot, and my primping process hasn't been interrupted. I opt to wait in the den. Lip-syncing *So Good* as I walk down the hallway, I smile to myself. Like Dove Cameron, I am feeling good. Despite my occasional misgivings about our limited time, I'm happy, excited even. I haven't been told exactly what has been planned. But I do know we're going to dinner. As such, I've picked an outfit suitable for the occasion. Should I need it, I have an oversized blazer folded up in my bag by the door.

Sitting on the couch, I keep the playlist on rotation as I get lost in the unending, unyielding and ever-constant scroll of my phone. In what seems like seconds, though it's nearly twenty-five minutes later, I'm hauled out of my social media by a knock at the door.

"One sec," I call. As I stop the music and gather my things, a nervous tingle begins in my fingertips. The anticipation of what, by Nolan's account, is our first *real* date has birthed a new kaleidoscope of butterflies in my stomach. I feel like he's picking me up to go to Jameson Distillery all over again, except now the outing is truly romantic in nature instead of the feeling stemming from some inane notion, desire, or fear it may be misconstrued as such, which somehow makes the sensation better and worse.

As soon as I open the door, the rabble settles, waiting at their posts to resume flight at a moment's notice. The Irishman is there, standing on the threshold with his hands in his pockets. The confidence in his expression as he shamelessly studies me slashing through my qualms like an all-access pass at a security barrier. "Hi," he breathes. "You look nice."

"Thanks. So do you." I blush as I repurpose the compliment.

His already upturned mouth expands into a grin. "Ready?"

Accepting his offered hand, I shut off the lights, letting the door swing closed, double checking it latched behind me. "So, where to?" I inquire, hoping pressing for details in person will prove more fruitful than it had over the phone.

"You'll see," Nolan teases. He smirks at me, cool as ever, eyes twinkling. I narrow mine. "What?" he questions with a chuckle.

I wait until we've arranged ourselves in the elevator to answer. "You know, the last time you said that we ended up walking for almost an hour, right?"

He laughs. "This time, I have an actual address and a taxi."

46

Laurel

When Nolan said he'd hire a cab, I didn't think he meant he had already. Yet, as he held the hotel door, there it was, idling next to the curb. The bespectacled driver raised a hand in greeting before we were even off the landing, the attention an outward indicator of his social tendencies and alerting us to the friendly prattle he would keep up during our sojourn north. When we were fifteen minutes outside the city center and a great deal more knowledgable on the current underground politico-art scene than we ever expected to be, he deposited us out down the street from a large, glossy, white brick building which was eccentrically accented in aqua and coral paint. When I pivoted to thank him, he was already distancing his car from the sidewalk, doffing his cap and bidding a cheery farewell with his exhaust fumes.

"So," begins my date, reclaiming my attention over the ambient music drifting toward us as we meander closer to the black and gold signage of The Bernard Shaw, "we have a couple of options. We can either eat in the main restaurant. It's got a funky, disco, sports bar vibe–" I snort at his messy description, "–or since it's not too chilly... " As his fingers are otherwise engaged between my own, he swings a booted foot to the right of the restaurant's doors, sending a stray pebble skittering across the distance and into a spotlight shining at the foot of a small alleyway. My eyes follow the glow to its source: exposed bulbs screwed into the steel of seven blue carnival letters: E–A–T–Y–A–R–D. The well-lit path is framed by an extension of the building and unfurls into a communal space, the visible edge of which is dappled with different food vendors and a smattering of graffitied picnic tables. While the string lights running across the open-air expanse tally major points in favor of the smorgasbord-style eatery, what seals the deal is the directional post in the entryway. It's similar to those often found at theme parks, tourist attractions or tropical resorts, except the multihued branches do not denote nearby locations but instead comprise a sentence formed word by word: One good thing about music, when it hits you, you feel ok.

"Eatyard," I say, skipping ahead a few paces and facing him. "But, can we go inside and get a drink first? A "funky, disco, sports bar" is not something I can afford to miss."

Nolan squeezes my hand as he tugs me to his side in retribution for my taunt."If you can come up with a better way to characterize it, I'll buy you a drink," he wagers into my flyaways.

When the pink glass-paneled doors sway closed behind us, my ears take a moment to adjust to their new environment. The Bernard Shaw is louder than I expected but as lively and bright as the local's word choice made it seem. Winding though the sporadically placed teak chairs and bar stools, I'm shocked to see a literal disco ball and accompanying LED light strips hanging from the forest green rafters of the main dining area. Patrons in various states of inebriation light our path to the walk-up counter.

"And you would define this as?" Nolan questions while we wait our turn, gesturing to the room behind us.

"I would call it…a grounded yet eclectic go-go." As I'd hoped, my simple paraphrasing of his adjectives is rewarded with laughter. The musician tips his head back and lets the full-bodied sound fill the atmosphere. Without pause, my brain registers it as my favorite of his many laughs. The sudden discovery throws its weight into my chest like a champion shot putter, leaving me reeling amidst the blossoming sense of pride I feel for earning its issue on purpose. By the time the outburst has abated to a chortle, the bartender has backpedaled in our direction.

"What can I get you?" she asks, briefly wiping the area in front of us with a damp towel and tossing down two branded coasters.

Nolan sticks with Guinness, as expected. However, as I'm not in the mood for any of my usuals, I employ a tried and true tactic.

"What do you recommend?" I inquire. The mixologist flicks her strawberry blonde ponytail over her shoulder as she considers her available options.

"People usually go for our blended drinks, if I'm honest. Do you prefer sweet or spicy?"

"Sweet," I immediately reply.

"Grand. I'll have it right over. One tab or two?"

Nolan acknowledges her query while passing over his card. "One and close it out if you don't mind. We'll probably move to the bar downstairs."

We access Eatyard through this basement taproom. By the time we cross the threshold, the glass holding my frozen Pornstar Martini has gaps in its icy texture from my fingers.

"Do you want to try some?" I hold out my drink when we reach the apex of the double row of varicolored steel stands showcasing a selection of cuisines.

"Sure," Nolan accepts my thawing offer, imbibing a small sip. He closes his eyes as he swallows. "Oh, that's deadly. Here." The Irishman exchanges his beer for my slushy and enjoys a bigger pull from the cocktail.

"No!" I whine, half-heartedly. "We're not trading. Give it back."

"Hmmm," he muses, pondering my request. "What if we split what's left, then I'll go get you a new one?"

"Fine," I easily concede, starting down the runway.

"We can split the stout too, ya know?"

I convey my objection to this idea with the silent raising of my eyebrows, which produces a snort from the passion fruit glutton on my left as we pause to peruse the menu of a Chinese vendor called *Janet's*.

♥

Under the shadow of 'The Big Blue Bus,' a vintage double-decker now serving as an Italian eatery, my date and I made small talk and learned the makeup of each other's families. Visible pride manifested in Nolan's features when he spoke about his younger sister. The chestnut-haired spitfire is featured throughout his rotating wallpapers. The most recent of which is from a photo captured during her sixteenth birthday. Thirteen years his junior, he essentially helped raise

Croía after their dad split when he was fifteen. As a result, they are thick as thieves today, although puberty has made her sometimes deny it. We also talked more about my life in Los Angeles and his time in this city. While my desire to bring up his music only grew with each new fact I learned, the premonition that curiosity would kill the cat, so to speak, outweighed this compulsion. Overall, my ability to hold my tongue and the past couple of hours have solidified how much I actually like him.

Stuffed to the brim from the Saucy Cow's Hot Papi sandwich and waffle fries, I had reluctantly forgone a suggestion to split a chocolate brownie. But, as our Uber drives back into the city's center, I realize my food has settled. As it turns out, I absolutely have room for dessert. I clear my throat.

"Hey," I begin, somewhat embarrassed by my change of mind, "do you know anywhere near The Dean where we could get ice cream?" I direct the question to my date, but it's our driver who answers.

His fluffy salt and pepper brows furrow in the rearview mirror as he speaks. "I'm sorry, but do I have the wrong location? You're headed to Murphy's, correct?" he clarifies, confused.

"Yeah, mate. Crack on," Nolan chuckles. I connect the destination's name to the ice cream parlor I visited a few days ago after the record store. I look at the man next to me, eyes wide.

"How did you–" I marvel.

The busker shrugs, sweeping aside my awed silence. "I had a feeling."

"Nolan, I can't–" I'm grinning and shaking my head, failing again and again to finish my sentence. I don't regain the ability until after the car slows to a stop outside the blue storefront. In truth, I normally wouldn't have been quite this affected by the gesture, but the Pornstar slushies didn't come to play.

The parlor is shutting down for the night, so we get single scoops to go. I lag a couple feet behind, happily humming as I coat my tongue in raspberry sorbet, the tart farm fresh flavor tingling over my taste buds. When my shoes reach the barrier of cement and asphalt that marks the cross-section of Williams Street S, a sharp whistle yanks my focus from my dripping cone. Nolan is no longer in front of me. Instead, he's monitoring the situation from a nearby stoop, having veered away from the mainline shops while I was preoccupied.

"You eat ice cream like a psychopath," I call from the corner after watching him bite into his Bailey's inspired flavor.

"Well," he says smugly, taking his time to chew while I draw nearer, "at least I don't have ice cream on my face."

I halt just shy of the step, sure I don't feel any sticky residue around my features.

"Where—" I open in question as he reaches out and tips my cone up, colliding it with my nose.

"Was that really necessary?" I inquire, using my already messy napkin to wipe the berry puree off my face.

"If you're going to make fun of the way I eat ice cream? Yes," he deadpans, but his face soon gives way to its favored expression.

We eat in silence for a few minutes, playing phone tag with our gazes. I'm down to the final bite of my dessert when Nolan's presence warms my personal space. Every nerve manning my peripheral alerts me to the proximity of his lips before his words dance over the curve of my ear.

"Hey, Laurel," he voices softly.

"Yes?" I ask, leisurely lifting my chin to face him, attempting to ignore the anticipatory swell of hormones flooding by body.

He reaches forward. For a second, I'm sure he's about to touch my cheek. I'm anticipating it, waiting on bated breath for the final outcome. But his hand brushes past my skin and gently tucks a section of my hair behind my ear. He follows the strand down to the end, easing it through his fingers slowly, silently. My pulse speeds up in direct correlation to the delicate gesture. Finally, he whispers, "I think you have ice cream in your hair."

47

Laurel

I wipe the Dylan Suite's steam-fogged bathroom mirror before wrapping the damp towel around my dripping hair. My cooling scarlet skin pales when I press my thumb into my sore bottom lip, checking for signs of any bruising that may have developed in the last thirty minutes.

On our stoop, any embarrassment caused by my inherent messiness quickly subsided when my attempt to move away was met by a tender tug on the captured lock. From underneath my lashes, I watched Nolan's head incline quizzically. A small, sure smile played at the corner of his lips when I finally lifted my eyes to his face.

"Where are you off to?" he inquired calmly, using his other hand to brace the base of my neck. I melt into the steadfast warmth of his palm as he brings my face into his and kisses me.

And kisses me.

And kisses me.

The creamy toffee flavor of his dessert mingled nicely with the hints of raspberry left on my tongue until the lingering ramifications of the long-forgotten pornstar martinis had their Williams Street debut. Things got sloppy quickly. I'd dug my nails too hard into Nolan's clavicle. He'd bit down hard on my lip. We knocked teeth at one point. Finally, his finger caught in my earring, bringing a comical, if somewhat frustrating, end to our lustful pursuits.

The brief walk home is jovial enough as we attempt to hold a conversation based on what we hear eavesdropping on passersby. It never makes much sense, but we'd gotten into a rhythm by the time we reached The Dean. I'd gone in without much fuss after a prolonged hug and kiss to my temple.

When I can't find any signs of discoloration, I apply the finishing touches of my skin care, ending with a toning spray I'd left on the nightstand. When I reach the bed, my phone unlocks automatically from its vicinity to my face. A new calendar alert graces the screen, reminding me of Jenny and Pam's final reservation at a place I've called VCC. I click the link that loads Irene's itinerary email and locate the informational attachment on the restaurant.

At first, Vintage Cocktail Club (which is not an actual club but a speakeasy, thus escaping my dislike) seemed to be a surprising choice for my then-pregnant boss. But after

I scroll through the website and photo gallery, I understand the selection. While she might not have been able to consume alcohol, the bar is Jenny's favorite aesthetic to a tee. The three themed floors claim to be 'the epitome of 1920s chic'—filled with vintage trinkets and antique art and furniture.

I glance at the clock. We haven't been apart long enough for Nolan to have arrived home and fallen asleep, so once I'm snuggled under the covers, I give him a call.

"Remind me what hours you work on Mondays," I greet as soon as the interrupted ringtone signals I'm though.

"I knew telling you stories a few nights ago was a bad idea," he croons over the jingle of his keys. "And I don't, actually. A friend and I swapped days."

"Oh," I articulate from around the tip of my thumb. The knowledge of his foresight diverts me from my purpose.

"I knew it was your last night."

"I see. Have you ever been to Vintage Cocktail Club? I have a reservation for 8:00 PM."

"Oh, class," he interjects. " No, I haven't. But I've heard of it. Should I pick you up at 7:30 PM?"

I chuckle lightly. "No. No. It's closer to you. Let me Uber."

"Are you sure?"

"I'm positive."

"Let me know if you change your mind."

The line falls silent for a few seconds. "Hey Nolan," I reach into the void, placing the phone on speaker, "since I have you..." The sound of his laugh fills my room.

"Get comfortable," he instructs. I slide deeper under the covers and place his voice by my ear. "You're lucky Ireland has so many myths."

Once I've had time to prepare, the bard begins the tale of Fair, Brown and Trembling, a Gaelic variant of Cinderella.

I'm aware I've begun to drift as fragments of dreams snag on my musings. Made-up conversations mingle with Nolan's narration. Scenarios I often replay before sleeping blend with recollections. I recall the reassuring rise and fall of the storyteller's chest, keeping time with the *Leap Year* soundtrack, which hums from the turntable in the corner. *Right Time...Wrong Guy* is slowly overtaken by the underlying *tick tick tick tick* of Christopher Nolan's *Dunkirk*. The unsettling score growing louder and louder until it is blaring from the alarm clock next to my face. Startled from my unrest, I slam my hand into the snooze button, smacking it twice to end the unneeded cycle. In my euphoric state from the night prior, I had forgotten it was on. Flopping onto my stomach, I shove my face into a pillow, trying to shake the sound of impending doom—*tick tick tick tick*—rattling my brain. It's 9:30 AM, which means my time in Dublin has dwindled to just over 24 hours.

In an effort to assuage these feelings, I locate my phone in the disarray of bedclothes, temporarily bypass the three texts I'm sure are from Taylor and navigate to VCC's Instagram account. After scrolling enough to get a sense of the speakeasy's atmosphere, I roll over and open my text chain with Nolan.

> *Since it's my last night, want to dress up?*

I follow the message with the account link. He responds right away.

> *Like fancy dress or formal attire?*

> *Not necessarily with the theme, but nice.*

> *Is this an attempt to get me in a suit?*

> *If you dress up, I dress up. Take it or leave it.*

> *Obviously, I'm taking it.*

Good Morning, by the way.
Did you know you talk in your sleep?

Yes, actually. I like to delineate my dreams.

I roll my eyes, assuming he's joking, but as I have been known to exhibit this parasomnia on occasion, I check my recent calls. 15 minutes. I'd been awake for roughly ten, so he didn't stay on long enough for me to enter a REM cycle, but he hadn't hung up as soon as I'd stopped reacting.

I should market the discovery as the miracle cure for nightmare hangovers. My approaching EOTD (End Of Vacation Depression) is repelled by a wave of unreasonable giddiness, which sends me and my socked feet skidding down the hallway to grab a to-go cup for my coffee. For the first time since I got here, I'm in need of a new outfit.

48

Laurel

As I schedule my taxi, I notice Vintage Cocktail Club is only two blocks from The Auld Dubliner. I smile at the bittersweet yet fitting realization that my trip will end so close to where it began. The lobby of The Dean is not too crowded. A young couple has stationed themselves at the bar across from a group of college-aged co-eds who lounge piled around their suitcases.

"Well, don't you look nice, miss."

I respond to the compliment from the front desk, surprised to see Rosie manning the post for the first time since she checked me in. "Thank you. I bought it today. It has pockets!" I shuffle closer as she leans over the counter to see my hand can indeed disappear into the lining of the full red skirt. The high waistband is fastened securely with a bow, making the hem hit right below my knees. It's part of a two-piece dress, the top of which rests about an inch under my breasts.

I smooth the wide strapped square neckline crop under her appraisal. Although, the skin-tight linen doesn't leave much room for wrinkles.

"What's the occasion?" she inquires pleasantly.

"It's my last night," I preen the words, but the delivery is contrasted by the needle someone has stabbed into my voodoo doll's heart.

Rosie beams, "You're sure to catch a fella going out like that. I'm telling you."

Blushing with gratitude, I tuck one side of my straightened hair behind an ear. Before I can vocalize my continued appreciation, her co-worker, a striking woman with dark violet balayage and constantly matching lipstick who I've seen more regularly but never spoken to, interjects.

"Oh, she has one, Rosie, love. Have you not gotten to see him? He's a right mount." My skin brightens further to rival my clothing.

"AMELIA!" Rosie shouts, slapping her friend in the arm. The handful of heads in the room snap in our direction.

Unfazed, Amelia shrugs. "What?! I'm just sayin'." She lowers our conversation's volume so that it remains encased in our bubble. "Slap me again once you've seen him if you don't agree."

My phone dings, indicating my car has arrived. I wave goodbye to the two women, who continue jovially prattling among themselves.

Confirming which ride is mine, I scuff the bottoms of my new shoes on the pavement, tan heels identical to my beloved black pair, and slide into the backseat.

The Uber is scented by an on-vent air freshener, and sealed plastic water bottles fill the cup holder by my ankle, which my driver lets speak for themselves. No words pass between us besides mandatory inductions, the silence forcing me to stew in my unavoidable simmering emotions.

I'm still *in Ireland. I* can *live a little.*

I'm **still** *in Ireland. I* **can** *live a little.*

I cling to the mantra, repeating it over and over as I try to not pick at my nail polish.

When I've reached a few hundred iterations, the vehicle pulls over in a spot adjacent to a tattoo parlor and The Old Storehouse Bar. I make my exit, careful to place my heels outside of the divots in the worn cobblestones.

While I know we're on Crown Alley, I don't see any street numbers or signage indicating where the speakeasy may be.

Unexpectedly, I hear the sound of the descent of a car window from among the usual nightlife ruckus. "It's the door tucked in the black building there," my driver directs through the newly made opening, pointing to an unadorned facade. "I went last week. Craic was great. Just ring the bell when you're ready."

"Oh, thank you," I stammer, stunned by his sudden loquaciousness. He merely grunts, reestablishing the tinted barrier as he accelerates away.

"Well, don't you scrub up well."

In a magic act of his own making, the removal of the taxi reveals Nolan crossing the street. True to form, he's already grinning and right on time.

While the man is still at a distance, I fully appreciate the well-tailored three-piece he's chosen to wear. The accompanying black oxfords glint in the surrounding neon signage as they bring him near. "I could say the same about you," I answer.

His responding smirk is paired with a coy shrug. "Eh, it's nice to dust this thing off every once in a while." His eyes spark conspiratorially as he speaks, the grey tweed of his ensemble bringing out their more achromatic tones.

"You look beautiful," he states plainly, grasping my fingers and bringing them to his lips. The Edwardian-era custom steals the air from my lungs. "Shall we?" he suggests, interlocking our hands.

We're a tad early for the reservation, but after clearing my throat, I step up to the unassuming entry and alert those inside with the buzzer. There's a loud kinetic noise, followed by the thud of a freed deadbolt granting us access. Nolan reaches past my body and engages with the rust-covered door, allowing me to guide us through.

My first impression is that it's dark. Even adapting from nightfall, my eyes need a minute to adjust to the low lighting of the hallway.

"Welcome to VCC," a shadowy feminine outline purrs from behind an antique desk. "What's the name?"

"Cole," I reply. When I'm finally able to make out more than her general shape, the hostess is revealed to be a slender brunette in a fitted black dress.

"Grand. I have you here. As long as you don't mind the roof, we are able to seat you now if you'd like?" I glance at my guest for confirmation.

"Fine by me," he approves.

The receptionist leads us through the classically-wall-papered main room of the restaurant and up a staircase. We emerge onto the top floor. The landing is partially exposed to the elements, allowing the twilight breeze to waft through the gilded bronze-covered area. Art deco tile patterned in pink, orange, and blue compliments the velvet fuchsia seating thrown in among the mostly wicker furniture. The arrangement contrasts nicely with the wide red and white stripes that accent one wall. I catch my reflection in one of the small mounted mirrors as we are led closer and seated at one of the many tables dotted along a lengthy upholstered booth. While Nolan settles into a high-top chair, I hop up onto the pink cushion opposite, assuring the hostess we are comfortable.

"Your server will be right with you," she promises and leaves us to our evening.

No truer words have ever been spoken because she's not even reached the staircase when a young man materializes next to me.

"Good evening. My name is Cian." He introduces himself with genuine pleasure as he places a pitcher of water and two glasses on our table. The orange glow of the lamp above my head coppers his dirty blonde, matching scruff and full mustache while highlighting his deep brown eyes. "I'll be your server tonight. First things first, are you dining with us, or are we only here for the cocktails?"

"Dining," Nolan and I say at the same time, making the entire party chortle.

"Wonderful. The food menu can be found here." Cian flips the cocktail booklet in front of me to its final page. "Do we know what we want to drink, or shall I give you a few more minutes?"

I'm the first to respond. "I'm going to need a moment to weigh my options, sorry."

"Same, mate," Nolan follows.

"No worries. I shall return shortly."

When our waiter has vanished from view, my date pauses his study of the available libations. "Well, this should be fun." "What?" I question, inferring from the childlike glee in his expression that he isn't commenting on the evening in general.

His public joy wanes slightly when his eyebrows approach his hairline. "Laurel," He states incredulously, "you know he thinks you're a lash, right?"

"I'm a what?" I offer, amused by the slang.

"That you're fit, attractive."

I scoff at the observation, undertaking the daunting task of filling my cup. "No, he doesn't. He's just being friendly."

Nolan props an elbow on the table. "Do you seriously not see it? Petal, the man could not be any more obvious."

I shake my head. "I really don't–"

"Laurel," he interrupts before bringing his voice one decibel above a whisper, "he acted like I wasn't even here, rarely took his eyes off you, and, I'm pretty certain, mentally undressed you twice!"

My mouth falls open. "That's–, You–, I–" I stammer, floundering for reasonable justification. Eventually, the busker plays search and rescue.

"Pay attention when he comes back," he insists, assuredly resting against his chair and refocusing on the menu.

We've settled our order by the time Cian reappears. "How are we doing? Do you have any questions?" I begin to negate this, but Nolan clears his throat.

"Actually," he starts. The mischief in his eyes warns me I won't like what's coming. "She was having trouble choosing a cocktail."

In a matter of seconds, our waiter determining my alcoholic likes, dislikes, and preferences through a barrage of extremely specific questions, explaining the differences and similarities between the concoctions that have piqued my interest and offering advice on why I may not enjoy some of the others. I would chalk this up to him being a knowledgeable and helpful server if Cian wasn't practically seated next to me in the booth.

After a few minutes of back and forth, I stick with my original decision: High Tea, a fruity vodka-based drink topped with a cherry and mint spring. By the time we're alone again, Nolan is positively beaming.

"Believe me now?" he teases, head cocked insistently to one side. I nod, aware of the heat building in my cheeks. "So, I think I may need to sit closer. Thoughts?"

Biting back what I know would be an award-winning smile, I scrunch my nose. "Mmmm. That's really not necessary."

♥

Two rounds later, the Irishman had gotten his way, sliding into the booth and claiming our waiter's brazen neglect of his presence had forced his hand. Our third drinks are halfway gone, and while their alcohol content and the heat lamps placed around the room have helped lessen the effects of the dropping temperature, I'm grateful for the additional warmth his body heat and stolen blazer are providing.

"I have a question," I say, bridging the gap between our last conversation and this one. "Where do you record your songs?" The topic of music had flowed more freely this evening, but I'm still treading lightly, "Do you rent out a studio?"

Ice clinks against the tumbler as Nolan shakes his Whiskey Smash. "It depends. *Butterflies* is actually a demo. I recorded it in my spare bedroom. Over the last few months, Eoghan and I have worked on remodeling the space into a tiny studio. But obviously, when I can afford it, I prefer a more professional set up."

"Yeah, that makes sense." Sipping on my vanilla and hazelnut-infused Irish latte, I nestle into the crook of his arm. The drink wasn't on the menu, but when I inquired about a coffee-based cocktail, Cian delivered.

"I have three new songs I recorded in-house, but the sound isn't quite as crisp as I want it to be, so they need to be re-done in a real studio before they're ready for release." My eyes widen.

"You have more songs?" I gasp. He chuckles.

"Yeah, but they're on my computer. We'd have to go to my gaff for you to hear them."

"Can we?" I ask.

49

Laurel

"I don't see what the problem is?" I pester, crossing in front of Nolan on the sidewalk, "you've walked back to your place from much farther away than this." I can physically see the musician chew the quandary I've purposely created. His suggestion to get a Taxi as we left VCC was met by my outright refusal. When he pressed the issue and was once again shot down, I sensed his growing discomfort. Based on our past adventures, he is aware I am more than capable of traversing the distance between the two destinations, but—despite our near-constant time together—we haven't known each other long enough for him to be completely confident referencing my disability.

Just to antagonize him more, I spin on my heel and walk backward a few paces, the bottom of his blazer brushing the back of my thighs, "Come to think of it," I continue into the silence, "I've walked from yours all the way to The Dean, so why is this little jaunt bothering you?"

He sighs. "It has nothing to do with the distance. It's your feckin' shoes. You can't be comfortable."

I briefly examine my heels, furrowing my brow in dramatic extrospection. "I'm fine." I shrug and skip into a half-turn, hoping it covers for my near trip on a crack in the pavement. Using my left over momentum, I bound up the steps of Ha'Penny Bridge, pausing at the crown so Nolan can join me.

The urban skyline sparkles from all sides. At this hour and vantage point, the buildings of both old and new Dublin are awash in neon and the sounds of merry-making pub patrons. This was the real reason I wanted to walk. One last stroll to soak in the city.

When I've had my fill, I address the familiar presence waiting at my side. "I'm kidding. My feet hurt. We can get an Uber."

The Irishman peers down at me, an amused exasperation drawing lines across his forehead as he clicks his tongue. "You can be a very frustrating drunk. You know that, right?"

I recoil from him in offense. "Considering I have been "drunk" in front of you like four times now, and this is the first time you've voiced that very wrong opinion, I'll allow it. But just this once."

Nolan scoffs, reeling me back in by my wrists. His snort ruffles my hair as he settles one hand at my waist and uses the other to retrieve his phone from my jacket's inside breast pocket. The device's light contrasts his face from over my shoulder as I snuggle into his chest. "It should only be a couple of minutes." He announces after a few light taps.

Under my ear, his heartbeat increases its tempo. His hand at my side stops tracing the exposed skin there and squeezes lightly. The gesture is partnered with a tug on the lower portion of my hair, which forces my attention a half-step away from his body warmth and to his face.

"Hi," he breathes through a grin.

"Hi," I echo.

I forget about the growing evening chill when Nolan's lips find mine, once again pulling me close. My hands roam up his chest, up to his shoulders and around his neck. His glide gently over the small of my back and tangle in my hair. A trill of vibration rounds off the back of my skull from the phone still held in his palm, making me giggle. He uses the moment to sweep his tongue along my bottom lip and–

The blare of a car horn shocks us apart. From the opposite side of the bridge, the hazard lights of a beige minivan blink spotlights on the wind-blown waters of the river.

"That was faster than I expected," Nolan admits, double-checking his phone as he grabs my hand to dash to the waiting vehicle.

"Sorry to interrupt." The heavily-mustached driver apologizes with a bashful glee that suggests the opposite as we situate ourselves inside. "It may be a little hard in the seats you've chosen, but if you'd like to continue, I operate on an 'eyes forward' policy."

The two of us regard the space between the two middle seats for a beat too long, causing the entire car to break into fits of embarrassed laughter.

Obediently, buckled into my chosen purgatory, I can't help but wonder if our jovial-eyed chauffeur is purposely prolonging our journey. When I'm certain we've passed the same communal gathering of teens commandeering a street corner for the second time, I shift in my seat once more, no longer endeavoring to hide my near-constant fidgeting as I try to decipher the reason behind Nolan's latest bought of silent chuckles.

I'm about to make a brazen objection to this little game when the cab slows to a stop across from our destination's front door.

"So sorry for the hape of traffic." The driver states, shaking his head as he accesses the automatic doors, "I did my best to cut around it."

I roll my eyes, fighting the urge to drag my date the remaining yards to his apartment, but the Irishman has paused next to the car window.

"Have a good night, mate." He passes our driver a cash tip as they exchange final smiles.

"I'd say the same to you," the man replies, pocketing the funds, "but I don't think I have to."

As the minivan rounds the corner, Nolan rounds on me. "Is it too cheesy to start with 'Where were we?'" he offers, cocking an eyebrow.

There is a tiny, *tiny* faction of my brain that contemplates telling him it's too late, but before I've fully registered the option, I'm swept off the pavement.

"Hi," the busker summarizes again as my ankles lock around his waist. "I'm – sorry – there – was – so – much – traffic." He keeps up the ruse, punctuating each word with a kiss to my mouth and a step toward his home.

By the time he's fishing for his keys, face nuzzled in my neck, it's as if no time has passed at all. The door swings open easily, with our combined body weight already pressing against it, sending us stumbling inside.

Nolan feels for the light switch while I struggle to rid my body of his blazer, only for it to get caught in his grip around my thighs. It hangs there as we proceed farther into the living space, eventually falling forgotten to the ground when he transitions me onto the cool tile of what I assume is his kitchen counter. Stepping between my legs, the he leans into me. I shift backward, attempting to position myself more comfortably, but instead, my head violently connects with the handle to one of his cabinets. The crash is both hard and loud enough to immediately break the hormone-induced trance between us.

"Ow!" I exclaim, rubbing the impact point but giggling.

"Jesus," Nolan says, pushing off the ceramic surface and placing his hand over mine, "Are you okay?"

I grimace. "Yeah. I'm fine."

'May I see?" Once I give one slow bobble, he uses the hand still at my back to push me forward. I rest my head on his shoulder as he delicately parts my hair in search of anything other than a bump. When he reaches the impacted region, I flitch, inhaling sharply, surrounding myself with the remnants of his cologne: Rainy days. Warm blankets. Wool sweaters. Fireplaces.

Nolan stills. "Sorry," he comforts. "I just want to make sure you're not bleeding."

"It's OK," I promise, permitting him to proceed.

I know he's certain I don't need professional medical attention when I feel his deltoid muscle relax. He extracts his hands from my hair, covering the offending hardware with one while bringing the other to my chin and using it to angle my face this way and that. "I think you'll live," he finishes. I simper under his exaggerated inspection. "How about some water?"

I blush. "Yeah, Water is probably a good idea." He uses one finger to stoke my nose before releasing his hold on my jaw and helping me off the checkered surface.

"Make yourself at home," he directs while indicating the other rooms with a backward bow. "I'll be right there."

As I walk into the den, I note that while the living space isn't sparkling clean, it's not a biohazard either. What I'm most impressed by is the amount of decent and complementary decor. It's so well done I can't help but wonder if Roisin had a hand in the interior design. The rustic hardwood floor is partially covered by a black and white geometric rug on which a cluttered brass-topped coffee table is centered. It perfectly complements the brown faux-leather couch and dark-washed credenza that bears a mid-sized flat-screen TV. The various shelves around the cream-colored room house photographs, books and other sentimental trinkets. There's a keyboard in the corner, next to a currently empty guitar stand. I'm scanning the area for the missing instrument when Nolan enters the room.

He quickly reorganizes the coffee table, making space in front of the couch for the glasses he brought with him, and sinks to the most-used cushion. He drinks his water, watching as I come to sit beside him. There's a small pile of aspirin next to my cup.

"I wasn't sure how many you'd want." he references, "But you should at least take a couple. There's a pretty serious bump back there, even if you don't already have a headache."

I fish two from the edge and swallow them. "Thank you. Now, as for why were here..."

In answer to my pointed stare at the piano, the musician groans. "And I thought I'd properly distracted you."

"Blame your kitchen cabinet," I snort.

"Trust me. It and I are going to have a serious discussion in the morning."

My stomach tightens as Nolan locates his laptop. *In the morning, I'll be gone.*

After a few moments soundtracked by typing and keypad clicks, he twists toward me, his computer resting gingerly on his knees.

"Remember, these aren't done. So, listen gently," he conveys easily as he prods the space bar, but I can tell he's nervous. I slide closer as the first melody reaches my ears.

Listening to the new tracks, which have unofficial titles, I understand what he meant at Vintage Cocktail Club. While these versions are fine as they are, the songs sound empty, like there's space waiting to be filled between the words. When the final song ends, its creator hits his space bar again, reviving the light on the screen. The clock widget in the corner reads 12:01 AM. *I leave today.* But Nolan's looking at me expectantly, which hauls me out of my head.

"They're great, really," I agree. "But, you are right. They don't sound completely finished."

He grins. "They're kind of hollow, right?"

"Yes!" I agree. "Exactly. But, for an early demo, they are still really good. I've definitely been sent worse." I fill my lungs with a steadying breath. If I don't do this now, I may never get the chance. "Nolan," I ask cautiously, "why do you not want help growing an audience?" Next to me, he instantly stiffens. "I'm genuinely curious. That's all."

He clears his throat, handling the moment with care. "If I ever have any kind of commercial success, I want to say I made it on my own, by my own merit and my own decisions."

I place an understanding hand on his arm. "A little help or outside insight won't take away from that. If you let...I don't know...Colin posts your stuff on his Instagram story or Twitter every now and again, some of his followers might listen and tell their friends, who tell their friends and so on and so forth. It'd be exactly like it is now, except it'd maybe speed up the process." Nolan sighs, but I push on. "It's not like you'd be paying someone who doesn't actually like your music to promote it, and if & Then Some's fans don't like what they hear, they won't stay and listen. Anyone new would still be there because of *you* and *your* music." I'm about to add I'm only offering advice because I think he has great potential and actual talent when he interrupts me.

"But that would just be the beginning. If I amass a fanbase quickly through external avenues instead of hard-work and effort, someone like you comes along offering to make use of my "viral potential" to mold me into some kind of industry money machine. If I don't take the time to figure out what people like most about *my* music, then suddenly, it won't be mine anymore." I'm more than startled by this response. The Irishman wasn't yelling, but his voice was sterner than usual.

"That's not–Is that what you think I do?" I inquire, offended, unintentionally creating space between us."Is that what you think Capitol is going to do with & Then Some?"

Nolan shrugs, "I guess we'll have to wait and see."

"Have you even talked to the guys about it?" I reply, harsher than I mean to, "All I'm helping them do is enhance what they've already been doing. It's not what we're able to do with every artist, I'll admit to that, but when the artistic vision is already there, which I know you have–"

He scoffs in response. This time, there's nothing friendly behind it. It's a mean and derogatory sound. "Enhance is a fancy word for dictate, right? If they already have an artistic vision, why is your job even necessary?"

I stand. "I refuse to sit here and defend my job to you, but there's more to it than what you're considering, and I suggest, if you really do want to "make it" at some point, you talk to Colin because rarely does that happen without a record company. It might not be Capitol for you, but it will have to be somebody." I step back, careful to avoid colliding with any furniture. "It's late. I should go."

50

Laurel

An instant hush falls across the room. In the time in which an obligatory pin could drop, Nolan and I stare at each other. His eyes instantly soften at my movement, and he issues an immediate retraction statement.

"Laurel, I'm so sorry. I'm not trying to belittle you. I know how much the band appreciates you and what you do for them. I got flustered and defensive, and I shouldn't have said that. Please, sit back down." He reaches for my hand, but I step back a few paces, letting the coffee table create a concrete barrier between us, chest heaving, adrenaline ready to power a fight or flight response.

"No, I should go," I say.

Confused, Nolan removes his computer from his lap, brow furrowed over apologetic eyes. "Laurel, c'mere to me. I didn't mean it the way it sounded, honestly. I don't think that at all." There's sincerity to be found in every inch of his face.

My pulse slows. "I know," I reply with a small smile, "I still need to go. I have a plane to catch." Before he can stand, I make for the door. I'm a few feet from his house, heels clicking quickly over the cement when I hear him behind me. He catches up easily.

"Stall the ball! He cries, stopping in front of me and placing a hand on my chest. "Are you actually leaving right now? Like this is it, leaving."

My eyes fill with moisture as his run disbelieving circles around my face: Right eye. Lips. Left eye. The last thing I want to do right now is cry, so I take a shaky breath, steeling my response, "I was always leaving. We knew that."

"Come back inside, just for a bit," Nolan pleads, hands cupping my face and catching errant tears. "I'll put the kettle on, sober up, and drive you home." His face is so earnest. I want to tell him yes.

I'm still in Ireland. I can live a little.

But I'm not really. I leave today. One foot is already out the door.

I can feel my heart breaking as I shake my head. "I shouldn't," I reply, voice barely above a whisper, water fully streaking down my cheeks. "It'll make it harder to go. Plus, I already called an Uber. Don't worry."

He doesn't speak for a moment, thumbs working like windshield wipers on my face. "I don't want this to end."

"Nolan," my voice cracks on a sob. "This was always–"

"Maybe for you. Not for me. It was at first. Ten days. Pretty girl. Barely a Summer fling. But it hasn't been since Guinness Storehouse. The moment you told me you got up at 3:00 AM to talk to Taylor because there wasn't any other option, this became something that could work. We can figure it out. Tell me you don't want that too?"

I fold into his chest. "It's not the same."

"Why not?"

"When would I actually see you again, realistically, and for how long?"

"I don't know," Nolan confesses into my hair," I could come to LA. See you, go on a bus tour to the Hollywood Sign, and visit a mediocre brewery."

I chuckle, "And after that?" Discussing the reality of our situation is a sobering experience. "It's easy to promise now that we'll fly back and forth." I create enough space between us to place my hand on his cheek and attempt a small smirk. "To make those promises. But in a week, two, three, spending that kind of money won't seem sustainable. It's not, no matter how much I wish it was."

"Laurel, can we try, please."

I shake my head, sniffling. The singer's tear-filled eyes mirror mine. "This isn't what I expected it to be ten days ago. It grew into something real and intense that I haven't felt in a long time. I want to remember this—you—as it has been. Like it still is right now. I don't want it to become some muddled and muted version that fades over FaceTime calls and alternate timezone texts until one of us inevitably uncovers a reason to move on. I know this is the easy way out, but a clean break is for the best."

As I distance myself, the car I ordered slows to a stop a few inches in front of us. Nolan unlatches the door. "When's your flight?" he asks.

"Early," I acknowledge the inquiry as optimistically as I'm able after buckling my seat belt. My busker nods, stepping back onto the sidewalk. I watch as he runs an arm across the top half of his face and disappears from view.

51

Laurel

Back at The Dean, I consider calling Taylor but settle on crying myself to sleep.

52

Laurel

As I wait to board flight BA 845 to LHR, I can't believe I went and got myself in the exact mess I'd wanted to avoid in the first place. I'd told the Irishman my flight left early this morning without actually knowing the exact time, but my assumption was correct. It's currently 10:15 AM, meaning I've been at the airport since 8:30 AM, said goodbye to Rosie by 7:00 AM—who blessedly did not comment on my puffy and bloodshot eyes—and had roused from my alarm at 6:00 AM. When I woke, I hadn't gotten any calls or texts and haven't since. I'm not expecting any. Thus far, Nolan has been nothing but respectful of my wishes. I'd be surprised if that changed now.

I meant every word of what I said outside his apartment. I don't regret any portion of our time together, as painful as parting may be, and I don't regret my decision to seal the memories away in a box with a well-tied bow, leaving them there to revisit when the "what-ifs" are lost to time instead of the entire relationship. When push comes to shove, I'm thankful the evening deteriorated when it did. Yes, in the moment, the blatant disregard for and disparaging of my career had hurt. But, he is not the first nor will he be the last artist to hold that opinion. For that reason, I'd forgiven him the second an apology came out of his mouth. Yet, his words had broken the spell which had somehow survived midnight. I was reminded that, like it or not, Cinderella had a plane to catch. I saw an exit ramp, and I took it.

As soon as his door had slammed behind me, I'd known. Had the circumstances been different, I would have let the moment pass. I would have set out to prove him wrong. And sitting in my taxi this morning, watching the city speed by, I recognized my unwelcome career advice was not unselfishly given. It was my declaration on the sidewalk, my last-ditch effort to make it work, to light a match and try to find the end of the tunnel. If Nolan was willing to grow his audience by using his network, then maybe he'd eventually have a reoccurring reason to come to The States, which was independent of a desire to be with me. If I could hold on to the possibility that down the road, the necessary trips across the Atlantic would be held together by something stronger than an invisible string, I would have raced back to his landing. It was a long shot either way, but it was the only hope I had.

I know all of these things, so why is there something akin to remorse gnawing away at my insides? I flop down in my assigned seat and endeavor to take stock of my feelings. I'm heartbroken, disappointed, irritated, annoyed and angry... all at myself. I have no one to blame for the way things turned out but me. Even at the end, Nolan never did anything but exceed my expectations. *I knew on this day, at this time, I'd be sitting right where I am now. I was the one who had made* the repeated choice to spend so much time with an Irish busker in spite of this fact. It's all on me.

I stuff my headphones into my ears and put my playlist on shuffle. It's all-female and specially curated for times when my emotions feel jumbled. I almost backtrack when LYRA comes up first. I click past to Nell Mescal, another Irish local and recent addition, and then once more to land on Gracie Abrams. I let the LA-based singer/ songwriter soundtrack my takeoff.

53

Taylor

I know Laurel's landed before her texts chime through to my phone because her Spotify status changes. It's not unusual for her to be listening to Charli Adams. But the playlist itself is essentially my personal bat signal. "Shit," I exhale but then steady myself with a calming breath. Maybe we're not Code Red. Maybe she's just sad about leaving.

I stow my laptop and steer the car out of the LAX cell phone lot and into the dreaded arrivals loop. Luckily, I don't have to go far to reach the entrance to the parking garage closest to the Tom Bradley International Terminal. I steer Laurel's car into an open space, hang her disability placard on the mirror, grab my supplies, and head inside. As neither of us has ever traveled internationally, it would be remiss to not take full advantage of this moment.

Standing at the arrivals gate, I'm dressed in an almost exact replica of Anita Miller's (Zooey Deschanel's character) stewardess outfit from *Almost Famous*. While it is not my favorite film, Laurel is absolutely obsessed with it and has been for as long as I've known her. On the occasional Halloween where we've been too busy to come up with costumes, she always has a Penny Lane ensemble prepped and ready to go. I couldn't think of a more appropriate way to welcome her back to California. As we're a go big or go home household, I'm also donning a similar hat, travel bag, and hairstyle.

Strangers cast wary glances at my pink and red retro attire, but I don't mind. Laurel is going to love it. As passengers begin funneling out of the tunnel, I'm almost giddy with excitement. I've missed having my best friend a room away. After what feels like an eternity, I catch sight of her. I wave to get her attention. By the time she reaches me, she's beaming.

"Taylor, oh my goodness! This is amazing! You're Anita!" Laurel exclaims. We embrace, laughing. I pull away first.

"I'm so glad you're back!" I cry, "I've missed you! How were the last two days? I know you have updates."

She chuckles as we walk through the airport doors. "You could say that. It was a really good trip overall."

I pause—both mentally and physically, as we have to wait at the crosswalk—and really examine Laurel's face. She's purposefully not making eye contact, but I can still see the small pool forming over her bottom lashes.

"Hey, woah," I ease, shielding her from passersby and invading her space, placing my hands on her shoulders. Immediately, she shakes her head, face contorting the way it always does when she's trying not to cry. "We don't have to talk about this here. We'll run through In-N-Out on the way home and get you some food. Then you have to tell me what happened, ok?"

Laurel focuses on the pavement beneath our feet, pulling herself together enough to finally look at me. "Okay," she agrees.

♥

As soon as we walk through the door, I tote our dinner to the kitchen, plating it and pouring our drinks into more suitable cups. By the time I return, Laurel is seated comfortably on the couch with a plethora of items surrounding her. "What's going on?" I inquire, scanning the unexpected scene.

There's actual light in her answering simper, "I'm giving you your presents. The ones on the table aren't yours, though. They're for my parents. I just laid them out, so I don't forget to take them with me tomorrow."

As we eat, I let Laurel distract herself as she fills me in on the backstories behind each of my gifts. The main item is my favorite Hozier album on vinyl, purchased from what my friend describes as an absolute dream of a boutique record store in Dublin. At each of the stops on her infamous bus tour, she picked me up a trinket as well. Providing me with new earrings, a vintage-style postcard featuring Cliffs of Moher, a soy candle, and a small antique keychain.

Our burgers gone and beginning to digest, I set aside the trinket from Ivyleigh House and place a pillow on my lap. "Ok. You've avoided it long enough," I push, patting the cushion to firmly indicate a shift in the conversation. "Tell me everything."

Laurel groans, placing her head in her hands and flopping sideways into the newly dedicated space. "It's not that big of a deal," she deflects, rolling onto her back, "But I'll miss him for awhile."

"Oh, girlie," I murmur, brushing her travel-matted hair out of her face, "you'll see him again soon. How many days is it going to be?" The bridge of my nose crinkles as my friend silently shakes her head. I inhale deeply before slowly prying her palms from her face. The eyes they were shielding are once again wet and adorned with smudged mascara. "What do you mean? Last time we talked, you were so happy. What happened?"

Laurel steels herself with a resigned sigh, catching a runaway tear with the sleeve of her Taylor Swift sweatshirt. "What I always knew would happen. We ran out of time."

"I thought you wanted to see where things would go," I prompt, still puzzled. "What changed?"

"Nothing. Nolan was—is— great and wonderful and caring and charming and lovely, but when all is said and done, I live here, and he lives in Ireland. It would never work long term."

"So, you decided to be friends?"

My words are met with a grimace, "Not exactly. I asked for a clean break."

I don't think my eyebrows had been properly introduced to my hairline prior to this moment. *"You did what!?"* my brain screams. Thankfully, my lips compassionately request the full story in their stead. "Can you start from the date? I need to fill in the bits and pieces you sent over text."

As Laurel recounts her final two days in Ireland. I console and comfort her until her tears are flowing at a less rapid and regular pace.

"And then I got on the plane," she concludes with a shrug.

I pause, exchanging her now sodden Kleenex for a fresh one, and proceed gently, "Laurel, babe, I love you so, so much, and this question is coming from the most adoring place, but I need to voice it because I'm trying to be as empathetic as possible." My roommate peeks up from her place of solace, eyes red-rimmed and puffy, waiting.

"Well, spill," she eventually concedes my purposeful silence with the weakest of laughs.

"Why didn't you want to at least see how you guys functioned apart? Why'd you decide to cut him off completely?"

Laurel's labored inhale causes me to quickly clarify, "I understand exactly where you were coming from. I'm only curious because you seemed to really like him."

"It's *because* I liked him so much."

Laurel sits up to emphasize her point. The frustration sketched across her features underscoring how much she means it. When I knit my eyebrows together, she goes on to explain. "If I believed there was any chance I'd see him in person again anytime soon, I would try to keep in contact. But I really don't see a point. If I keep talking to him, then I keep liking him. If I keep liking him, then I can't move past him. If I can't move past him, I'll end up in my fifties, hoping he walks into my highly-rated-and-locally-loved boutique hotel!" The tail end of her sentence is lost to an intense renewal of tears, but as I corral her back into my lap, we both chuckle at her *Love, Rosie* novel reference in which the Irish characters are reunited much later than their British film counterparts.

If Laurel is making pop-culture jokes, we may win the night yet.

"I get it. I do," I relay, stroking the sniffling mess on top of me as I mobile order our favorite pints from Salt & Straw. "I just wanted to know for sure."

"I don't know why I'm this upset," she says. "I really only knew him for a week. That's an embarrassingly short time period."

"Hey," I respond in the delicately stern tone I usually reserve for actors fighting the end-of-day delirium of particularly repetitive press junkets. The word forces Laurel to rotate her head and face me properly. "Don't do that to yourself. Seriously. Love is weird. The amount of time you've known a person isn't directly correlated to how much you're allowed to feel for them."

A small smile tugs at the corners of her lips as my words soak in. "Thank you," she manages, reaching for a tissue. There's not much light behind her eyes, but she inhales fully for the first time since landing on American soil.

Now that Laurel has regained the ability to bear her own body weight. I make my way over to the record player. "So, who do we want on first, Lorde or LEON?" I question coaxing her into what I know is the mourning process's next necessary phase. Fortunately, her grin grows more sincere.

"LEON," she replies, finally picking up her pink lemonade instead of our quickly dwindling supply of water. Watching her confidently gulp it down, I wince.

"Taylor!" she cries, small droplets of the drink clearing her airway as she rallies from what I know is an unexpected taste. "Did you put tequila in this!"

54

Laurel

The night has progressed past crying over boys to dramatically lip-syncing songs about crying over boys. And while it did briefly regress for the amount of time necessary to go through one brand new Kleenex box, it eventually transitioned into watching a romantic comedy featuring a woman who learns to cry again because of a boy (The Holiday), a choice we did not properly consider for various emotional reasons and ended up changing to a enemies-to-lovers romance featuring the safe topics of pizza, baseball and incorrectly delivered salads (Set It Up).

The past hours of crying, laughing, and exorcizing emotional demons have culminated in Taylor and I heaped upon my bed with an insane amount of pillows and blankets, both covering and fencing us in, psyching ourselves up for the night's boss-level event.

"Are you sure you want to do this?" My friend asks for the umpteenth time in the last 20 minutes. "There might be a way to repurpose it."

I chuckle. Taylor and her last long-term boyfriend, the one who had dumped her, giving rise to the unremarkable kennel of Dobermans, had met at a Florence and the Machine concert. The day after their breakup, I found her in our backyard, lighter in hand, prepared to burn an effigy of all the band's albums and merchandise she owned. Once I talked her off the ledge, we instead spent the night driving circles around the city. The band's songs blasting as loud as my car would allow. From that moment on, it has been written law that as far as breakups are concerned, whenever possible, we exchange a negative action for a positive one.

"Unfortunately, this is not an FATM opportunity," I begrudgingly admit. "Plus, it's not like it can't be undone, and he won't know. I'm the one who wanted space, so I need to make sure I stick to my guns, at least until I'm not at risk of changing my mind. It wouldn't be fair to him for me to suddenly reach out."

Taylor cocks her head. "I guess it could be seen as emotional manipulation...in a certain light...if you squint."

I angle my body away from my friend's, spearing her with a sullen glare.

347

"Ok. Ok," she relents. "You can make your own decisions. I am here to provide a non-judgmental environment and support...until you are in the correct headspace to hear otherwise." As she tacks on the qualification after I've rearranged to get comfortable, I knock her arm with my shoulder in retaliation, unable to stay my exasperated eye roll.

"Right," I press through an anticipatory breath. "Let's do it."

Taylor gapes as I mute Nolan in every way, shape, and form on every social media front, including Spotify. It'll be better this way, for now. When there are fewer emotions involved, if I want, I can check in on the musician.

The task complete, I plop back onto my pillows, physically, mentally and emotionally drained.

"Love you, babe," Taylor says, snuggling in next to me and placing a kiss on my temple, "Wake me up if you need me, even if it's just because of jet lag."

55

Nolan

Songs are written in many different ways. Sometimes, they start as concepts. Sometimes, as melodies, you can't get out of your head. Sometimes, a line comes from something you overhear or from a moment in a dream. Some songs never see the light of day. Some take months to perfect. There isn't a formula to follow to guarantee success or even reliability. But, for me, the songs I'm proudest of, the ones people seem to connect with the most, are the ones that write themselves. The ones I can't get down on paper or into a voice note fast enough. Some songs feel like they were always there waiting for just the right moment to be brought to life.

56

Laurel

NOVEMBER

"Taylor," I groan, haphazardly knocking my knuckles on the plaster making up our shared wall, "It was 100% your turn to check the record player last night.

"It was not," she harrumphs weakly through the thankfully thin barrier.

I pull my blanket over my head, hoping its dark golden color will shut out the light seeping through my curtains while instantaneously willing the upbeat refrain of The Aces' Daydream a slow and painful death. It's halfway through the next verse before I finally accept I haven't acquired mind control powers overnight and begrudgingly tangle my toes in the fabric of my shag rug. The hardwood floor is cold to the touch as I pad into the living room to silence the singers, so I locate my cable knit socks from where they were abandoned when Taylor suggested pedicures as last night's additional activity. My ruby red toenails wiggle gratefully from inside the added warmth, thankful for their newfound shield against the even colder tile I know I'll encounter in the kitchen.

While LA never freezes over, there is a more than slight chill to the early morning November air that trickles in from the open window next to the coffee pot. I go ahead and switch on the brewer, allowing the promising aroma to dispel any lingering drowsiness. When I've summoned the energy, I return to my bedroom to shut off my upcoming alarm, poking my head into my roommate's oasis of total darkness in the process.

"There will be coffee in a minute if you want it." I prod, "Is it okay if I go ahead and jump in the shower?" I interpret the disgruntled sound that escapes the jumble of bedclothes as assent.

I'm not usually one for morning showers on a workday, but with an additional thirty minutes now being added to my schedule, I can't come up with anything else to do.

When my hair has been washed, blown dry and styled into simplistic waves, I throw on a pair of high-waisted jeans, canvas converse, and a vintage sweatshirt. Finally ready for my morning dose, I'm surprised to find Taylor, makeup done and jewelry chosen, seated at the table in the breakfast nook.

"We need to talk," she begins ominously as she passes me a pre-made cup.

I choose the adjacent chair, eyeing her suspiciously as she takes a cautious sip, all at once knowing where this is headed and hoping I am wrong.

"Are we seriously not going to go tonight?" she asks, still holding her mug in front of her face, a physical obstacle between us. I sigh and slouch against the wooden back of my seat.

"Taylor, we talked about this literally all night. My answer is the same." I wish I was guilty of exaggeration. This month's roomie date had been punctuated repeatedly by the aforementioned discussion and finally cut short when Taylor and I finally decided to call it after getting as close to fighting about it as we'd ever come. I'm displeased to be accosted by this continuation but not shocked she hasn't let it go. "I already told you. They don't need me there."

"It's not only about that," she admits quietly. "Yes, it is absolutely ludicrous that you aren't going to see & Then Some play the Troubadour. But, I'm forcing the issue because it proves something I've been worried about for awhile."

I raise my eyebrows over the cooling coffee's steam while Taylor exhales a preparatory breath.

"I'm saying this because I love you. I have tried to be sympathetic and give you time to figure this out on your own, but you haven't. Or, maybe you have, and you're not talking to me about it, which, frankly, would make me even more worried if I'm honest, but that isn't the point. Again, please don't be upset. I know it's not the best delivery, but now I've started talking, and I can't stop." Ironically, she resorts to a momentary pause to collect her convictions. "Laurel," Taylor tears her eyes from the table and forces them to meet mine, "you're not happy. I don't think you have been happy since you got back from Ireland. You've distanced yourself from so many things you used to love. I'm not claiming you don't still enjoy them, but nine times out of ten, it feels like you're 80% there at most. There used to be this vibrance around you. It's not obvious to everyone, but I can tell it's dimmed."

As my jaw has dropped during her speech, I stammer a response. "What? What do you mean?"

Taylor sighs, her eyes softening. "Last week at Fonda, you were on Instagram during the opening act. I know my Laurel Cole cardinal sins."

"I was just having a rough night," I insist under my blush. "Nothing has changed since Ireland. My life is the same. I love living here with you. I love my job. I love–"

"Damn it, Laurel." Taylor's gentle indignation reignites with a fury, propelling her to stand. "Nolan happened. You can't pretend he didn't. He changed the way you relate to all of this, and I can't watch you shove that to the side anymore! Yes. You might be fine. You're content. But you are my best friend. I need you to be happy. I miss you happy. I understood—partially—the need to block him on socials and get past him, but it's been two months, and you've stopped fully engaging with anything that reminds you of him at all, which is a lot of your usual activities. This isn't the life you deserve."

I sit up straight, readying my oral defense, but Taylor holds up a hand and continues.

"It's because it hurts. I get it. I've been there. But don't you think there might be a reason it still feels so raw after all the time? You're calling this healing, but it's not. You're not you. You haven't been for a while. I need you to see that too, so you can get to the actual recovery process."

I blink back the tears that have begun to line my eyes at her fair, if surprising, appraisal. "Taylor, I–" I look to my lap, endeavoring to complete a calming breath, but my voice breaks, "What am I supposed to do?"

Compassionately, Taylor kneels in front of me and brushes my hair out of my face. "Take baby steps. Do the things you used to, even if they remind you of Nolan." At my cocked eyebrow, she clarifies, "I mean really doing them, not lingering in the background. Know it is going to hurt, and I will be here when it does, but it will get better. If it doesn't, maybe unblock the man, reach out and see if he's in the same boat. If he is, there's your answer."

My friend translates my anxious expression and smiles. "I've known for a while it was going to take something big— something special—to shake you out of your excuses. Maybe this is that. If I'm wrong, I will buy out the entire Ben and Jerry's freezer at Ralph's, and we can play *Leap Year* on the blow-up screen in the backyard and boo at it like in *The Princess Bride*."

A light chuckle makes its way past my lips. "Can I think about it?" I question.

"That's all I'm asking," she affirms as she wraps me in a hug. "Now, go fix your makeup, or we'll both be late."

While we're no longer walking on eggshells around each other, today's commute is quiet due to the emotionally draining morning. I've merged into the North Gower traffic by the time my passenger grabs my phone from the cupholder between us and finally utilizes Spotify.

"Taylor," I say as & Then Some's newest song fades in, "don't."

"Laurel," she replies in the same teasing warning tone, "stop being stubborn." She proceeds to turn up the music and cover the volume dial with her hand. "I'm simply helping you consider your options while there's still time to get tickets." I roll my eyes. *Speaking of stubborn.*

As promised, I entertain the scenario. Although The Troubadour is one of my favorite venues, and I very much love and miss the band, I can immediately summon five reasons why I don't want to go to the concert tonight, each one having to do with a single specific person.

1. Someone mentions Nolan, and I realize I'm not ready to talk about him

2. No one mentions Nolan, and I find I actually do want to talk about him

3. Nolan does come up, and the band assumes we've kept in touch, and then I have to awkwardly illustrate why that isn't the case

4. We do discuss Nolan, and I discover he's completely moved on (while I'm here, still not sure whether or not I even want to talk about him)

5. I learn Nolan didn't mention anything that happened between us to the band and am left in this weird acquaintance limbo

I am completely aware all my reasons are unabashedly hypothetical. However, I still think it's best if I sit this one out. I agreed to baby steps, and the & Then Some Show seems like a very big leap.

As the song ends, a red light keeps us from arriving at our final destination. I hold my hand out for my device. Taylor begrudgingly places it in my palm. Before the light can change, I select Julia Michaels from among my recently played artists and regard my friend.

"I need to sit this one out. But–" I strongly interject when she begins to protest, "–I can see if there's any room for you and Jeremy on the guest list." I watch Taylor imitate mulling the offer over, pretending I didn't see the way her eyes widened at the mention of the guest list. Taylor likes being on lists. I don't blame her. I do, too.

"Are you sure?" she asks, scrunching her nose as we slow to a stop in front of the studio. "Won't it be weird if we go without you?"

I smile and shake my head. "Not at all. Plus, then you can FaceTime me if they put B-sides back on the setlist."

"Deal," Taylor replies with a grin, pleased with my compromise. Exiting the car, she pauses at my door. "Bye, honey. Have a good day at work."

"You too," I extend in return, letting our past twelve hours of disagreement get carried away with the passing breeze. When she's crossed the street, she spins around. "Are you absolutely positive you don't want to come? We'll miss you."

I laugh. Taylor is nothing if not persistent. "Yes, I'm sure. I'll send you the details when I have them."

57

Laurel

In the ten minutes it takes to reach Capitol Records, my anxiety about the day has risen significantly. I'm not sure why. Nothing has changed in terms of my daily schedule. I'm not second-guessing my choice to stay home. Yet, something is setting me off-kilter. Walking through the doors, there's a palpable heaviness weighing on the base of my skull. The sense of unease travels down my spinal cord and into my palms as Daysie wishes me a happy Thursday. I wipe my hands on my jeans and struggle to recall what I have obviously forgotten, but only come up blank. Maybe I've simply had too much caffeine and not enough calories.

"Fourth floor, please, Paul," I say when he beats me to the elevator.

By the time my breakfast burrito is halfway eaten, I'm feeling much better. Not quite well enough to risk another cup of coffee, but as the voracious butterflies in my stomach have finally settled, I press into my waning sense of peace. I've decided I'm going to spend the evening with my ever-growing pile of demos—on which I've been procrastinating—when Irene knocks on my door. With Jenny on maternity leave, her assistant has been more than instrumental in helping me bridge the gap.

"Morning!" I greet her as I wipe my mouth on my solitary and, per usual, overused napkin, "What do we have on the schedule for today? Is there anything besides that last piece of prep for Maggie Rogers' session?"

"Nope," she chirps cheerfully. "It should be an easy day, which is good since you need to leave by 5:20 PM for the & Then Some show."

"Oh, I'm not going. Jenny okayed Nessa and Morgan covering, remember?"

"I know. I just assumed that changed since…," she trails off, giving in to her confusion when my knit eyebrows clearly convey I'm not following. "Honestly, I don't know what I'm saying. I haven't had coffee yet. Sorry," she laughs.

"No worries," I smile back, "I've been there."

She spins to go, then backtracks, accomplishing a 360-degree twirl in the hallway. "Actually, I'm about to run out for a matcha. Do you want anything?"

"I'm OK, thanks," I decline. "I'm feeling a little over-caffeinated today. But when you get back, can you see if you can add Taylor Avalon to tonight's guest list, please? And give her a plus one if there's room."

Irene nods. "For sure. That shouldn't be a problem. The one I sent over last night was pretty small. I'll make the addition on my walk over. Is Avalon A-V-A-L-O-N?"

♥

I've finished listening to about three-fourths of the demos when a voice makes me jump. It's barely after 6:15 PM, but most of my team went home half an hour ago, leading me to believe I was alone with my thoughts and recently delivered dinner.

"What are you still doing here?" I'm even more shocked to find the words belong to Nick Miller (Yes, his name is the same as the *New Girl* character's, a fact he is quite fond of), one of my department's executive vice presidents, who is grinning congenially in my doorway. "Aren't you supposed to be at The Troubadour in–" he pauses to check his watch, " –

well, basically now. The supporting act should be on in forty-five minutes, maybe an hour."

"Sorry. No, sir," I explain from behind my desk. "Jenny said it was fine for Nessa to go since I saw & Then Some play in Dublin."

"But, what about the new guy?" he questions, tilting his head. "Oh, what was his name? I wasn't super involved. We signed him on Monday in New York on recommendation from the UK office. The kid basically blew up overnight. He released a song that went viral over there. Noah something? I think. Irish." Nick's flippant mannerisms are a profound parallel to my blazing internal struggle. "Anyway, his name will be correct on the marquee. At this point, there won't be enough time for you to talk to him ahead of the show, and this probably won't be his ideal audience, but try to make it over there so someone can see what we have to work with.

"Of course," I squeeze the affirmation over the heart that has lodged in my throat. "I'll head to the venue now." Standing, I work with shaking fingers to pack up my desk.

The executive chortles as he leaves. "Sorry about the short notice. I bet Pete forgot to CC you on the email."

As soon as he is out of earshot, I dial Irene. She answers after the first ring.

"I didn't forget anything, did I?" She sounds almost panicked. I feel bad for alarming her.

"No, you're fine. But I have a quick question. This morning, when you felt like I needed to go to The Troubadour, was it because we signed a new artist?"

"Yeah?" the assistant confirms with a syllabic emphasis that suggests I've lost it.

The muscles in my throat begin to tense. "What was his name?" I ask on bated breath, struggling to calm myself.

"Nolan O'Kelley, she replies pragmatically. "Laurel, is everything okay?"

I bob my head a few times before I realize she can't hear me. "Yes. Yes, Irene. Everything is fine. Have a good night. I'll see you tomorrow." The call clicks to a close. As this was the last thing I expected, my entire body is shaking with adrenaline. I force down a few deep breaths and am eventually able to croak, "Hey, Siri. Call Taylor."

I'm relieved when the AI puts through my strangled request.

"Did you change your mind?!" Taylor ecstatically inquires in place of a greeting.

"Nolan's the opening act," I respond hastily, hand to my burning esophagus.

There's such a sudden and immense silence on the other end of the line I'm worried the call dropped. Eventually, four deadpan words slip through the static. "Wait, are you serious?"

"Yes," I swallow. "Apparently, he had a song go viral, and then we signed him. But I wasn't on the email, and since I muted him on everything, I haven't–"

"WHAT?!" Taylor screams over top of my informational relay. The direct delivery into my eardrum sends the phone flying from my ear. Despite the distance to my auditory nerve, I can still make out her frenzied prattle, "There's a new song?! Have you listened to it? What's it called? Is it about you?" As the string of questions continues unanswered, I contemplate the last one I registered: Is the new song about me? *Am I currently considering the possibility? Yes. Am I hoping it is? Yes. Do I have time to really think about this right now? No.*

"I don't know," I choose to close all her queries at once. "I found out because Capitol signing him means I actually do need to go to the concert since Nolan is a new artist. He goes on in like forty-five minutes, and I am not prepared for this at all. I mean, for starters, I like this outfit, but I dressed cozy today since it was chilly this morning, and you and I kind of had a fight and I was stressed. So, I'm not in a like, 'Hi, it's nice to see you after two months, man I definitely had and still have feelings for and made out with a few times' outfit." To my complete chagrin, Taylor laughs, a response I find most distressing. "What's funny about this?!" I demand with a chuckle of my own.

"I'm sorry," she says, laboring to work past her giggles, "but if you would take a breath long enough to let me get a word in, I would be able to tell you I packed you an outfit last night in case you changed your mind. The real challenge was getting your makeup to your car this morning. But, I am the best, so it is there."

"Taylor Marie Avalon, you absolute saint." I marvel, beaming into the receiver.

"That is what they call me," my friend replies with marked smugness. "Go change. I'll Uber to you now and drive us over."

Lines form over the bridge of my nose. "What about Jeremy?" I wonder.

"Eh. He can handle himself, "she assures me blasély. "I'll tell him to meet us there. He's stuck at work, and given the circumstances, I'd rather not miss anything." I can hear the smile that spreads across her face. "Besides, you don't really seem like you're in a fit condition to drive."

I grin back. "Ok, if you're sure. Let me know when you get here." I'm about to end the call when Taylor's voice pops through the speaker.

"Wait! Laurel!"

"Yeah?" I rejoin, almost to the elevator.

"Don't listen to the song until I get there."

58

Laurel

Taylor speeds down Santa Monica Boulevard as I do my best to put the finishing touches on my makeup. We have approximately half an hour to make the usually twenty-one-minute journey. I pray the Los Angeles traffic gods to show mercy, promising to work on my road rage—either by diminishing or increasing it, whichever he, she, or they may prefer—and that moving forward, I will always allow the cars that properly signal room to merge in front of me. We're covering the miles in a mad dash because while we will still be allowed entry if we're late, I'm hoping to have at least a few minutes to get both emotionally and physically settled before Nolan's set.

The outfit Taylor stowed away in my back seat is all at once perfectly me and 100% her. The camouflaged duffle contained my black lace bodysuit, a pair of my high-waisted black skinny jeans, black ankle boots, and a cropped multi-colored suede jacket I'd recently acquired at the Studio City

Crossroads. It's not entirely work-appropriate. But, in her defense, when she packed it, I wasn't technically going to be working.

"Not to rush you, but are you ready yet?" she practically whines. Taylor was a little more than disappointed to climb into my car and discover I was not anxiously awaiting her arrival with my finger poised perfectly over the play button of Nolan's new song.

I reply as best I can while my mouth is agape, its position assisting in my mascara application. I take advantage of the stoplight to lightly coat my bottom lashes. "Literally two seconds....okay done. How's this?"

"Honestly, it can't even tell you did it in the car," she says, leaning closer than usual in order to properly scrutinize my face from the driver's seat. "I'm impressed."

"Ok, good." I exhale and smile, trying to seem a little less nervous, "That part is done. What's next?" I locate my phone. "Should we listen to the song first or check socials?"

The light changes to green as I make my inquiry. Pedal to the floor, Taylor utilizes the moment to square up to and pass the bus we've been stuck behind for a block and a half, as she flies in front of it, she shrieks, "If you do not play the song, I'm going to pull this car over and park until I've heard it at least twice! Hurry up!"

"Okay. Okay. Calm down," I laugh. "It may not even be about me." I voice the stipulation more for my benefit than hers. In response, the Formula 1 trainee spears me with an exasperated glance.

I open Spotify and use the search bar to get to the proper page, unmuting the musician as I go. His latest track, *Reimagine*, was released on September 15th. I tap on the artwork, a photo of Nolan with part of his face sketched in pencil, which loads the single. One more light touch on the title, and the song begins to play.

For an entire three minutes and forty-two seconds, I don't breathe. I remain rapt and motionless, not even so much as peering at Taylor even though I can feel her consciousness, and intermittently her eyes, boring into the side of my face. The new song is good, a stand out amongst the others. While it's vague enough to stay relatable, it is also specific enough for me to identify myself among the notes. The lyrics describe old places becoming new because of who you're with and how burgeoning relationships can make you rethink the kind of person you want to be. The pictures are painted along a familiar balladic melody, a string of notes I first heard as sound waves reverberating through Nolan's chest, now repurposed from their Ivyleigh House lullaby. As the final seconds fade to silence, I exhale around a growing grin.

"Well???" Taylor releases in a pinched squeal, "is it?"

I face her, nodding sluggishly, my smile in full disbelieving bloom, "I'm in there."

"Damn," Taylor replies simply. *Butterflies* fills the packed silence that follows, a second in which nothing and everything is said until it is drowned out by our giddy screams. As our enthusiasm gives way to laughter, Taylor slams her hand down on the steering wheel several times. "I knew it. I knew it. I knew it! I knew it!" she says. "Look at you. Just sitting pretty over there, a muse incarnate. Living the dream."

I giggle in response. "Daisy Jones would be so disappointed in us." I navigate to Nolan's Instagram and then Colin's. As I expected, & Then Some was publicly involved in the promotion of the track. I try to keep my emotions from turning even the slightest amount smug. I'm not sure what changed his mind, but in the end, he had listened to me. He doesn't owe me anything, but it feels good to have my assumptions validated and know my parting advice contained value.

"You're okay, right?" Taylor follows up, her voice coated in minor concern now that I've grown quiet.

"Yeah. I'm okay." I set my phone aside and allow her to read my expression as droplets of my anxiety begin to transform into excitement. Taylor reaches into my side of the vehicle to squeeze my hand and puts a little more pressure on the gas.

As the The Troubadour comes into view, the clock on the dashboard reads 7:03 PM. Luckily, it's a few minutes fast. Taylor skids my car into a miraculously free meter a few stores down from the historic venue. "Can we park here?" I ask, endeavoring to read the three separate signs bolted to a nearby post.

"If we can't, I'll pay the ticket. Let's go." Before I can protest, Taylor is out of the bug and at my door. She wrenches it open, hauling me onto and down the sidewalk. We secure two of our three wristbands, use my work badge to convince the young girl in the window to list Jeremy's under his name, and finally, walk through the doors.

The club is filled to a higher capacity than I expected, which is good for everyone involved. It's not sold out by any means, but the floor is decently full. There's some walking space, but not ample amounts. I notice the ADA section is still empty. I'm not usually one to seek out ADA seating, mainly because I don't really need it but also because the view they offer is typically mediocre at best. At The Troubadour, however, this isn't the case. Right by the stage, the venue has a marked-off section of the floor reserved for people with disabilities and their guests. If no one else needs it, that's usually where my friends and I would go. However, since I'm working, I lead us toward the balcony.

"You go find seats," Taylor directs in my ear, barely loud enough to be heard over the intro playlist. "I'll get us drinks."

Picking my way through the upstairs crowd, I'm thankful when Nessa catches my eye and waves me over.

"We saved you some seats," she says, sipping what I know is a vodka cranberry.

"Irene called and said you might be coming," Morgan adds with an amused scrunch of her nose.

"Thank you! I appreciate it." I have to almost shout for them to hear me, as we're next to a speaker, but they both smile good-naturedly in return.

I scan the room for other friendly faces. I don't recognize many people here, but I spot a familiar shaggy head near the foot of the staircase. Michael Malley beams up at me and takes the steps two at a time.

"We thought you weren't coming!" He declares, claiming space in the row behind mine. "It was minus craic backstage for more than a minute because of it, if I'm honest."

"Sorry. I didn't think I could get away." I can't help but grin at the manager even as I lie through my teeth.

"You'll come say hello between sets, yeah? Everyone back there will be buzzin' you've made it." He goads, tucking me into a hug.

Once I'm released, I step back so I can meet his eyes. "I promise. It's the least I can do since I was so late."

"Bang on," Michael cheers. "I have to make sure Nolan's ready. But I'll grab you after." As he goes, I catch his sleeve.

"Would you mind–," I start, not fully believing the words flowing from my mouth, "–not telling him—sorry, I mean them—I groan inwardly at my Freudian slip and restate the request in full, "Would you mind not telling them I'm here?"

The manager's sideways smirk widens. "Ah. If that's how you want to play this, fine by me." With a knowing wink, he's back down the stairs and disappearing through the back-stage door.

Not even a full thirty seconds later, Taylor materializes next to the seat I've flopped into, hoping to make myself small enough to hide my quickly increasing flush of embarrassment. "I wasn't sure what you were in the mood for," she prefaces as she slides down next to me and hands me a Jack and Coke. "But, I figured this was a whiskey situation." I gulp down a forth of the contents before thanking her. "Who was that guy?" she inquires. "And what in the world did he say to you? I could pick up on your mortification from a level away."

"Band manager," I reply, assuming she means Michael, "and likely Nolan's now too." With a sigh, I fill her in on my faux pas.

Taylor doesn't respond because the music fades and the lights dim. For the first time, I watch Nolan O'Kelly take an American stage.

59

Nolan

My set went ok. Actually, I don't have to be modest. As I wipe the sweat from my forehead, I know I smashed it. The audience definitely weren't legends or anything, but that was to be expected at the American shows. Michael keeps insisting my only goal as support is to play well and be engaging enough to pique the & Then Some fans' interest. If my twenty-five minutes on stage can convince them to go home and stream my music, he's adamant the majority will come around with time and exposure. I did notice a group of girls in the front row knew the lyrics to *Reimagine*, which was class and something that didn't happen in New York. I automatically wince. I don't like dwelling on the Bowery gig. It wasn't my best go, probably because I was practically shitting myself that the Capitol people were watching.

Granted, there are people from the label—from *my* label, a quantifier I still find absolutely mad—here as well. But the group doesn't include the person I thought it would.

I can't determine whether or not I'm bothered by Laurel not showing. I don't want to be. I've made every excuse for her absence I can think of. As I make my way backstage, I run through the growing list.

    a. It's possible she's too busy.

    b. Although I'm aware this likely isn't the case, maybe she doesn't know I'm here.

    c. She might have chosen to not show because she hates the new song. But, based on what I know about Laurel, I also can't imagine this would be true.

    d. There is a chance she hasn't heard it.

I sigh as the crowd's final cheers fade, and I mount the steps. There's a simple remedy to this final hypothetical. I could send the song to her. It's something I've almost done with every iteration. In our text chain from August, I've typed out the lyrics, pasted the voice memo, inserted the demo, and now could send the Spotify link. But it always made me feel like a tool. Laurel asked for a clean break. I need to give her that even if I can't give it to myself.

"That felt absolutely savage," Eoghan says, alerting me to his presence by smacking my arse. When Colin and the gang had invited me to join the tour, my acceptance hinged on the one necessary condition that Eoghan be signed on as my drummer. Often, he's the last to leave the stage, basking in the glow of the spotlights as he doles out his drumsticks to a lucky few. In New York, one recipient was Roisin, as my friend wanted to both interact with the audience and hold on to the keepsake. Tonight, his girlfriend was not to be found intermingling with the fans, choosing instead to stay in the dressing room. No one is more disappointed than I am in regards to Laurel's absence, but Roisin might be a close second.

As we walk through the entryway, I inherently step aside, expecting the redhead to pounce on her boyfriend the way she usually does. But the air around the opening remains still. Confused, I force my focus back on my surroundings. Roisin is standing across the room, arms flung around a petite blonde woman.

Laurel Cole's brown eyes flit to mine as I advance a few cautious steps into the room.

"Now, we're suckin' diesel!" Colin exclaims from his place in the American's receiving line, "Look who's here!"

60

Laurel

"Now we're suckin' diesel! Colin shouts over the collection of noises that fill the dressing room, "Look who's here!" There is genuine joy laced into the words, but the almost imperceptible restraint in his tone has me wondering if they were meant to double as a warning. From his angle, the frontman can't tell Nolan and I have already locked eyes. With the brief emotional contact, I strive to convey the mess of feelings I can't currently name. I'm sure Roisin was made aware of the new arrivals by the accelerated and syncopated beat that began pounding in my chest.

I wriggle out of our embrace and meet Eoghan halfway as he barrels toward me, beaming. I was thrilled when I recognized the drummer on the small stage and excited that it meant I would get to see him again. At present, however, I am struggling to voice even the simplest of greetings because closing the distance between him and me meant relinquishing some of the space separating me from my busker, who, aside from a small shuffle past the doorframe, has remained glued to the scuffed tile. Eoghan's hug sweeps me off my feet. When I touch ground again, I've been conveniently placed in front of the newly-signed singer. With the rest of the room behind me, I have no choice but to give Nolan my full attention.

Seeing him under any circumstances would have been nerve-wracking enough. In my haste and surprise, I had not accounted for the fact that the version of him with which I would reunite would be fresh off the stage. The time he's spent under the spotlights has left him flushed and sweaty. He hasn't gotten a haircut since this Summer, meaning the waves I knew were prone to curl around his ears and forehead now manifest as soaked ringlets plastered to his skin. As his lingering adrenaline fades, the slowing rise and fall of his chest is easily traceable through his damp fitted t-shirt, which started the set tucked into cuffed jeans. It's a look that more than suits him, making it a struggle to keep my gaze within his unwavering eye line. Yet, neither of us moves. The boundary I set has physically manifested before me.

"Hi," I try, painfully aware of how stilted this welcome is when compared to the others I received.

"I didn't think you were coming," Nolan states plainly, tipping sideways to prop his guitar against the couch.

Despite his constant eye contact, I cannot get a read on the musician's emotions. Without any hint into how he is feeling, it's hard for me to know what to say next. At first, I wasn't sure if I was glad or annoyed this meeting would have a large audience, but it's proving to be more of a nuisance than anything else. As if reading my mind, Michael clears his throat.

"Ok, everyone," he begins, "if you're due on stage in fifteen, head to the VIP Lounge for a warm-up. If you're finished for the evening, go have a drink on me." The proclamation increases the tension in the already riddled atmosphere tenfold, but it does the trick. In less than a minute, Nolan and I have the small room to ourselves.

I watch the musician's weight shift as he prepares to take a step in my direction. My face falls as he reconsiders and abandons the impulse with a heavy sigh.

"Maybe we should sit?" he suggests, gesturing to the sofa.

There's a tender yearning to the sound that reaches my ears. The note of sentiment douses my relieved answer to a whisper, "Okay."

We arrange ourselves much like we had in his apartment—him on the edge. Me atop the middle cushion—save for the valley that spans between us. I study it as I speak.

"I didn't know." Those three small words are both the most basic truth of the matter and the only initial sentence my brain formulates. "I didn't know about the song, about the signing, about any of it until just over an hour ago."

"Wait. Are you serious?" His brow furrows over soft eyes as a strain I hadn't previously noticed vacates his shoulders. He shifts into the leather ravine. I interpret the motion as an invitation to bridge it fully, placing a hand on his knee.

"Yes," I gravitate even closer. I can't help it. Now that Nolan is once again tangible in my universe, I don't know how I ever found the wherewithal to ask for space in the first place. "I was never angry with you. Before my plane even took off, I knew I was solely to blame for how things ended. By the time I landed, I felt like reaching out too soon after telling you I wanted a break wouldn't be fair to you, so I muted you on everything. I did a full social media detox, including Spotify. I didn't see a single post or get a new release–" I trail off at a rate directly proportional to the grin spreading across the singer's face.

"You did a detox?" he clarifies, signature expression out in full force now. "Are you saying I'm a drug?" A lightning-fast wink accompanies the second question. My stomach flips as I realize how accustomed I had grown to the gesture and how much I had missed it. Somehow, I still manage to roll my eyes.

"No. But I didn't want to be tempted to reach out while my feelings were still fresh. I wanted to give myself a fighting chance to get over you and give you an opportunity to do the same." Nolan's smile fades substantially.

"And were you successful," he asks hesitantly, "with moving on?"

I hum, pondering the inquiry and ignoring how our faces have gravitated within inches of each other, "Even if I was, there's this one song that puts me right back in the thick of it."

The Irishman brings a hand to my chin. "I still want to apologize," he says, "I shouldn't have said the things I did about your job." Like last time, I can tell he means it.

"You already told me. I forgave you in Dublin."

"Please, let me finish. I talked to Colin and the guys about how it'd been working with you. I told them everything you said about my music." He pauses fondly in memory. "As it turns out, you were right, and I was an arse. They completely agreed with you on every point." I can't hold back the boastful curve of my lips. In response, the knuckle of Nolan's pointer finger begins to pace languidly across my bottom one. "I played them a voice note of some lyrics I'd been piecing together since...honestly since we went to Jameson Distillery." Heat builds in the apples of my cheeks. "We all messed around with it, recorded a new version in their home studio and well–" he gestures to the dressing room. "–you can put together the rest."

"I'm glad you came to your senses," I gloat. He smirks at me, trailing his touch along my jaw as he leans in. I almost groan when I press a halting hand on his chest. He places one of his on top of it.

"I need you to know I used what you said as an excuse," I continue our apology circuit, wanting it all out in the open. "I knew how close I was to leaving, and I knew I didn't want to be trapped in an unending long-distance relationship, so I used what you said about my job as an out. It was immature. I'm sorry, too." The entire time I was talking, Nolan's eyes stayed locked on mine. I'd forgotten how good he was at eye contact. Once I've finished, he takes a lap of my face–Right eye. Lips. Left eye.–weighing my words ahead of speaking. My nerves begin to creep back to the surface in the expanding silence.

"So I'm not permanently relocating or anything," he announces, reclining onto one elbow while entwining our touching fingers, "But I'm set to be in Los Angeles for three weeks after this to work on an EP and periodically after that. There would still be times when we would have to be long-distance. Is that okay with you?"

"Absolutely." He straightens slowly, bringing his chest almost flush with mine.

"In that case, are you going to let me kiss–" My lips are on his before he can finish the question. Caught off guard by my momentum, Nolan falls back into the sofa, pulling me on top of him. We chuckle into one another's mouths until my fingers tangle into the still-damp curls at the nape of his neck and tug him back to me. Aware we do not have all the time in the world, I push off of the faded cushion sooner than I'd like.

When my partner props himself up and raises an eyebrow, I explain, "You kind of smell. You know that, right?"

"Cons of dating a rockstar, I guess," he grins and lightly nudges my chin with his knuckle in an attempt to lead my face back to his.

"Oh, so you're a rockstar now?" I tease, trying to not melt back into the kiss, "and here I thought I wouldn't have to worry about your ego."

The Irishman preens as he backs away, "I'll admit it's a bit inflated at the moment because this time you *definitely* kissed me first."

61

Laurel

Using the faint reverberations of *SUPERLIKE* by The Academic as the signal our friends are about to take the stage, Nolan and I vacate the dressing room. As we relocate to the balcony, we stop briefly at the bar to order a round of Jack & Cokes. Jeremy has arrived during my time backstage, claiming my vacated spot next to Taylor, but there's still room on the upper level as my group of co-workers and friends have dutifully guarded the empty seats on our row. Jackets, coats and bags are hastily gathered during our approach, allowing us to slide into the freed-up seats without causing a scene.

"Laurel, hey! Thanks for this!" Jeremy gratefully greets me from around my roommate. "Oh, hi. "I'm Jeremy," he continues, seeing Nolan and sticking his hand out in the Irishman's direction. I risk a side-glance at Taylor, impressed by her boyfriend's feigned lack of knowledge on the subject at hand, certain he had been filled in during my absence, if not earlier in the day.

Nolan shakes the outstretched appendage, "Howya? I'm Nolan."

"Cheers." The two men clink their plastic cups, bringing Taylor and me into the exchange.

I nudge my already fawning friend forward, " Nolan," I begin, "this is Taylor. Taylor, this is Nolan." I watch them greet each other, heart full.

"I really liked your set," Taylor says.

"Ah, class. Thanks!" The Irishman beams. "I'm glad to finally put a face to the name. I've heard a lot about you."

Taylor smiles wearily, "I hope Laurel hasn't made me seem like a crazy person."

"Not at all," he confirms, "just someone worth waking up at 3:00 AM for." While I definitely hadn't expected this answer, I'm somewhat used to the musician's charms. Taylor, however, is not. I giggle at her momentary loss for words and the rosy hue creeping into her cheeks. When I peer up at Nolan, he winks at me.

For the second time this evening, the lights dim, and the cheers grow louder. Our group quiets and faces forward. But Taylor, somewhat recovered, takes advantage of the roar to whisper in my ear, "One, 'oh my gosh.' I got it before, but now…congratulations to you." I snort, pleased. "Two, you can totally tell you've been making out. In case you were wondering." Due to the snicker sneaking past her lips, I lightly shove her into her boyfriend. She sticks her tongue out at me as he stabilizes her, but I uphold an aura of innocence, sipping my drink as *All I Could Do* opens the show.

62

Laurel

Once the venue has cleared out, I return the favor &
Then Some showed me in their city. As I promised, we continue our evening after the gig. There are plenty of tourist trap
bars within walking distance along Santa Monica Boulevard,
but I march us up Doheny Drive and down The Sunset Strip
instead. Our merry band of revelers does not complain about
the incline, using the brief journey as an opportunity to bond. I
stay at the head of our party with Nolan, Dylan and Rory. I act
as our guide, the only person who knows both the path and the
destination. Taylor walks with Roisin and Stephanie, happily
listening to their accented exchange and adding her own rele-
vant commentary while Eoghan and Colin interrogate Jeremy
on The States' obsession with football and lack of enthusiasm
for rugby. The kind-hearted American seems almost relieved
when I veer into Rock & Reilly's, a music-themed Irish Sports
Bar.

I've been here a few times and feel like my visitors will enjoy the gastropub's atmosphere. Given our large number, I bypass the already crowded main floor and climb the sturdy wooden staircase that leads to the loft. Luckily, it's empty. The new space somewhat dulls the chatter blossoming below, but not enough for conversations to be heard across the room, so we gather at its center. The group splits, collecting on the two dark velvet couches. When that alone is not enough, the boys coral a matching armchair and three red dining chairs from around the area.

"This isn't too bad a choice," Colin muses, messing with the large foosball table behind us. "Of course, it's not exactly like home, but I can see the emerald isle inspiration."

"I figured it would make a good first impression," I chuckle. "I can show you some other places while you're here if you'd like, but Rock & Reilly's has live music on the weekends."

"Oh, that's class," Rory says from his spot next to Dylan.

"And weekly karaoke," I finish.

Piled on each other in the large wing chair, Roisin and Eoghan beam at me.

"Should I sign us up?" I question.

"Sorry," Roisin simpers at my raised eyebrows, "It's not karaoke. It's pure quality we get to see you again, that's all. When you left, I assumed that was it."

I answer her honestly, "Me too."

"I mean, we missed you and all," Eoghan continues, eyes glinting impishly in his friend's direction. "But, I'm mainly glad you're back because now Nolan might stop all his bloody whinging." The intended recipient, along with everyone else, laughs in response.

When we've collected ourselves, Steph asks, "Do we order drinks at the bar? I'll get the first round."

"Oh, yeah! Sorry," I respond. "I wanted to make sure there was room for all of us first."

Roisin wriggles out of her boyfriend's grasp, "I'll help you carry everything," she adds.

Jeremy steps forward, as well. "Me too. You'll probably need a few pairs of hands."

As the threesome disappears down the stairs, Colin calls out from a far wall. He's bent low, peering at the bottom shelves of the floor-to-ceiling bookcase, which runs along a small section of the room, "Anyone up for a board game?"

"Ah! Now that could be good craic," Eoghan exclaims.

Beside me, Nolan shakes his head contentedly. "You'll have to find something we can play in teams, mate," he instructs his friend, "We have a hape of people here."

After narrowing down our options, Colin sets five choices on the table, grinning ear to ear. Dylan immediately nixes two possibilities with an intensity that suggests they were included as an inside joke.

"Thoughts?" & Then Some's drummer queries Taylor, who perks up on my other side.

"I haven't played *Trivial Pursuit* since I was a teenager," she responds.

Dylan smiles at her. "Same."

"*Trivial Pursuit* it is, then," Colin dictates. He and Nolan begin the unboxing and setup as Jeremy hands off the first set of drinks.

"I need to go back down, but Taylor, here's yours, mine and Laurel's," he says, passing her the glasses.

Rory halts him, standing, "Have a seat, mate. I've got it."

"Oh. Thanks, man." Jeremy claps the musician on the back as he settles into his spot next to Taylor.

As she looks between us, Taylor squeezes my hand. There's a warmth practically radiating from her.

As she happily taps her temple on my shoulder, Nolan kisses the top of my head. I simper up at the Irishman in response. When he repeats the gesture, I chortle.

"What?" I question.

"Nothing," he shrugs, stealing a drink of my cider and winking at me.

I scoff and take the glass back. "No, what is it?"

"I'm trying to get used to the idea this is my life now. That's all," he shrugs.

Now, it's my turn to mime indifference. "Get used to it," I reply. By the amused yet puzzled expression on his face, I can tell he is expecting me to finish with a cheesy cliché, something along the lines of 'because there's no way I'm letting you get away now' or some other final scene one-liner. "You've already signed the contract," I remind him with a smirk.

"Feck off!" Nolan exclaims, but the fact he kisses me in the same breath makes me think he may not mean it.

As the rest of the libations arrive, my friends gather around the board game, paring off into teams. And, from the speakers overhead, I can make out the faded intro to Bruce Springsteen's *No Surrender.*

THE END

Irish Slang Glossary

A good day for drying – sunny weather

Arseways – to make a mess of

Aye – Yes

Bags; to make a bags of something – make a mess of something

Bang on – good

Banjaxed – if an object is banjaxed, it's broken beyond repair

Boyo – the Irish equivalent of the British term "lad."

Buckled – drunk

Bunk – skip

C'mere to me – come here

Dander – walk

Deadly – good or great

Delira and excira – Dublin slang, delighted and excited

Eejits – an idiot or a fool, but more often, it's used in an affectionate manner

Fair play – well done

Feck off – go away (polite version)

Gaff – house

Give it a lash – to give something a go

Gobshite – idiot

Hape – quantifier meaning lots

Haymes – complete mess

How's she cuttin'? – a greeting, how are you?

Jammy – lucky

Lash – attractive

Leg it – run away

Lift – elevator

Lob the gob – kissing

Mad – crazy

Mill – fight

Melter – annoying

Minus craic – a situation that isn't very fun

Mot – girlfriend

Mount – an attractive person

Petal – term of endearment

Petrol – fuel

Pram – stroller

Pure – quantifier meaning very

Quality – good

Quid – money

Rubbish – trash

Ructions – when two or more people have a huge argument about something.

Scratcher – bed

Sham – friend

Shifting – kissing

Sound – an affirmative response to something

Spitting – light rain

Shite – Shit

Stall the ball – wait or stop

Suckin' diesel – doing well

Sure look – it is what it is

Taking the piss – joking around with/ making fun of

Thanks a million – thanks very much

Tool – someone you're less than fond of

Topper – term of praise

Author's Note

Growing up, I never felt like I wasn't represented in the stories being told. Except for a brief time in Middle school, I never considered myself "disabled." I obviously knew I had cerebral palsy. It was a huge part of my life, but I was raised around other strong, confident disabled individuals, so I never saw it as a limitation. It wasn't until I was older that I realized there weren't really any characters in books, movies or TV like me, that what other individuals looked to the media for, I was lucky enough to see represented in peers.

Disability in the media is rarely portrayed as a part of a whole. It has gotten better in the few years since I first wrote this story, but often, when a character is disabled, that is the story, that is the plot point, and it must be healed, fixed, accepted or overcome. That is not my story. It has never been my story. Cerebral Palsy is not who I am. It is simply something that I have.

Laurel is how I see myself. She was born out of the music I listened to, the people I knew and some of the experiences I have had. I grew into her—a woman with a full life that simply includes having Cerebral Palsy. If you are reading this and you have never felt or seen yourself as someone capable of having a whole life, if you have been told that something that is just a part of you is your entire story, I'm giving her to you. I hope you find somewhere in these pages a bit of yourself and the courage to write your own story, real or fictional.

Acknowledgments

When I say getting this book to the point where you are reading it now was a process, I mean it.

The first time I wrote it was in 2020, when a global pandemic was keeping everyone in their homes. Right before lockdown, I had gone to Ireland for the third time, and the PTD (post-travel depression) from the trip hit ten-fold with the newly enforced and necessary restrictions. Eventually, all my newly found free time allowed me to pick up an old hobby from my high school days. I started reading again. In tandem with my best friends, we began to pour over romance novels, passing them around like the jeans in The Sisterhood of the Traveling Pants. With each book that we read and hour that we spent on Zoom giggling, gasping and swooning over our favorite parts, I began to remember how much I love stories. Whether they jump off a page, are projected onto a screen, are sung through a melody, or are relayed at lightning speed over a bottle of rosé, there is a magic found in stories that is integral to humanity as a whole. I wanted to be a bigger part of it.

So, I started to think about what kind of stories I could tell, what kind of characters I would craft. Nothing felt right until I was driving up Laurel Canyon with In-&-Out in my passenger seat, listening to Selena Gomez' Rare on repeat. Somehow, the lyrics and the melody melded in my brain into the theme song for a headstrong and spunky protagonist. And thus, Laurel was born. Once I had her, everything else fell into place.

(You could almost say the book wrote itself.)

As this is my first novel and I was just writing to see if I could, Laurel is a lot like me. She's obsessed with music, is overly protective of her best friend and fell head over heels for a boy with a microphone and an accent in a matter of days. So, the plot was built around my dream version of her unplanned vacation and, like Laurel herself, was pushed forward in part by the artists I was listening to at the time. You can find them all on the novel's playlist, so their thanks will remain in auditory format.

However, I do want to thank in writing everyone that I actually know who helped me make it what it is today:

I have to start with my parents, both for your endless support and encouragement, Mom for all of your proofreading and copy edits and Dad for your marketing advice. I would not be me without you, and by default, neither would Laurel.

Thank you, Geneva, Laura, and Lindsey–my original beta readers–sorry, I kept moving the ice cream scene. I hope you like the "bonus content" in this version.

Thank you, Anna, Cameron, Chris, Parker, Shelby S. (soon to be R.), Shelby T., and again Geneva, Laura and Lindsey, for all being my versions of Taylor in one way or another. I love you all with my entire heart and currently miss you dearly.

Thank you, Devrie, for being the first person who didn't know me to read this story and for championing the manuscript as hard as you did. Your kind words and encouragement came at a time when they were desperately needed.

Thank you, Danielle Stewart, for all of the self-publishing advice. You made the final step in this process feel far less daunting.

Thank you, Ashley Santoro, for bringing Laurel and Nolan to life on the incredible cover and for the stunning interior. Seeing it for the first time made this all real.

I would like to give a shout-out to Google Maps, Dermot Kennedy's 'Some Summer Night' – Live From Natural History Museum and the Irish Mocha at Pricilla's in Toluca Lake. It sounds silly, but the book would not be the same without those three things.

I would also like to use this space to pat myself on the back. Not only because I managed to, not only put 66,000 words on paper, but then came back when time allowed to cut it to 50,000 and then a year later added an additional –and needed– 26,000, but also because I got over "the way I wanted things to happen" and figured out what needed to happen, which for my personality was a hell of an obstacle to overcome. No matter how many books I write, which I am hoping will be many, this one will always be special to me. It taught me a lot and continues to do so.

Lastly, I want to acknowledge you (especially if you made it this far). Thank you so much for reading my book. It means more than I currently know how to articulate. I really hope you liked it. But, if you bought a physical copy and don't plan on keeping it, do me a favor and put it in one of those free libraries on street corners. Maybe it will find its way into the hands of someone who needs it.

Books are magic that way.

Printed in Great Britain
by Amazon

30850462R00229